THE CULT OF
QUIETUS

THE CULT OF
QUIETUS

CONRAD TYCKSEN

Ordering Information:

BookTrail Agency
8838 Sleepy Hollow Rd.
Kansas City, MO 64114

Printed in the United States of America

Contents

CHAPTER ONE
DANIEL & CHRISTINE

The *Vaieli* was a dark place to those who wandered from the naturally made trails. Old oak trees stretched their branches wide as they fought for the rays of light shining through a dense canopy. Thick underbrush filled with prickly thorns scattered the ground making it near impossible for living creatures to cross. A deadly environment where even trees fought one another was only more apparent by the many dead or dying branches that snapped all around.

Few dared to venture these paths as the unforgiving forest tended to gobble up human invaders with little remorse. Though small, taking only a day and a half to travel, it had an insatiable appetite for all who stepped across the threshold of thorns. Once crossed, a person would be lost to an unknown fate as none return to describe the interior. Staying true to the trails made by the forest itself was the only safe passage for man. The thick smell of wet dirt and moss filled the air as a small group of companions were greeted with silence as they invaded this temple of loss.

Daniel and his company had been traveling for some time. Their journey home now brought them through the *Vaieli* as it was the shortest path. Entering had been a simple thing as the road of packed dirt held no barrier. Slouching trees provided great shade which chilled the late winter air. The only sound they could hear was that of the creaking wagon and soft steps of horses. Having traveled this route many times before, he knew what to expect upon entering, but there was a feeling of uneasiness and a strange presence that had settled around him. He held tight to the reins and kept vigilant watch as they continued steadily.

Daniel Evergreen was not exceptionally tall. His hair was jet black and kept short. He had a stern face, but his eyes were as calm as gentle rain. His unkempt beard sprouted wild hairs that poked out at odd angles as though he had slept face down in the dirt. Despite the cold, he wore no gloves. His calloused fingers, far thicker than those of his palms, had shown the build of an archer; gloves would have only been in the way should he be needed. He wore a short sword on his side that shone brightly from little use. His preferred weapon of choice was the bow, and with him, he always carried two.

The first was made of maple and carved from a tree that had fallen across the road he now traversed. These woods were bizarre in that of the lumber itself. Logs drawn from here burn longer, craft stronger, and grow faster than any forest across the continent of Breathwood. Even the sap contains elements of healing that are coveted by the alchemists, and the leaves were used in every salve produced this side of the Arrowed Mountains. He crafted the bow with his own hands and twined the string from a sapling oak that sprouted nearby. This bow was well worn, and Daniel trusted it.

The second bow however was special in a way, and it was the only one of its kind. It was an Elvish make and crafted with various metals that even blacksmiths from Darvonian, city of Dwarves, were unable to identify. It held the shape of a recurve however the bow did not bend when used. The string was made from a very rare silk produced by the spiders of the Dying Forest far north of the mountain borders. Elvish runes and writings covered the weapon, and the words themselves were imbued with enchantments. Named after the Goddess of Magic, the bow's signature had been carved near the riser. *Magi Elo,* or Breath of Magi. The vast many enchantments made it near impossible to use. Daniel was a strange exception to this.

He had been present when the bow was discovered. Its near-perfect condition baffled them as it had been crushed beneath heavy stones of caved ruins. Wishing to test its ability, he attempted to fire an arrow; a feat that nearly left him unconscious. Others on their expedition had tried and failed to replicate the endeavor witnessed. Only Daniel could pull out the bow's true potential. This Elvish weapon, properly cataloged and gifted to him, was able to fire arrows made from the wind. Vast turbulence would amas around the user as the string was drawn; release would send a roaring cyclone towards its mark and rip it asunder. The impact of course made it impossible for hunting. However, this deadly weapon was perfect for war. Records indicated no use during the Great War. Such a weapon would have caused devastation to the united armies of man, dwarf, and lizard folk as they fought to free themselves from Elvish rule. Both these two trusted bows were as companion to him as the women he rode beside.

Christine Evergreen was slightly taller than her husband. Her hair was a dark black so long that, tied up, reached her waistline. Her figure was rather frail, and her skin was exceptionally pale. Despite this, she sat with a straight back and firm eyes. Daniel best described her beauty as a calm ocean before the crash of a raging surge. Comparatively, her looks were only matched by the first princess of the kingdom; Daniel looked a vagrant near royalty on the shared bench of the covered wagon. She did not wield any special weapon as he did, but her unusually strong sense of smell made her a peerless hunter. If not for her tendency to fall ill, she would have been the breadwinner of the pair. She had been often left home as a simple cold could end her life.

Riding under the canopy, was a young scribe by the name of Stephanie Monger. Her hair was thickly curled and shone as red as the sun; a feature shared by many along the western coast. Taller than the couple who carried her like cargo, and with a slender frame, she was sought after by many of the men where she had learned the pen. She was only sixteen years old and had just recently graduated from her training. This was her first real mission and she had been quite nervous through most of it. Daniel found it annoying as he hated useless company, but Christine seemed to enjoy the young girl's presence. The pair often rambled in aimless chit-chat; Christine seemed particularly interested in the baker's apprentice that was infatuated with Stephanie.

The last two of the group were a couple of experienced adventurers. One had the grey of wisdom in his well-trimmed beard, while the other was fresh-faced and as young as their scribe. Despite his youth, his life had been blessed with many travels that made his experience unparalleled. Together, their knowledge could even guide a babe through the western providence nearly of its own ability. Their strength was great, but Daniel

initially felt it was unneeded. After visiting the affected cities, they were
hired to inspect, he worried their strength would not be enough.

They departed from their hometown of Pneu and traveled first
to the western city of Kend. Here, animals had gone missing without
a trace. It would have been blamed on thieves, but a footprint left in
blackened earth had turned Daniel from this idea. He had never seen
such markings, and Christine's remark of smelling ash, made them
all question the nature of these events. At each farm with a reported
incident, charred grass and the smell of ash were present; a fact they used
to connect each report. Stephanie was vigilant, making sure to detail
each mark and account within the pages of her journal.

They continued further west to the port city of Round Rock. Here,
fishermen had been making claims of cursed water as diseased fish were
being shipped in by the netful. Upon their arrival, they were taken to the
mass pit that had been dug to burn the fish. Even with daily lightings,
the smell of rot filled the air, and masks had been worn in hopes of
preventing the spread of the unknown ailment. Due to the rot, no fish
could be brought with them, and Stephanie took additional time to draw
the looks of it. Strange bubbling from beneath the skin caused scales to
turn to algae. An unknown breed of it that would eat away both the skin
and guts of the fish while releasing a putrid smell. This occurred whilst
alive and no doubt in pain. All boats worked tirelessly in effort to clear
the water and stop the spread. Massive nets and buoys had managed to
quarantine the affected schools. Only one case had been reported in the
citizens, and it was due to the man consuming a diseased fish; fortunately,
he lived, and great care had gone into the prevention of spread.

They next traveled Northeast, taking a detour to avoid the dead
city of Harrington. This road brought the company to Lake Town.
Here, entire silos of wheat had been found rotten despite being
stored appropriately. Even worse, early planting to soil test, showed
malnourishment as though it were barren dirt. The city had salvaged
enough stored food to make it through another season, but if the earth
had turned to dust, they would have nothing to last the next winter.
Stephanie worked hard to describe the wheat, and from here, they were
able to collect some samples to return with. Just south of Lake Town
was Pneu, and between the two was the forest they now journeyed.

He once again noticed the strange presence felt upon their first arrival. An eerie chill caused his instincts to go on alert when Christine had shifted slightly next to him. She gently rubbed her arms as the cold visible nipped at her, and his worry moved from the forest to his side. "You should cover-up," he gently handed her a blanket that he had retrieved from behind their seat, "you are just getting over being sick."

"I'm ok for now," Christine's voice was soft, "I'm enjoying the breeze…"

"I won't allow you to get sick again." He attempted to shove the blanket to her, "Take it." Daniel quickly regretted his choice of words as fury fluttered across her face.

"And who are *you* to think you can just order me around like this?" Her words were like venom as she forced the blanket back into the wagon, "I told you that I am fine."

"See there, Ben, once you finally marry you should take note of how not to talk to yer wife." The older adventurer, Grant, let out a burly laugh as he poked fun at Daniel's marital tongue lashing. "You know Daniel, I've been married quite some time. I can always give you advice should you need it."

Daniel grew red in the face as the two laughed behind him. He even heard a small chuckle come from Stephanie. Before he could say anything, Christine had cut in. "Since you seem so knowledgeable on the workings of a marriage, Grant, perhaps I should have a little chat with your wife about how much you drink while traveling."

With her retort, Grant's face turned pale as he withdrew. Tension soon broke as the entire party began to laugh. Daniel preferred traveling alone, but this party wasn't unfavorable to him. He knew that he would not win the argument with her, but he truly did worry for his wife. Needing to clear his mind, he turned his attention to the young scribe.

"Stephanie," his sudden spark of conversation made the girl jump, "based on what we have seen, what ideas do you have about these events going on?" Daniel didn't know himself, so he didn't expect her to find an answer, at least not on the road.

"Well, it could be a disease we've never seen before. Or maybe some kind of poison was released in the area?" she sounded unsure with both of her answers. They sounded reasonable, but the distance between the villages made it unlikely for either. Before he could reply she had spoken up again, "I can't help but think of a passage from the Book of Corruption in the Common Faith. 'They were like poison to the land. Their steps marked by black earth as soil turned barren in their presence. Animals were of little sustenance and devoured whole. They did not crave food but rather souls. Souls these being no longer possessed. Demons were the soldiers of the fallen one, and they were a plague to a world now foreign.'"

This answer took Daniel by surprise and responded in kind, "True this is, however, the Gospel of Zosen continued 'Go forth my reapers and bring me the souls of the lost. None should suffer in the absence of he who abandoned his duty. My wish is for all to sleep peacefully in my care, and ye are my subjects to make it so.' Thanks to the agents of Zosen, demons shouldn't exist anymore."

Stephanie face began to redden. "They don't. It was a stupid guess, I'm sorry." She began to hang her head.

"There's nothing wrong with thinking in your own way. Sometimes the answer is what you would never expect. Don't be ashamed of thinking about things in a different way even if others look down on you for it." Daniel did his best to console her, even though he had never been good at speaking. Focused on the trail, he couldn't see that his comment did bring the girl's smile back.

Christine had been sick at the start of their journey however she had recovered before they reached Round Rock. In her pleasant mood, she decided to strike up a conversation of her own. "So, where did you live before Pneu?"

Stephanie had moved towards the front of the wagon to talk easier, "I lived in Round Rock! My family are all fishermen there." She gently brushed the locket resting beneath her collar. "They were all helping with the cleanup, so I didn't get a chance to say hi while we were there."

"We could have made time for you to see them. I'm sure it has been a while."

"It has, but they were against me coming to study. I should have taken up the family business with my siblings, or so my parents felt. It's fine I didn't see them. I wanted to wait until I had some real stories to share before going to visit."

"what made you come here to study?"

"I just wanted more than fishing in my life. I wanted to see the world and maybe see things no one else has. For now, I'm stuck at that Library, but after this mission, I can go to the capital and look for more work with my education. Hopefully, that too can take me somewhere new!" Her eyes were far away as she spoke, dreaming of all the places she hopes to see one day.

Christine was now turned around in her seat as she spoke, "that was a really big move. Do you regret it?"

"Not one bit." Stephanie was cheery as she spoke.

"Well we are glad to have you with us now. You are a lot more fun than the last scribe who came with us. He was so stiff I could have planted him as a tree!" The two girls shared a laugh.

As Daniel listened, the earlier presence had returned; his experience screamed of caution. "Quiet!" He snapped so that he could listen to the forest. Stephanie looked embarrassed as she thought that he was annoyed by their chatting. Christine had gone as stiff as a hunting wolf; she had picked up the scent of blood nearby. The smell permeated from all around them, and she couldn't find where it was coming from. The experienced couple now halted their wagon as they took stock of their situation. With little wasted time, he looked back to talk with the other escorts, and the sight of a rider-less horse drew his attention. "where is Ben?" Grant turned and was visible shocked to the absence of his companion.

"He was here just a moment ago. Ben!" Dismounting, he grabbed the reins of a horse which didn't seem to notice the absence of its rider. He shouted as he moved towards the edge of the road. A dark presence enveloped the remaining members in a sense of dread that beat heavily against their own sanity, "there is something moving out there, Ben!"

"Let's go!" Daniel shouted after Grant. He felt that this was wrong and standing still only made the threat grow. Stephanie withdrew in fear as Christine now leaned over the girl as a mother protecting her cub. Daniel eyed his bows quickly before peering back to Grant moving slowly towards the thorny barrier. If there was something out there, it wasn't Ben. "Get back on your horse, and let's move." He made no effort to hide the fear in his voice.

"But what about—" Grant had turned to look back at Daniel, and the next moment happened faster than they could process the incident. Two trees had been shattered to splinters as black arms embraced Grant. He attempted to scream out, but rotting fingers held firm to his neck stopping any sound from escaping. Without stepping foot on the road, both the creature and Grant vanished into the growth opposite the trees still falling. The terror of this was in the absolute silence that remained as two horses now stood with no sense of what had occurred. Stephanie looked on in horror as Daniel whipped the reins hard which caused the wagon to lurch forward. The young girl slid some while Christine had braced herself to remain unmoved.

The couple watched the tree line as they raced away from the sight just witnessed. A shape moved swiftly in and out of view as it neared them. Daniel handed the reins to his wife and climbed into the back of the wagon; the two moved seamlessly and without word as if moving of a single mind. Her face had already hardened as she pushed the horses faster. Holding tight to his maple bow, he looked to Stephanie, "I know you are probably scared, but I need you to try and draw whatever this thing is. Do you understand?" She looked as though she would pass out, but she managed a quick nod. He smiled at her as he unlatched the canopy to lessen their drag and give him clear sight for aiming.

He had hunted every known animal in this region; he knew their patterns well as this meant life or death when on the road. No creature, known or read, moved as this one did. As they quickened their pace, he could see the creature jumping through the trees in pursuit, gaining speed to match their own. It moved effortlessly and made no noise as it traveled. Unfortunately, in the darkness of treetops, he could only make out the shadow of the thing.

He was kneeling in the back of the wagon as he took aim, and he let the first arrow fly. Cutting through the air as though it were insubstantial, the tip connected with the beast and shattered. "Christine! We need to move!" He shouted as he readied the next arrow. He steadied his aim and fired. The arrow struck the creature again, but it fell away as though striking solid stone. He reached forward to grab his elvish bow as the creature leapt across the road. It continued its pursuit and was close enough to drop into the wagon with them.

As it leapt once more, he was able to clearly see the creature's body. It seemed roughly four feet tall and was disproportionately built. It's arm-span was nearly six feet wide, with a large chest and shoulders to support the creature's sizable limbs. Its legs folded in reverse, much like a bird, and they were folded beneath its body as it moved from tree to tree. He couldn't get a clear look at the creature's face as it passed.

Daniel drew the string on his bow. As he did, a roaring sound raged in his ears as the wind began to blow heavy around him. A spinning gust began to form in the space where an arrow would have been. He focused all his thoughts on striking the creature as he readied his shot. He felt the pull from the bow signaling that it was ready, and he loosened his fingers. The cyclone shot away as quick as lightning. It hit several feet ahead of the beast and as it did, a powerful surge sent trees and plants flying.

The creature managed to avoid the blast as it hopped back across the road. Daniel could hear Stephanie crying as she watched it, but he gave himself little chance for fear to settle. He quickly drew his bow again. As he did, he felt his body growing weak. The weapon was strong, but it pulled strength from him when used. He never fired the bow more than once. As the wind began to draw around him, he could hear Christine's attempt to protest. He couldn't make out what she was saying through the roar of the wind.

He felt the pull from his bow again and fired. The creature jumped out of the trees as he did and was struck in its abdomen. The wind began to unravel, ripping the creature in two. While the lower half fell away, the rest of its body managed to land in the wagon. Stephanie cried as she attempted to pull herself as far away from the thing as she could. Daniel stared into the creature's eyes, and his blood ran cold. The head was deformed with its lower jaw sitting wider than the crown. The creature lacked eyelids and lips with one eye nearly protruding from its skull, and its other eye was dilated to the point that it looked solid black. The muscles around its jaws were bare and looked strong enough to bite through a tree.

The creature held itself up by heavy arms and let out a horrifying scream whilst staring at Daniel. At least, it should have been a scream. The creature's mouth was open wide, but only silence escaped the beast.

Not even where thick hands splintered the edges of the wagon, was a single sound heard.

Daniel's mind was blank as his instincts took over. His body was incredibly weak from already firing two shots, and he knew that a third might be his last. This creature was ready to kill them, and he was the only defense between this *thing* and Christine. The string took little strength to draw, but his arms were weak. He lost feeling in his hands, and the smells around him faded. His vision tried to blur as he fought back the exhaustion. *I must make this shot* was the thought he kept repeating. Losing his sense, he lost his way to know if the shot was ready. Trusting his instincts, he loosened the arrow.

It struck the creature in its chest. As it did, the wind unraveled and ripped the creature to pieces as it flew away from the wagon. He was amazed that the wheels were still intact as the rear of the cart had been savaged along with the being. He had lost his vision now as he collapsed in the cart. He could tell the girls were trying to get his attention, but he wasn't able to hear what they were saying. The muffled murmurs of the girls trying to speak to him were the last things he could sense before he passed out. Trusting that the work was done, as the world faded to black, he thought only of his wife and prayed her a safe return to Pneu.

Chapter Two⊙

ELIJAH RETURNS

*S*outh of the *Vaieli* fused two rivers. Flowing West from the Arrowed Mountains was *Riela Sendai*, red river, and South from the northern border, the *Andor Sendai*, Andor River. *Riela Sendai* formed the second greatest river through the continent of Breathwood; second only to *Broethen Fistese*. Along the *Riela*, the river ran so wide that one shore could not be seen from the other, and ships could pass one another with space to spare.

This route provided quick transportation from the coast of Round Rock to the city of Darvonia, making both river and ocean fish an easy trade for all in the West of Breathwood. Although the mouth of the *Andor* merges with the *Riela*, the river flows strong enough to keep its height even in rainless summers. Rich soil brought farmers' fortune to all who planted near their banks, and this place of mergence became the city of Pneu.

Despite its capability of creating economic significance, the city's vast history bled red as war often found this place. Citizens struggled continuously, and the inability to cultivate proper fields led to poverty comparable to the slums in the city of Breathwood. Steady currents allowed riverboats to move troops freely, and the city was often left with the task of recovering the bodies of men, naming the river to match. Misfortune built upon the people until one building broke ground to usher in an era of growth.

From the west, a road crossed the *Andor* by a bridge that had been mounted with ancient Elvish statues. The two marble monuments featured the Goddess Esprit and represented heartfelt greetings to all. A stone wall had been erected to surround the current borders of

Pneu which now stretched across the *Riela*. Two massive draw bridges expanded across the great river to allow both passage and ships to flow freely through the city with a large port existing to the East of the city.

In the West of town, a large building stood several stories high, and it was the one responsible for the city's rapid growth. Made of stone and hardwood, this place was home to Breathwood's only known facility to specialize in the recovery of lost Elvish knowledge and had been named The Library. As it stood, all coming from the West would be able to marvel at its splendor, and all those coming from other routes would quickly find their way to see as well.

To the north, creviced between the two rivers, was the old town of Pneu with the old church at its center. The building itself was the only one left from before The Library and stood strong as the second-largest building in the city. Twice a day, the bells from the twin spires would ring out in hymn to praise the Goddess Esprit. The area between the church and the library was filled with homes of mixed stone and wood as several streets flowed through the varied dwellings. All roofs had been tiled with either red or blue, and there were several shopping courtyards where larger roads would meet. North of the church was the road which led out of the city, and into the Vailed Forest.

The eastern side of the city, across the *Riela,* is where the city had grown the most. There were many shops that lined the streets in this part of town as well as a new market square with many stalls selling their various wares. Three more large buildings existed in this part of town however their designs were all unique.

The first, resembled a large cabin and stood along the southern wall that now bordered the town. This was home to a rather new idea birthed within the city and spread rapidly back to the capital. The idea was that of an organization. Dedicated to the protection of people and free from the politics of fiefdom. Their sole purpose was to provide services for the citizens; they were excused from military drafts, but in exchange, they served as militia forces for the city in times of crisis. It was called The Adventurer's Guild and had been founded by the local lord and the former sword master to the king. *A nation's army is strongest when the citizens are protected* was the thought of King Dol which allowed this idea to come alive.

The roads North of this guild were lined with merchants, armorers, and blacksmiths as their work was high in demand. North would lead to the market square which rested near the King's Road. This highway provided the most direct route to nearly all major cities across the nation, and it had taken nearly ten years to complete. The second larger building within the city, arched over this highway and connected to the market. This building had flat edges and stood in perfect symmetry. This building was the trade house and local bank which housed the Merchant's guild local branch.

The last of the larger buildings rested near the banks of the *Riela*. It had been made of various stones and wood which resembled a house more than a business. This was home to the Trade's Guild who handled all specialty trade work within Pneu. Most of its members had come to the city during its great expansion and founded their guild instead of returning to their former homes.

Sitting atop a little hill near the border of the *Vaieli* was a simple and exceptional old oak stump. Named Yaris by the elves, its extraordinary long life was spent in solitude watching as the world changed. Sitting on its little hill, Yaris existed even before the forest which it now neighbors, and the city which took root below. It loved seeing all the creatures that grew and changed both around and below it.

Over the years, many creatures blessed the old stump with their presence, both from the city and the forest. Of all the creatures to visit, none made it feel as welcomed as the Elves. They had a way of connecting with nature that other creatures could not. Those long and wonderful years ended too quick in the stump's view as their city had ended and the humans built their own. Very few came to visit after the Elves were gone, but it still enjoyed the presence of man when they did. However, after many years, otherworldly beings began to visit as well.

Those visitors brought sickness to the old stump. Rot finally began to afflict it, and the stump felt the many years wearing on its old roots. The sickness which had grown into the hill, brought terror to the humans. The stump overheard once, that its hill had been named the Reaper's Perch. The stump felt cold. It once had many friends, and it now existed as nothing more than a legend of terror for the humans it so greatly loved. Being left with nothing but old memories, and its home being treated as a disease, the stump wished for the first time that its long life would end.

There was one special day though when the stump was visited by an old friend. The human had been resting with his back against the stump for several hours without saying a word, but his presence was enough to sooth the old stump's core. Despite the sickness in the earth and the fear that other humans had for this place, the man came to merely enjoy the same view the stump had loved all these years.

Elijah was twenty-three years in age by the human calendar. He was originally from Pneu, and he had no family name to take. He was a tall man who walked with a slouch from what appeared to be a heavy bag now resting near him. His dark blonde hair was just long enough that it covered his ears however stopped just short of his eyes. His face had a light dusting of hair and appeared to be trimmed this way. He wore a traveler's cloak over his dusty clothes, and he was enjoying the cool breeze of the late winter weather.

The stump watched as he had removed his gloves and rolled back the sleeves on his shirt. It felt a deep flood of horror seeing the condition of Elijah's hands and arms. In the palms, were many thick calluses, and his wrists were marked by deep scars. Along his arms, it was apparent that he had been cut, scratched, and even burned many times. The wounds didn't appear to have healed well if at all. Yaris wondered how much its old friend had endured until now.

Thanks to the elves, the stump learned how to sense the emotions of any who touch it. Elijah, as a child, was always filled with warmth and excitement. Now, he harbored fear and anger. Had the stump not known the human most of his life, it may not have even recognized him anymore. The stump was moved to try and help its old friend.

All things that existed in nature had a way to share energy with one another. Unsure if it would help, Yaris flowed as much energy as it could to Elijah, but the stump was old, and it had little to share. Even if it was only a little, the stump wished to give its old friend as much peace as possible. No creature could sense the earth since the elves. It knew Elijah couldn't know, but if he felt even the slightest amount of peace, the stump would be satisfied. Elijah took in a deep breath. Eyes still closed; he spoke directly to the stump.

"There is truly little left from the time of the elves. Even less than that exists of the nature they were able to bring to life." The stump was awestruck to discover that Elijah *could* sense it now. "I don't let my guard down around others. You must be a very old spirit to be able to move energy like that. Thank you."

The stump suddenly felt an overwhelming amount of energy begin to flow into it. More warmth and power than the stump had felt in a long time. The energy spread from its bark, to its roots, and even through the soil around it. Soon, the stump was unable to even feel the sickness of the earth as it was pushed back into the *Vaieli*. "A gift for you my old friend. May that give you enough strength to live many more years." The stump was astounded by how much this human had grown.

Elijah had reached into his sack and withdrew an item which the stump could tell was made by the elves. The object was a bronze sphere covered in dials, symbols, and markings of ancient Elvish. It wasn't quite right though, or so the stump thought. Perhaps, it had been the many years since Yaris had last seen Elvish which made it seem foreign.

The elves spent many years writing and reading here upon this hill, something seemed off about this sphere. As if he could sense what the stump was thinking, Elijah had spoken again. "This artifact is unlike anything else I have seen by the elves. I don't know what it is though. I wish I didn't have to return here, but I'm told this is the only place I can find someone to decipher it."

Elijah had been so entranced by the town that he had nearly merged with the earth in presence. A small herd of elk had wandered nearby, most likely due to sensing the poison having left the hill. The stump realized that Elijah must have grown aware of the herd as he remained in a statuesque state so not to disturb their foraging. The moment Elijah moves, the elk's peace would be broken, and they would wander off into the forest. Like the herd, the stump could sense that Elijah's peace would be disturbed soon. The stump once again attempted to flow peaceful energy into Elijah as he sat there.

The sun was setting, and time was up. He turned his head so that he could catch a glimpse of the herd. As he moved, a large bull turned his head to face Elijah. For the briefest of moments, the two stared into each other's eyes. The bull was large, and the antlers on his head held more points than the stump could recall ever seeing. Soon though, the rest of the herd had become aware of Elijah's presence. Without a thought, they bounded off into the forest. Before long, not even the large bull could be seen, and just as their peace was now gone, it was time for Elijah to continue with his own journey.

He rolled down his sleeves and covered his hands again. As he stood, he realized the stiffness that had filled his body. He returned the sphere to his bag, and interlocking his fingers, he stretched his arms towards the sky. He continued to stretch out his stagnation as he took in one final sight of the city.

Soon he will be back within its borders, the stump would have to watch him as he moves forward into something that brought much fear and anger. He shouldered his bag and looked back on the old stump. Without a word being said, the stump could feel the generous smile Elijah gave to it was a thank you. His smile faded though as he turned away from comfort and peace and headed for the unfamiliar city that he once called home.

Alone, the stump was left with the warmth his old friend had given him. The sun was now setting beyond the church, and Yaris allowed some of its energy to release into the cold night breeze. It hoped that the energy would find its way to Elijah and give him peace should he find himself in need of it.

The great elk from before had wondered back to the hill. Yaris was confused why a forest creature would be drawn here for a second time, but as the bull approached, the stump felt another old presence. One of the beautiful things about the elves, was the way they adored nature. Granting long life and consciousness were only a couple of the gifts the elves would give.

The elk was now standing beside Yaris, and it could sense the elves' touch on its soul. The connection they had through the elves' gift allowed them to commune even without being able to speak. They stood in silence as they watched the sun set entirely. It was the bull which broke the silence first.

I had thought it was an elf returned when I felt the sickness leave. Who was that human? The stump could feel the confusion and disappointment within the bull. It must have lived nearly as long as Yaris to have remembered the elves and gifted greatly to be able to communicate so efficiently.

The stump could only communicate its emotions, but it hoped the bull would be able to feel the affection the stump had for the human. Perhaps this great elk spirit would be able to help Elijah should he ever need it. As destructive as humans can be, the stump loved them for everything they are.

I can feel your love for the human, but as the named Elk Spirit by Angeli of the Elves, I could never lower myself to help a human being. The stump could understand how the Elk had felt. If not for the humans, Elves would still be here with them. Still, Elijah was different. *For you, Yaris, I'll keep watch over him should he cross through our forest again.* The stump was relieved that such a great spirit would help keep watch over Elijah.

I found the source of the sickness that was plaguing your hill. The Elk spoke out. *It comes from both the northern lake and from the dead city in the west. The rot is different from each place, but both threaten this forest and everything in it. Soon, some of the animals may start to go mad from it.*

Both Yaris and the Elk Spirit could feel a chill in the air. Not a chill that was normal for the cool nights of a fading winter; a chill that they had felt many years before. The same chill that carries death upon its breeze as unnatural creatures once again walk the Earth.

CHAPTER THREE

KATIE

Within the city, a single building served as the pride of Pneu. The building was crafted by some of the best masons that could be spared from the capitol, and they were handpicked by the king himself. This building was as beautiful as any that could be found within the inner city of the capital, if not more beautiful than most. As magnificent as the building was, its name was simple, The Library. It had been over eight-hundred since the Elves had disappeared, and it had seemed as though all their wealth and knowledge disappeared with them. As more of their lost knowledge was brought to life, it was a wonder that they had been overtaken in the Great War. As humble as she tried to be about it, the credit for all The Library's success lay with none other than a simple girl.

Katie was lost in thought as she peered through a nearby window. The sky had turned various colors of oranges and reds that only a painter could truly describe. The waning sun cast its reflection on the flowing *Riela* which danced and sparkled in brilliant lights. In that moment, Katie had felt as though she could stay forever and forget everything else that existed in the world. A warm cup of coffee turned brown from cream had been placed before her. The rich aroma flooded her sense of smell as her mouth watered to the welcomed invasion of her trance.

A luxury which came from the far south, even further south than the City-State of Breaking, and beyond the tribes of Lizardmen, the Free-Trade Company had managed the amazing import with ease. A bitter treat that none in the kingdom had tasted until ten years prior when an expedition of Lizardfolk found the beans and had no taste for them. Katie ran through all memories she had of coffee as the sweet taste of the hazelnut graced her lips upon first sip.

Through the window, many streetlights were being lit as she returned her attention to *The Tales of Andor the Giant*. The book chronicled the life of Andor who rose and led his people against the Elves during the Giant Rebellions. Twelve-hunderd years had passed since those skirmishes. Twelve-hundered years since their extinction, and the genocide of his people sparked others to fight for their own freedom.

Katie had always longed to know more about the elves. Strong, intelligent, wise, cruel. Despite all their *wisdom,* they saw themselves as Gods. Mercilessly, they treated others as livestock, tools, dirt. So much so, that she believed there may have even been other species drove to extinction besides the Giants. All the longing in the world though couldn't reclaim lost knowledge.

She stared at the book which she had read many times over, and she wondered as she always did what the giants truly looked like. What did they sound like? Did they have their own beliefs, their own language, their own songs? She pitied the elves. So much power yet they couldn't even see how much they destroyed. It was a wonder to her how the God's could have ever considered them the chosen race.

"Lost in the clouds again, are ya?" Her thoughts had been interrupted by the baker who had placed the cup before her. A plump woman, later in her years, with graying hair. She had spent most of her life living in the capital with her husband who had been a baker as well. During the civil war, her husband had been drafted into the King's army and died for it. She had sold the bakery she ran with her husband and moved to Pneu as The Library began to gain its fame.

Despite her short time living within the city, Katie felt as though she had been there her entire life. She brought her focus to the baker and smiled. "Mistress Thelma," Katie spoke in her soft charming voice, "I don't think there has been a day your bakery has disappointed me." She took another sip from her cup, "your blends get better every time I visit you."

"Aye, councilwoman," Thelma had sounded sure of herself as she spoke, "With all the new business here, I have to find my own ways of standing out." She stood taller as to show her pride. "*The Long Way*

Home will always stand above any other shop! Whether it be the capital or anywhere else for that matter."

Katie's smile never wavered as she listened to Thelma speak. She had heard the old baker tell her many stories of pride many times before, but she always loved listening to them. Always she spoke insults of her late husband, calling him things like lazy or fool and a few times even claiming he had probably taken a nap somewhere and forgot to come home.

No matter how poorly she spoke of him, she always found a way to point out that even in his death, he was still taking care of her. During his time in the King's army, he had made many connections. Surely, his intent was to bring additional business to their bakery, and he often wrote to her speaking of all the dreams he had for their little shop. Thelma always claimed his drive for success was so he could sit back and become lazier than he already was.

Those connections he had made, held true to their word, and brought her such exotic ingredients and ideas that her bakery's name was well known throughout the kingdom. The agreement he had made with all those connections almost had the feel as if he knew he would not come home from the war. Through her many jokes and insults of her late husband, Katie could always see the tears Thelma would hold back.

The sun continued to fall as the colors changed to shades of black and blue. Thelma did not carry on the way she usually did before she had come to the part of her speech Katie always dreaded. "Councilwoman, you really should find yourself a husband soon." Thelma spoke assuredly, "It'll be easier to find one now while your beauty is in its prime. Wait too long, and you'll be left with only pig heads and fools."

Katie was still rather young, only twenty-three years of age. Her hair was a dark brown that barely passed her shoulders. She was prettier than nearly any other woman her age, and it was recognized by nearly every single man in Pneu, even some married ones. She was neither tall nor short, and she stood to the shoulder of most men. Her lean appetite was reflected in her figure, and Thelma always pushed her to eat more.

"You don't have to call me that," Katie spoke with a small chuckle, "I'd be rid of the title of councilwoman if I could." Katie had only been given the title due to her position as the figurehead of the library, and she was expected to be a part of the city council. She would rather just focus on her books and leave the leadership to others. "Besides, all men are pigheaded and fools anyway, if I'm to believe all your stories."

"Hm…So you do listen to the rantings of this old woman I see." Thelma spoke with a delight in her voice, "Men still have their uses though." One of her young shop keeps had been sweeping nearby. "If only I had been a bit younger, perhaps I could have worked my charm on that one over there." She joked as she pointed to the young man.

"Even in your age," Katie was laughing as she spoke, "I wouldn't put it past you to try." The two women had laughed for a moment. Katie finished her drink in a single gulp. A decision she had regretted as the hot liquid burned its way down to her stomach. "I should be getting back to the library before someone comes looking for me." Katie collected her book in folded arms across her chest, "They're always worried I'll run off again."

"Ah burn them," Thelma stated, "If you decide to do so, you'd probably return with even more fortune for the lot of them anyway." It was no secret that Katie would get wild urges to run away. Often, they would find she had packed in the middle of the night and disappear for weeks or months. Always she returned. Always with new relics and knowledge. Sometimes it wouldn't even be Elvish. The Library served as a collection of knowledge for the entire Kingdom, a title it shared with the Citadel in the capital.

Katie would often gather traditions and histories of random cities or villages so that their culture could be preserved as well. She loved knowledge, and she wanted to preserve as much of it as she could. If she ever tried to plan one of her trips though, she would always be expected to travel with others. She enjoyed her solitude, and she always learned more from people on her own as opposed to having companions.

Katie smiled to the old baker as she prepared to leave. The two said their goodbyes and she left the old baker to her shop. The cold breeze fell on her quickly. She thought of the coat she had left sitting in her study back at the library but knew the fault was her own for not bringing it. She exchanged many greetings as she moved away from the bakery. She was recognized by nearly everyone within the city, and she enjoyed being friendly to so many. She did her best to remember as many names as she could, but the city had grown so much that it was difficult at times.

The bakery was in a little square of the old town, and it sat near the church she had once called home. The square was busy as many people were coming from mass, and the bells sung their usual evening prayer to Esprit. A hauntingly beautiful sound that wrought pain along with the grace that was childhood within. She thought back to her many years living there, and all the other kids she had grown up with. A welling stirred within her chest as she thought about them. A few were still here in the city, but her heart longed for the ones she had lost. Her vision blurred as tears filled her eyes and she fought to push the memories away. An icy wind had licked her face as cold tears rolled down her cheeks.

To distract her from thoughts of regret, she decided to eavesdrop a conversation between two women that happened to be heading in the same direction as she. They seemed rather tense with their conversation, and Katie had recognized one of the women from Lake Town. Elizabeth and her husband had a large wheat farm. The two were nice enough, but around the city, Elizabeth was known for being a rather promiscuous woman. Even here in Pneu, these rumors were known, and women were often cautious with their husbands around her. The lady that Elizabeth walked with had a similar reputation although Katie could not remember the woman's name, and the two often walked together when Elizabeth would visit the city.

Katie listened in and could hear them talking about unusual things that were occurring in the north. Elizabeth spoke about how several of the farmers around Lake Town had silos of diseased wheat, and there were concerns of the coming year's crops. She spoke about how the mayor grew more concerned by the day of these things. Katie had met the man a few times. He was a reserved man who didn't like to announce his concerns to others, and she wondered how Elizabeth had gotten the tight-lipped man to tell her of his worries.

Elizabeth talked about how she came with her husband to request help from the guild. Their two cows and all their chickens had disappeared without even a feather being left. As she spoke, the worry was apparent in her voice. From what the mayor had told her, again Katie wondered how she got him to speak, there were other villages to the west that had similar events. Elizabeth became aware of Katie standing nearby and offered a warm hello. Katie greeted them both feeling slightly ashamed as she thought about Elizabeth's reputation. They were both kind women, and Katie had no reason to put any real stock to the rumors around the two.

"I couldn't help but overhear," Katie spoke quickly in hopes that they couldn't interpret her thoughts, "is there some trouble out in Lake Town?" Elizabeth repeated a lot of what she had already overheard. Katie listened without showing any expression, and she tried to think if she had read anything that could explain these events. "That is perplexing to be sure." Katie was baffled at the full detail of incidents.The three women were all standing there silent. As many books as she had read, Katie couldn't think of anything useful to this. After a moment, she looked to Elizabeth, "Why don't you go see the guild *and* the church. If there is something abnormal going on, Father Bernard should be able to make sense of it." Katie was smiling again, "Tomorrow, I'll be meeting with the council and will bring this matter up. I will also see about sending some aid to your village as well."

"Thank you, councilwoman," Elizabeth stated with a bow. Katie hated that more than even the title. "When can we expect you to visit again, miss? The kids always love to hear your wild stories."

"I probably won't make it out there until after the spring festival," Katie spoke with sincerity, "I promise to give the kids a good story though should you all come for it." Katie knew better. The spring festival in Pneu was such a large event that most of the villages within a week's ride would come for it, Lake Town bringing more people than most.

"We'll be here for sure, miss, you can count on that!" The three women gave short goodbyes, and they had gone their separate ways. Katie had succeeded in pushing away the troubles of her past, only to bring new ones. A gust of cold wind reminded her that she needed to get home, and she began to make her way out of the square. From the corner of her eye though, a strange figure moved.

She turned to look for it, but as the square had mostly emptied now, she couldn't see anything that looked unusual. From an alley, her eyes focused on several shadows that sent chills through her body. Unsightly shapes of horror took form within the confines of darkness that peered upon her with empty eyes. A cold breeze sent a quick chill to break the hold her imagination had placed on her, and the feeling of unease had dispersed as the alley seemed to be as empty as the square. She decided it was time to get home and turned quickly to keep walking. In her hurry, she happened to bump into a man who stood so firmly that she had been knocked back several steps; the book in her hands had fallen to the paved street.

Katie began to apologize to the man when their eyes had met. His eyes had a dark brown color to them that would almost be mistaken for black. Those dark eyes stared at her in anger, and a chill ran down Katie's spine. She took time to look over his features. His dark blonde hair was unkempt and nearly covering his eyes. There was the faint remanence of a scar across his left cheek. His jaw was clenched as though he were holding back several cold remarks. Her initial response to the man was of unease however after observing him, he almost felt familiar to her.

Without realizing it, she had begun to lean in closer to him. *Why do I feel like I know you?* This question was burning her curiosity, and all she wanted to know is who this man was. "Do you mind?" his words were sharp and made Katie jump as she took several more steps back. He picked the book up from the ground and extended it for her to take. The gesture though was not a friendly one.

"I'm trying to get to the library, tell me the fastest way there." The man was not smiling and looked as though he wanted nothing more than to be away from her. Katie knew it was rude to have bumped into him, but she didn't understand why the man was so angry. His sleeve had pulled back some as his arm extended, and she caught sight of several deep scars. After she took the book, he pulled his arm back as in disgust of her.

"I...I'm" Katie's voice quivered as she spoke, "I'm the head of The Library. If there is something you need, I can help you."

At first the man did not answer. He stared at her with eyes that looked as though he wanted to scream. She didn't understand what she may have done to make him hate her so. He clicked his tongue as he spoke, his words were like knives. "I'll find my own way. Meet me there tomorrow morning." Katie was taken aback by how rude he was as he turned to walk away. She could hardly feel the cold as anger rose in her.

"If there is something you need, I can help you now." She spoke sternly, "I don't plan to make my day around some rude traveler that can't even find his way around the city." She lost all her courage as the man turned back to her with a dark glare in his eyes.

"I have an artifact," he said shortly, "I need someone to decipher it for me. I'll leave and go somewhere else if you aren't there tomorrow." The man stormed off leaving Katie with many questions. She has visited many places now, including the capital, however, she had never met anyone as abrasive as this man was. Despite that, she couldn't help but feel as though she knew him.

Her thoughts went to a boy she was once very close to. This boy took care of her for many years but just vanished one day nearly ten years prior. She pushed the thought of him from her mind as she told herself that couldn't have been him. The boy she remembered had never been that rough, not with anyone.

Through all the questions she had, his name was the one that had bothered her the most. Her fists were clinched so tightly that her knuckles had turned white. She watched as the man disappeared around a street corner. He had mentioned an artifact. It wasn't unusual for artifacts to be brought to her. She was known around the kingdom as being the expert on anything that had to do with Elves. For a man like that though to have something seemed unlikely to her. Whatever it was he had, she didn't think he had come by it honestly.

She had finally reached the foot of The Library. As many times as she has seen the building, it had never ceased to awe her with its beauty. She had one of the higher studies converted into a bedroom for her so that she never had to be away from her research. A presence pulled her once more. She quickly turned however there was nothing to see. Her eyes examined every person and object. From one of the alleyways nearby, she had thought a shadow had been staring at her again. After staring for several moments, it appeared to be nothing more than her own paranoia. She figured she needed to rest if she was jumping at nothing, and so she entered the building hoping that the morrow would bring her some answers the man had left with her.

9

CHAPTER FOUR

JOHN

"And let us go from here with the words of our Goddess Esprit, 'Be ye safe in your journeys as the world is cold to those who have lost their way. I am your guardian, but only in faith can peace be found. Trust in me as I have trusted in you, truth beyond which can ever be known.' Amen." The old priest's voice echoed throughout the stone chapel. "Let us all live a life she will find pleasing upon her return and may you all have a blessed day."

John stood in solace as he listened to the words of his surrogate father. Comfort was the only word to describe the way he felt as Father Bernard began a hymn signaling for people to rise from their pews. A few scattered souls remained in their seats with folded hands and closed eyes. John wondered if it were through love or tragedy that left them in deep prayer. The familiar temple had been filled with John's prayers more than any other within the city, and he can attest that the Gods are no longer listening to them.

The church was an old building. It had been the only one left from his childhood. According to Father Bernard, it was built shortly after the city had been razed by the Elves near the end of the Great War. Many secrets laid within these walls, and the old priest was cautious of them all. Shortly after John had moved in to one of the upstairs rooms, he had wandered into a spire office and found a book which contained information on nearly every person who lived here at the time; a mere thirty souls. The priest had been furious with him as he had instructed all the kids not to enter *that* room. It had been Elijah's idea, honestly, but John had played along just the same as the others.

He stood in awe of the chapel. The coarse walls and beautiful stained-glass were worship in themselves. Each pane spread around the hall, told the story of the Goddess Esprit. Her Gospel described it best in stating, 'My work was arduous, yet the people were worth it. Though I must go now to slumber, I pray that the sacrifices I have made will be for their betterment. I am tired, Angeli, please give them my words as I will return once more to guide them forward.' As the evening service concluded, the setting sun cast light through the western windows. The fires sent forth from the fallen god were brought to life, and John had felt a chill as he started at the terrified people being guarded by Esprit from the flames.

People began to walk past him, and he was met with a multitude of greetings. A man named Douglas was in service. He was an armorer in town and specialized in heavy armor which made John a regular. John was a large man, standing a head over most, and anyone who saw him had no doubts about his strength. Douglas had to peer upwards to see into John's emerald eyes. His bright blond hair was kept short, and his face was clean shaven. He maintained a strong posture, and he kept a strong smile that hid anything he may have felt. "My Lord!" The man shouted out, "I haven't seen you in my shop lately. You must be taking it easy around the guild finally." Douglas had given a small chortle at his own joke.

John belted out an echoing laugh, "No one around the guild has the skill to make sparring worthwhile anymore. Armor isn't much use when no one can touch you." His burly laughter could draw the attention of a deaf man through its thunderous boom.

"Well I'm sure no one wants to accidently hurt you now do they, my Lord?" His eyes moved from the two swords John carried with him. A short sword which looked more like a dagger on his waist. Made of steel from a blacksmith Douglas had recommended. The blade had been named *Thelle Lo,* or great knife. The second was an Elvish blade that had been recovered by Katie during one of her expeditions. Enchanted to change its weight with the wielder meant it could be used by any. The name inscribed near the hilt was *Thel Law,* or Law Bringer. It was gifted to him on the day of his knighthood into the Cololomo family with his own name of Limoux. This had allowed him right of lord over the Western Providence.

"You talk as though they are holding back," John smirked as he spoke, "there isn't a man in town able of scratching me anymore. It's almost too boring around here if you ask me. I haven't been able to leave this stuffy town in quite some time now. I'm growing rather bored around here." He sank his head to feign depression.

"I would consider this peace a blessing John, or have you already forgotten your childhood?" The priest spoke with a quiet voice that could easily be missed. Douglas caught on that this conversation was going to become uncomfortable. He offered a quick goodbye and followed in behind the others to depart the church.

John's smile turned sincere as he greeted the priest, "I think your sermons are getting duller as you age old man. You should consider turning the church over finally."

"And if I did how would you get your weekly naps then?" The priest gave John a stern look and sarcastic smile. The two men let out a small laugh as John wrapped his arm around the priest's neck in a familial embrace. "Let's go back to my study. I'm going to assume you are here to talk about something important." John's smile wavered some as they moved into the small room near the pulpit.

Once inside, John took quick notice of several books laying open on the desk. The first was a book tracking all the birth records from here in town. *Katie Harthwood* was the name that caught John's attention. Katie was one of John's closest friends, and it was curious that the priest would be looking into her family. He attempted to read some of the book however the priest had become aware of John's attention and quickly closed it.

"Is everything alright with Katie?" John's voiced expressed concern.

"Oh yes," the priest replied, "everything is quite alright. She had been here earlier today to ask about her mom is all. As you know, she lost her parents that night, and she had been wondering if she might still have family somewhere."

"Does she?"

"If she does, we have no record of it. It's quite bizarre. There doesn't seem to be any record of her mother's family until Katie was born."

"Have you requested the citadel to help?"

"Why yes, I have, that's where things became extremely perplexing. Apparently, the name Harthwood had never been seen until the day Katie was born. There is no record of that family from anywhere within the kingdom." The two sat in silence for a moment, "Anyway, I'm sure you didn't come here to talk about Katie's family. What can I help you with?"

"Yes." John straightened himself as he had been brought back from his thoughts, "I've received a few unusual requests through the guild over the last few days. In three different villages to the west, animals have been going missing and crops have been dying out."

"Unusual? It sounds as though bandits are causing trouble again. Isn't this something for your guild to handle?" The priest seemed confused as to why John was bringing this to him.

"That was what I thought too however a couple had arrived from Lake Town with some of the diseased wheat. I've never seen stored grains to rot as this did. They claim that the soil has grown barren as well. They also reported there being no signs of the animals that disappeared. Not even tracks."

The priest sat there with a quizzical look upon his face. After a moment, he finally spoke up, "I do have a few thoughts of my own, but my Lord, you are the man in charge now. What do you feel this could be, and why do you feel it is important to include me?"

"I feel as though I'm being paranoid, but I don't think that this is something natural nor do I think this was done by people. Earlier today there were even rumors that someone was sitting up on Reaper's Perch. The events and the timing of everything I fear are making me question if a demon may have spawned."

"A demon you say. You know there hasn't been a demon in the world in a very long time. Besides, when a demon hunts, it tends to leave signs such as scorched earth or charred trees. Did this couple report seeing this?"

"Well no."

"And demons are wild without intelligence. It wouldn't hunt in three different places. Just one. So, either three demons have shown up after all this time, or this is the work of something else. If I were you, I would have someone go back out and take a closer look. I think you may have missed something."

"You may be right," John bowed his head to the priest, "I think my listlessness has me jumping at nothing. Daniel is out making a run of the villages. I'll wait for him to return with anything he finds."

"And keep me in touch with this case too if you don't mind. I do agree that these reports are a bit unusual." The priest smiled at John, "Is there anything else that might be troubling you?" Seeing John's face turn slightly red at this question made the priest curious, "Perhaps trouble with a woman?"

John's head shot upright to this question, "Well I wouldn't say trouble exactly." John attempted to hide his embarrassment around the question, "it's the girl I told you about. In a few months when I return to the capital, I intend to ask her to come home with me."

"Now you know I can't approve the two of you living together. Unless of course you are trying to ask me to marry you once you return?" The priest was now smirking. John had much difficulty when it came to his romantic life, but he recently acquired some secret affair with a woman from the capital.

"Actually, what I'm going to ask of you might be breaking a few rules." John gave a scheming smile, "It's nothing too bad I promise, but there are a lot of people who would want her to be married there in the capital. We both want to be married in the same church as my parents."

The priest thought over his request for a bit before answering, "The capital may not be too happy about it, but I'll do this for you. Now, will you finally tell me the name of this woman who has you rebelling tradition?" John leaned over the table and whispered the name into the priest's ear. Shock went across his face after hearing the name. "Now this is interesting." His voice sounded distant as he spoke, "I can't wait to meet this lady."

The two men exchanged their goodbyes. As John headed for the door, the priest offered one last piece of advice, "You have a bright future ahead of you John. I have a feeling that something big is about to happen though. Take care that you get to be around for all these plans you are making." John nodded and left the study.

The warning Father Bernard had given him sat heavy upon his mind. There was a feel of uneasiness setting around him, and John couldn't help but think these events to precede something worse. John stopped in a little square just South of the church as a strange sight had caught his eye. On the other side of the courtyard, Katie had been talking to some stranger. John didn't recognize the man, but his friend seemed to be on edge. As he carefully looked the stranger over, a pit began to rise in his stomach. He may have grown over the last ten years, but his face was one that had burned into John's memories. *With everything else, why show up now?* The boy from his childhood who had left so much unsaid, had returned after ten years, and John's blood boiled at the sight of him, Elijah.

CHAPTER FIVE
ARTIFACT

The cold stones of her study and lack of fire within the hearth chilled Katie's room as she was unable to sleep that night. Her heart stirred with anxiety as the towers of books around the room felt restraining and massive. She felt claustrophobic as horrid nightmares once again plagued her slumber, and the biting she felt ran deeper than the temperature of the room.

Sunrise greeted her like an unwelcomed visitor as exhaustion tore through her body. Small slivers of light now illuminated her room, and she decided that it was best to begin preparing for *another* unwelcomed visitor. Katie groggily threw the blankets off as the frigid air shook away the rest of her drowsiness. She hurriedly dressed in some simple white britches and a red blouse. An intricately designed shawl she had been gifted on her last trip to Kend had been draped around her as she turned her attention to the fireplace.

It took her only a moment to get the fire started once more as she cursed herself for not maintaining the flame through her sleepless night. She took another look around her study as she made mental notes of how unorganized she had allowed it to become. Her desk was almost buried as papers, books, and artifacts covered the thing. Her bookcase overflowed as several shelves bowed under the weight, and more stacks lined the floor around it. There were even documents laying on the bed most likely getting a better rest than she. A simple mirror hanging over a wash basin in a corner was the only organized place within her room. She made use of this as she washed her face and combed the sleep from her hair.

Still having time before her usual appearance in the halls below, she turned her attention to the desk where she would likely be working most of the day. Her goal was to simply organize the material spread about, but in her usual fashion, she had been distracted by the various gadgets. The first was an elvish sextant that had been recovered from an ancient city found on the western coast. Discovered on her most recent excursion to the south, John had been furious she had taken off on her own again, there had been a cellar filled with tools, maps, and degraded supplies.

The city itself was a harbor, built on the Southwestern coast of the Poinet Ocean. The Elvish name was *Onesius Pon Et,* Pon Beast's Ocean. Pons were a sort of fish that were as large as cities; although none have been recorded in human records, Elves spoke of them often in seafaring tales. The sextant was accompanied with various maps detailing currents, star patterns, some scattered islands, and several more to help with navigation. What had struck Katie's curiosity was the map of the coast of what appeared to be a new continent across the ocean.

Humans had no ships worthy of making the trip if she understood the charts correctly, but the Alchem Empire had been quickly working on several vessels capable of such an endeavor. Katie had been approached to join their maiden voyage as there was chance of encountering elves in a new land, and she was likely to take their offer. When she had sent news of her discovery, the Citadel had sent a massive excavation party to assist her, and their work lasted nearly a full season. Her work was great, and she loved it dearly. She stacked the documents neatly beneath the sextant before moving on.

She next came to a report and map that she had been working on in private for some time. It had come about due to her curiosity of discoveries made in secret in the ruins near Kend. Secrets kept between her and the dead would stay as such whilst she searched for places of shared interest. This search is what had led her to the Elvish harbor however she had not found what she had hoped. As she read through the paper, she turned the charm she wore around her neck. The charm too had come from the place of secrecy which she had found upon her first adventure. The truth's she had learned about in that place were the source of her nightmares, and she had destroyed this private research on several occasions out of fear of discovery.

A gentle knock came from her door which brought her back from the thoughts. She quickly wrapped up the report in a leather binding and stashed it in one of the lower drawers of her desk. "Enter!" A young man around fifteen entered the study. His frame was rather small, and his skin was pale. The boy was one of Katie's students and he had helped her with many of her research assignments. He was one of only three people who even knew about the secret report she had been working on.

"James, you really should get out more. You'll become ill if you spend all your
time inside."

"Thank you for worrying about me." He smiled brightly at Katie as he spoke, "My place is with the books though."

"You won't be able to enjoy books if you ruin your eyes." Katie jokingly expressed towards him. "Well what can I help you with so early James?"

"There's a strange man here saying he has a meeting with you this morning. I told him that you didn't, but he rather forcefully shoved his way into the library saying he would wait for you there." James rubbed his shoulder briskly as if still hurting from the apparent forceful entry.

"I actually did agree to meet with him, although I didn't expect him so early." Katie could see James begin to worry and smiled, "Don't worry. I think he is just trying to find the value of something he found. I'm sure he is kinder than he seems."

"I seriously doubt it. You should give him a poor appraisal for being so rude."

Katie laughed, "You know I can't do that. Well, I better not keep him waiting or he might trash the place." With a smile, the two left her room. The study was located in the Northernmost corner of the third floor. This floor had been dedicated to offices, studies, and classrooms for those wishing to learn reading and writing. Passing by a room with the door cracked slightly, Katie could hear them reviewing formal letters. They made their way down the stairwell, descending past the second floor which had been dedicated to artifacts, and was a museum of sorts.

The first floor had been made in three parts; two of which branched away from the main building. Centered, was an atrium where people were greeted and guided to where their needs may be. The first branch had been divided into bedrooms where scribes and trainees could live should they need a place to stay. There was an open room at the end of the hall that served as a dining room for the tenants as well as a connected kitchen. The second branch was the library itself. Shelves of books rowed in perfect symmetry lined the open hall with a small study area centered in the middle of it.

The books available here were free for the community to use. Books for farmers, merchants, various household needs, as well as history of the country, or the best they could do with what remained after the Great War. There was also a multitude of fictional works. Katie loved the idea of exploring since she was a child, and the fiction had been a collection of stories and legends she had gathered in all her journeys. Although the literacy rate was still low in Pneu, she offered the free classes above to help improve it. Knowledge was everything to her, and she wished to share it with everyone.

When she had reached the first floor, the stranger was not present in the atrium. She shared a worried glace with James as they moved to the library. Quickly searching through the rows of books, she had found him reading a fictional piece. He appeared softer than he did the day before as he was fixated by the book. His posture was relaxed, and he almost appeared to be smiling. A glance at the cover had her face turning red. The book he was reading was one that she had written. It was a fictional tale about a boy and girl who ran away from home to see the world. She had based the characters on her own dreams that she had shared with a childhood friend.

He suddenly snapped the book shut which made Katie jump. She took notice that he was wearing gloves still. They were old and worn, but he moved his hands in ways to ensure that his skin would not be exposed. He placed the book back on the shelf and began to approach her. As he did, she felt her heart race. He looked past Katie as he spoke. "I want to talk to you in private." His brisk voice sent chills down her spine. She didn't know if this was fear or something else, but at the moment, Katie felt uneasy around him.

"James is one of my most trusted students. I think he could provide some valuable insight on whatever artifact you have found." Katie didn't know if she could trust being alone with him.

The man brushed past her and began to head toward the exit. "If we can't talk alone, then our business is done." His words were short and cold.

"Wait!" She shouted after him. He had stopped to look back towards her. His dark eyes felt as though they were piercing her. "Come with me to my study. James can wait down here." James attempted to protest, but Katie had cut him off. She turned to face the stranger, "Before anything else I need to know your name. Who are you?"

The man looked as though he was thinking hard. Katie began to wonder if he even knew his own name. Finally, he answered, "Just call me Let for now." His face remained stone cold as he waited for her response. Katie let out a sigh as she turned to walk him to her study. She knew this wasn't his real name, but it was the best she would get.

Once they reached her study, she closed the door behind them, and she turned to Let. He was staring at her bed which was unkempt, and she began to feel embarrassed. "I haven't had a chance to clean anything up. You never told me when you would be here, and you've been rather rude since I met you. Now if you don't mind just show me what it is you found and be on your way." Being in her own element, she felt bolder than she had before. She began to wonder if it was a mistake to do so. She knew nothing of this man, and he appeared to be dangerous.

He didn't speak. He simply unshouldered his travel bag and from it, he produced a dark metallic sphere. It was nearly too large for him to hold in a single hand, and the sphere was covered in elvish writings and glyphs. From the one side that was facing her, the writings didn't make sense. Of the three elvish languages, she was fluent in two of them and had a rough understanding of the third. No one knew elvish better than she however these writing didn't seem to match any one of them. He stretched the sphere out for her to take, and as she lifted it, she realized how heavy the artifact was.

As Katie turned it in her hand, she became even more curious about it. The sphere had several gears inside which allowed for all the glyphs to rotate. As she spun the various wheels, a glyph lined up that she recognized. The writing was bizarre because it was not elvish. Her heart began to race as she realized what this was, and for this man to have found it seemed almost impossible to her. "Where did you find this?"

"Where I found it holds no importance. What is important is whether you understand this thing? You are the *expert,* or so I'm told." His words were piercing, and this statement angered her. She found that courage she briefly had the day before. This time however it did not fleet. She stood and held eye contact with Let. After seeing she was not backing down, he began to speak again. "The old ruins you had discovered several years back. I was working a job there and found this."

Katie felt uneasy about his story. She could tell he was lying but knew calling him out wouldn't do any good. The language upon the cube is that of the God's, *Piet*; a root language that Elvish stems from. Very few know of its existence and even fewer can read it. An item like this could have only come from one part of those ruins, and Katie ensured that it was buried and hidden before she had reported her findings. This object as well as the secrets she buried is something humans should not know and was the source of the research she had moved from her desk moments prior.

"I searched those ruins many times over several years. Something like this should have been discovered already. Do you mind telling me exactly where you had found it? There may be more like it." Katie tried to hide her distrust with curiosity however lying was never a skill she had.

"If you doubt my story, I can take the artifact to the capital and have someone else decipher it." Let and Katie stared each other down for a moment. Their eyes like daggers filled with doubt and accusation of each other. Katie broke away first and returned to her chair.

"If I am going to try and decipher this, I need as much information as you can provide about it. I'm not trying to insult, but all you have done since we met is belittle and lie." Katie laid her head in the palm of her right hand while her left began to trace the glyphs on the sphere, "If I don't know what you do, then how am I supposed to interpret this for you?" Katie felt defeated. There was no getting through to this stubborn man.

Let's face softened some as he spoke, "You already know that this isn't Elvish. As rude as I may be, you are the only person I can trust with this artifact. As far as I am concerned, the less you know the safer you will be. All I need from you is your help figuring out what this is so I can leave." Let spoke with sincerity, "The most you need to know is that I found this in the ruins by Kend, and the longer I am here, the more danger you are in. Now, will you help me?"

Katie was caught off guard by his sudden change in approach. She didn't know what he meant by her being in danger, but she could tell that he knew this was Piet. *Who is this man? How could he possibly know so much, and why am I the only one he can trust?* She took a moment to stare into Let's eyes. They were softer than before, and they were sad. He once again felt familiar to her.

"Have we met before? This has been bothering me since yesterday, but it feels as though I know you." Katie asked as she began to approach him again. He quickly turned his head away and hardened his face once more.

"If we have met then it was in passing." He buried his head, and Katie could tell he was lying. She wanted to press the matter more however a sudden knock at her door had made her jump. Katie answered to find James standing there with a stack of papers.

"I'm sorry to bother you Katie, but you have the city council meeting to attend." Katie felt her heart stop as she realized she had forgotten about the meeting completely. She quickly turned to begin gathering various papers from around her study.

She turned to Let who had already hidden the sphere again. "I can help you with it." She said quickly, "This afternoon, meet me here again. I'll help you understand what it is, but on one condition."

Let did not show any acknowledgement to her statement as he turned to the door. "You want to know our connection, don't you?" He spoke with a monotonous voice. "I told you before. The more you know, the worse it will be. I will promise to tell you anything you need to know. Will that suffice?"

"What if it doesn't?" Katie was becoming very upset with this man.

"Then that'll be very unfortunate for you." Let said nothing else as he left the study. He didn't even confirm if he would return. Katie had no more time to think about all of this. She was already late, and she had made a promise to bring up the concerns she had heard while in the city the day before. She finished gathering what she needed and set out for the meeting.

§

CHAPTER SIX

TOWN COUNCIL

The cool morning breeze of old town was filled with the smell of fresh-baked bread as John walked past *The Long Way Home* bakery. John was a regular patron of the establishment as Katie would insist to visit anytime the pair were together. A beckoning wave from Mistress Thelma pulled his attention as he quickly made his way to her. "Good morning to ya, my lord." She gave a small tilt of her head in respect to John's title, "I haven't seen miss Katie yet this morning, and I know how much she loves my sweet rolls." She had a small basket with her that John could tell was packed with more than just the simple treat.

"I know the two of you are heading to the council meeting this morning, and that girl is probably going to be late again. Do you mind bringing these to her? They always taste best when hot." She handed him the basket, but she had refused when he attempted to pay her for them. "Tell Katie to make sure she keeps visiting, and that will be payment enough!"

"I will tell her," John enjoyed the older woman's presence since her first arrival to Pneu. She always had a warm place for them to visit, and the best food anyone could ask for in town, "I will make sure we both visit again soon! You take care of yourself now." With a bright smile, Thelma waved John goodbye.

The wafting smell of sweet rolls and fresh bread only offered a brief reprieve of the concerns that weighed on him. The sight of Elijah brought hatred John long since buried. The events occurring along with his return seemed more than mere coincidence, and John intended to find answers to what the connection might be. Long strides provided quick passage from the courtyard to the church as a familiar voice rang out from behind him.

"John!" Walking toward him was the master of the trade's guild, Hugo Andiel. Despite his age, his body was strong enough to keep pace with any master builder. John loved the man for his wisdom. He guarded all thoughts and actions and moved with intent. The Master stonemason had come from the capital to work on the Library during its construction. He fell in love with Pneu during his stay, and he, as well as other tradesmen, chose to stay in the city and took on apprentices to help develop the city further. "Good morning to you!" His greeting a bit louder than intended.

"Good Morning, Master Andiel." John returned his smile and spoke slightly louder than Hugo did. "I suppose you already have your plans together for the festival?"

"I certainly do John! You know the spring festival is my favorite time of the year," He finally caught up with John, "and you know that you don't have to speak in formalities with me. Feel free to call me Hugo! You are the noble of this region now." He gave John a small punch in the arm.

"You know I could never do that!" he gave Hugo a strong pat on the back. "You've done too much for us to give you anything less than your due respect." John was back to his loud, exuberant self. "Well, shall we head in?"

"Of course, you know Bryant hates to get started late." The two of them shared a laugh as they entered the church. Bryant was the Master of the Merchants guild. *Time is the most wasted resource*; he will often say. Born in Pneu, he was one of the few adults to survive the raid during the civil war. He happened to be away on business when the city had been attacked, and although he can be rather abrasive, he carried a heavy weight since that day. He lost both his wife and daughter that night and turned himself entirely to his work after their deaths.

Inside the church, the pulpit had been replaced, and the priest was already seated at the head of the table. He looked rather amused as Bryant appeared to be going on one of his rants about the cost of some product that none of the others would have cared about. Bryant wasn't seated. He was pacing back and forth as was his usually when they would meet.

Bryant took notice of them entering the room, "About time you show up. I'd rather not waste any more time." He looked as though he was annoyed by some merchant who wasn't meeting his dues, "We need to hurry and finish this so I can return to my work. Time is the most wasted resource you know!" He was involved with as much as he possible could. There is little doubt he would be involved with every merchant stand and shop if it were physically possible.

He looked past John and Hugo quizzically, "Where is Katie?" John took notice that she wasn't there, and just as Mistress Thelma had stated, Katie was running late. He worried that Elijah's connection might be the cause, and a fire of anger began to rise within his chest.

"Don't worry." Hugo stated calmly, "I'm sure she just got caught up with one of her books. You all know how she is." He gave a small chuckle as he said this. It didn't give John much comfort. If that was Elijah, did he do something to her? Bryant didn't seem to have calmed down either.

"I don't care if she is wrapped up in some book, she is late." He looked as though he was ready to start throwing things, "If she isn't here soon than she'll just have to deal with whatever we decide." He threw himself into a nearby chair hard enough that it slid on the stone floor.

"I'll go and get her if your head won't explode before I get back." John joked with the man, but truthfully, he was worried about her. She was attached to Elijah like glue as children, and if it was him, he needed to check on her before the meeting. As he readied to depart again, Katie's voice rang out from the front door.

"Sorry!" She was out of breath as though she had run all the way to the church, "Sorry I'm late. I got caught up with…a project." She frantically fought to catch her breath as she leaned over to rest on her legs. Her travel bag was roughly put together, and John could tell she did rush to get here.

"Finally!" Bryant rang out, "Now can everyone please take a seat so we can start!" Everyone found their seat. Katie spotted the basket in John's hands, and she appeared to have regained her vigor from before her run to the church. She offered a quick thanks to John as she unpacked a sweet roll and began to eat before even taking her seat.

"Yesterday, I saw you with a man I didn't recognize, who was he?" Katie stopped with what looked to be a rather large bit of food in her mouth. She chewed slower than she did before as though looking for an answer. She managed to take her seat before swallowing. Out of an excuse to still her tongue, she finally answered.

"He was just some traveler. He was lost and asked for directions is all." She looked at him with that smile that always gave away her lies. "I didn't even happen to catch his name." He was worried, and the smile offered no reassurance. He wanted to pry a bit further however Father Bernard cleared his throat to signal their meeting was starting.

"As we all know, we are a few weeks out from the spring festival. Today's meeting will be to finalize the city's planning for the event." The priest's voice was raspy from his age, and he spoke softly, "Before we begin though, are there any concerns that you feel need to be addressed?" Even though the priest acted as the head of the council, it wasn't an official title. Everyone felt it was easier to allow him to lead their meetings.

Bryant was the first to speak up, "Yes I have some serious concerns." He spoke as though he had little time, "Merchants have been telling strange tales of the roads leading here from the North and West. One merchant came to me this morning claiming some sort of beast is traveling the forests and terrifying the animals." John wasn't surprised to hear this. His adventurers have been reporting the same.

"In place of the military and police your guild is supposed to fill in their role, *John!*" Bryant's voice was sharp, "What are you doing about this? Merchants are scared to travel this way, and I don't have to explain why this would be bad for the festival, do I?" There were times when John didn't enjoy listening to Bryant's rants. He was right though; it would be bad if the poorer villages and merchants couldn't make it to the festival.

"We've already been looking into these reports. Right now, Daniel and Christine are already investigating that as well as other incidents that have been getting reported." John spoke in his typical high-spirited voice. His calmness and excitement always seemed to bother Bryant, "I also had him inform the guild halls in each of those villages that the escort cost will be half to encourage using my adventurers to get them here and back from now until after the festival."

John gave Bryant a smug look. He looked annoyed with John as he spoke again, "Well, at least you are talking your role seriously. I still think you are too young to be here though." Bryant tilted his nose to John having nothing more to say.

The priest spoke up again, "This is something I had already talked with John about, and depending on Daniel's report, we will decide if further action needs to be taken. Katie, is there anything you needed to bring up as well?" Looking to Katie, she had several papers scattered about and she looked as though she had many things to discuss.

"Well, all the things I wished to bring up," she pointed to John and Bryant, "the two of you have already been looking into." She looked at the priest now, "Has the church decided to get involved? Talking with some of the villagers from those areas, it doesn't sound like any natural events that I've heard of."

The priest gave a smile of reassurance, "As with most stories, people tend to elaborate turning facts into fiction. We shall wait until Daniel has returned to decide on anything." He turned to Hugo who held his hand up to state that he had no concerns to discuss.

"Then let us be on with the planning for the festival." The priest spoke with excitement as they worked out all the details of their planning. Even Bryant couldn't hide his excitement for the festival. This was the biggest event of the year for Pneu, and rumors suggest that even people from the capital would be visiting. Inns were already being filled, and farmers were readying their empty fields to be rented out for anyone in need of a place to camp near the city.

Despite the excitement, John noticed that Katie was deep in thought through most of their discussion. She seemed to be bothered by something and kept flipping to some paper that she had buried. She would only turn to it for a moment, write something down, and hide the paper again. She always had a bad habit of losing her focus when there was something new for her to study. John couldn't shake the feeling that this new obsession had to do with Elijah, or whoever the stranger was.

After several hours, the council finally began to wrap up their meeting. "I'm sure that this year will be the best festival thus far." Father Bernard spoke with a delightful voice. Everyone agreed with his statement as they began to leave. Bryant wasted no time leaving the church however the others all stayed behind to chat. Hugo and Father Bernard were wrapped up in some discussion about possibly expanding the church over the next year, and John took advantage of this moment to talk with Katie more.

"I couldn't help but notice that something kept pulling your attention. Got a new expedition your planning?" John laughed as he spoke in attempt to hide his curiosity with humor.

Her face lit up as she was getting ready to talk about something exciting, but she restrained herself before speaking, "Can we speak somewhere more private. It's about that something I had left buried in Kend." Her face was stern as she attempted to save face with him.

John knew what she meant but still didn't understand why she didn't trust to talk in front of Father Bernard about it. He didn't really understand any of this research stuff she went on about, but they had been friends for so long that he didn't mind listening as she rambled on about these things. He pulled her near the exit of the church before speaking, "I still wanted to speak with Hugo some, but if this is private enough, I don't mind hearing whatever has you so excited."

"Well, an artifact came to me today. I'm pretty sure it came from that room I buried, unless of course, it came from somewhere else, like a second set of ruins!" Her voice began to rise slightly from her excitement, "If there is another set of ruins, it would be just like I thought. There could be even more all across Breathwood! If only Let wasn't so rude, I could find out so much more about all of it. Just think! There could be a God chamber for each of the Eight!"

"Hold on…Let?" John realized she must have meant the stranger she had met. As soon as John mentioned the name, Katie's face turned red as she realized she was caught in her lie, "I thought he didn't even give you his name? You know Katie, you were never good at lying." He gave her a smug look.

"I'm sorry for lying," she smiled to try and hide her embarrassment, "I'm just trying to make sense of all of it still. This stranger shows up with a relic I've never seen and shouldn't exist. Then gives me the name 'Let', which I know is a fake name. I just am not sure what to make of it yet. He seems familiar to me, but he keeps claiming that we have no connection. He is so frustrating that I just want to hit him with one of my heaviest books!" Although she was talking to John, somewhere in her rambling she turned to herself more than him.

John thought that it couldn't be a coincidence that he seemed familiar to her too. *It has to be Elijah,* John thought to himself. He didn't hear Father Bernard come up from behind them before his voice caught them by surprise, "Did I hear you right when I heard you say Let?" Katie was taken aback by his sudden intrusion into their conversation.

"I'm sorry, but I didn't mean to eavesdrop. It's just, Let is an old friend of mine, and I didn't expect to find him in the city." The priest spoke with much intrigue now.

"How much do you know about him?" Katie asked before John could.

"I know very little, I'm afraid. Our paths have only crossed a few times, and he rarely visits any cities. A traveling kid, yes that's what he is." John and Katie both were suspicious of his answer however Katie dismissed herself stating that she needed to hurry back to the library. As Katie left, she gave her apologies once more before striding off nearly as fast as she had arrived. John was not ready to drop the topic though.

"You said that you know Let? When I saw him yesterday, I couldn't help but think it was Elijah. Is it him?" John's face hardened as he waited the Priest's answer. "I just find it bizarre for him to show up when all these other things have started to happen."

"Very keen eyes you have there, John." He was pleased that John realized Let's real identity, "Let is the name he travels by now. If he is giving it here, then he must not want any of you to know that he has returned. I very much would like to see him again, John. If you see him, do you mind finding out where he is staying so I can pay him a visit?"

John was confused. For Elijah to disappear so suddenly, it was strange that the priest would know anything about him. Father Bernard seemed to read John's mind as he spoke, "Through my network with the other churches, I had located him, and learned his travel name a couple years ago. It had been so long that I didn't want to upset any of you with the information."

John was appreciative of his thoughtfulness. "I'll see what I can do about finding him for you." His hearty smile had returned. Before he could speak again, a young boy named Thomas came running through the doors of the church.

"John!" The boy frantically tried to catch his breath as he spoke quickly through gasps of air, "Its Daniel. he's back, and it's not good."

John could see the worried expression on the kid's face. He placed a hand on the kid's head, giving him a reassuring grin. John was best at maintaining a strong presence around his guild and most citizens. "Let's get back to the hall and see what has you so worked up." He turned to Father Bernard, "I'll see you soon!" With a wave, he set out with the boy back to the hall.

§

CHAPTER SEVEN
DANIEL RETURNS

Christine's lungs burned as she shouted frantically. The battered wagon felt ready to collapse as she pushed towards the gate of Pneu. Her raged breath let out thick clouds as the cold day gripped her tightly. She hoped their horse would last as she made out twitching muscles across its body. Guards seemed to finally take notice of her approach as they frantically cleared the gate. The guild was finally in sight when a loose paving stone gave their rear axil the final bump needed to snap it in half. The wagon dragged to a stop as their horse too finally reached its limit and collapsed from exhaustion.

Christine looked around as faces stared on in awe as she finally met eyes with a man named Hardin who worked for the guild along with them. The fear which had set deep on Christine's face had been accentuated by the channels running through dirt beneath her eyes from where tears ran heavy. "Harden! We need to get Daniel help fast!" As she shouted, she had already leapt into the back of the wagon to grab Daniel. Her word's shook Harden from his disbelief as he quickly joined her to help with Daniel. Christine felt chills run through her body as Daniel had turned cold and his breathing was unsteady. Harden, along with several others, was by her side to help move the unconscious man.

Christine took a moment to look towards Stephanie who held fast to her knees as tears soaked her face. Her breathing was frantic, and she did not seem to notice they had returned home. A sudden shriek came from her as someone had tried to touch her. Her face twisted as though she couldn't accept where she was, but Christine could waste no time to help the poor girl.

As they moved towards the guild hall, Christine took notice of Thomas who looked as though he wanted to help. "Thomas, I need you to go get John. Hurry!" With a silent nod, he ran off towards the church. "Harden, is Jolie here?" He nodded shakily as he continued to stare on at Daniel. Seeing him in such a critical state caused fear to spread, and word of this would move fast. Christine would leave John to handle the fear. For now, getting Daniel help was her only concern.

The infirmary of the guild was small, holding only four bed and was rarely used. Most times it was only needed after someone's hard night of drinking. The local alchemist, Madame Jolie, had been sitting at the little desk set up towards the large paned window, and Christine was joyous that she just happened to be by the guild to check on things when they returned. They worked Daniel to the nearest bed as Jolie shot up in shock. Upon seeing Daniel, Jolie immediately forced everyone out of the room apart from Christine. "What happened to this boy?" She quickly asked as she began to examine him.

"He used the elvish bow. Three shots he fired before collapsing. Madame, I can't sense his presence. He is breathing but I can't sense him."

"Aye, and he is lucky to even be breathing!" Jolie quickly ran to her medical cabinet as she began grabbing various herbs and bottles. "That bow uses his spirit to fire. Too many shots, and it starts to tear his soul." Her hands worked quickly as she ground herbs and liquids from bottles. "His soul is breaking away from his body. We have such little time."

"What do we do? I can't to lose him!" Christine had finally allowed herself to break. Tears poured down her face as she began to gasp for breath. Her head felt dizzy as she clutched his hand tighter.

"Before anything else, you need to breath! I don't need you passing out on me. I'm about to need your hands if I am to save him." The mixture Jolie had been working was now a fine powder which she had poured into a dark green leaf. "Breath I said!" She shouted to Christine whose breathing was still quaking.

Shaking, Christine managed to take several deep breaths. When she had composed herself again, she looked from Daniel to Jolie "What do I need to do?"

"You need to hold Daniel as still as you can. He needs to swallow every bit of this!" She had rolled the leaf to form a funnel that would allow her to pour the powder into Daniel's mouth. "Once I pour this in, he will begin to move and shake but he must stay firm on his back!"

Christine nodded as she positioned herself to hold his head steady. Jolie spoke again, "That won't do. You need to climb on top of him and keep him from moving at all. He will shake hard enough to break his own neck if you only support his head." She followed Jolie's instructions and climbed on top of Daniel. She placed her hands firmly on his shoulders and was pressing as hard as she was able.

"No matter what, do not let him turn!" Jolie took a deep breath, and Christine took notice to her hands shaking as she poured the powder into Daniel's mouth. As soon as the powder appeared to reach his tongue, Daniel's body began to shake. At first, the shaking was gentle. So much so that Christine almost relaxed her grip. Without warning, Daniel's body began to jerk violently.

He writhed beneath her with so much force that she had nearly been thrown from him several times. Tears filled Christine's eyes as she continued to force his shoulders to the bed. Jolie's voice nearly made Christine lose her grip as the alchemist began to chant in Elvish. Christine didn't see when, but Jolie had Drawn several glyphs on the floor as she spoke.

Jolie's chanting and Daniel's convulsing continued for some time. Finally, Daniel began to calm down and the shaking had subsided. Christine's hands were stiff, and she feared moving them again. Jolie had stood as she moved to get some water from across the room. Sweat was visible across her face.

"The worst of it has passed." Jolie's voice sounded hoarse as she spoke, "healing the body is easy but healing the soul is hard on everyone. He should be ok after resting for a few days." She returned with a glass of water. "This is for you. You can move your hands now."

Christine's hands were shaking as she reached for the cup, and she had almost dropped the water on Daniel as she tried to drink. Jolie laughed as she helped Christine off the bed. "The damned fool knows not to go firing that thing off recklessly. What had him taking such risks?"

Christine's eyes looked far away as she told Jolie the events which took place on the road. The alchemist listened without interruption until

Christine had finished her story. "Damned fool indeed." The alchemist repeated, "If he had just made the first shot, he wouldn't be in this spot, now would he?"

Christine was holding tight to Daniel's hand, and Jolie knew that she wouldn't leave until he awoke. "I'm sure John and the others will have a lot of questions for you two." Jolie was walking to the door now, "I'll go and let him know that you are here. He is fortunate you got here when you did. His soul was nearly ripped in two. I saw this once before while I was working in the Capitol. Should he do this again, I won't be able to save him from what comes after."

Christine looked at Jolie in fear, but the alchemist had left before she could ask what would happen. All she could do now, is wait for Daniel to come to. She would be sure to lecture him heavily for this when he awoke. As she sat next to Daniel, holding his hand, she felt the exhaustion finally catching up to her. Before she realized, she had fallen asleep.

When Christine woke up, it was already late in the afternoon. Her head was laying on the side of the bed, and she was still clutching Daniel's hand. Her body ached as she struggled to lift her head, and her vision was still blurry. She knew that she needed more sleep, but her mouth was as dry as sand.

She attempted to look around when a voice from the desk spoke, "You should sleep more." Her vision hadn't cleared up enough to see him, but she had heard John's voice so many times that she could recognize it in any state. "I heard you and Daniel had some trouble on the road. I'll be meeting with Stephanie soon for the full report so you should just rest for now."

As Christine's vision began to clear, she could see him writing something. There was just a dim candle on the table, and the setting sun was casting too large a shadow for him to be writing properly. "How is she doing?" Christine's voice was course from a dry throat, "I didn't get a chance to check on her when we made it back."

John placed his pen down and ran his fingers through his hair. After a moment's silence, he turned his attention back to Christine. "Stephanie was upset worse than I have seen anyone in quite some time." He was walking to the pitcher of water and poured a glass. "She's composed herself enough to start her report but hasn't finished it yet."

John walked back to Christine and handed her the glass. "Madame Jolie told me what you had reported to her. I'm about to head out and speak with Ben and Grant's families. I was hoping not to wake you before I left." Christine had never seen John this sullen before.

"I don't know if we killed it." Christine's voice shook as she spoke, "It could still be alive out there…I don't want to imagine what will happen if someone else comes across that thing." Whatever that creature was, Demon or not, it would be dangerous for anyone to find it alive.

"Once the report is finished, I am going straight to the priest so that I can request the church's assistance." John placed his hand on Christine's shoulder, "We'll have to make sure to give Daniel an earful when he awakes again."

She looked up to John who wore a great smile that was meant to comfort her. She was too tired to tell if she felt comforted or not. After she had finished her cup, she laid her head back down and was asleep shortly after.

John watched as the couple slept. They were his oldest friends, and his hands trembled as he watched over them. While he had been in town complaining about things being boring, his best friend had nearly died. He fought back the tears as rage filled him, and his mind put a fast link between their attack and Elijah's return.

"If you brought this on us," *I will make you pay.* John kept his voice silent so not to wake Christine. He silently gathered up his paperwork and left the couple to get their rest.

§

CHAPTER EIGHT
JOHN AND ELIJAH

John's mind was racing as he tried to organize his thoughts. He had been worried about all the things that were happening, but now two people had died. The demon had made things personal for him. Both were good adventurers. Ben was always a loner, but Grant had a wife and kid. John's heart broke as he thought about telling them.

As he continued towards the scribe hall, he tried to put all the different events into place. *Why would a demon show up now after eight-hundred years?* His mind kept going back to Elijah. John didn't know how, but he knew Elijah had to be connected to everything somehow. There was too much to do, and the day was well into the afternoon.

He reached the scribe hall, and inside were many rows of books. Most of the books were bound in leather; Katie hated seeing paper in wood or scrolls. The scribes assigned here provided a much-needed wealth of information to the guild. The idea was spearheaded by Katie although it was mostly a way for her to run away from her duties at the library. The scribes kept a running log of adventures and quests that the guild performed. They also helped gather and log the information in regard to wildlife, nature, and even put texts to the various forms of combat training, both of martial arts and of weapons.

This was of course no substitute to the training itself, but it provided a written text for new recruits to study between lessons. The guild had come so far from its beginning. This was not a time for reminiscing though. John needed the report so that he can bring it to the priest. He found Stephanie rather quickly since she was the only one present in the hall other than him. She had been so absorbed in her report that she didn't notice John's approach, "How is the report coming?" With a squeal, she accidentally dragged her pen across the page she had been writing, leaving a glaring mark across the page.

Nervously, she answered John, "I," her voice stuttered, "I'm sorry. I'll fix this right away." Her hands were shaking as she reached for a clean sheet of paper. "This was the end of my report, so I'll be finished quickly." John took notice to several discarded pages. That as well as her shaking voice and hands made it apparent how scared the girl still was from earlier.

John gently placed his hand on the girl's shoulder as she quickly muttered apologies. He gave her a gentle smile as he took the report from her. He mostly skimmed the report to ensure that it had the details he needed. The streak on the final page made the report less official than he would have liked, but he was still able to read the report despite it.

"This is good for now." He could feel the girl shaking, the incident still fresh to her, "you can write a cleaner version tomorrow, but tonight I want you to head home." She attempted to protest, but he held his hand up to silence her, "You experienced something rather difficult, and you did well to report as much as you have. This is enough for me to make my report to the church. Go and rest, you've done enough for today."

She didn't protest this time. She quietly put away her writing supplies as John headed for the door with her report. As he reached the door, she spoke up, "Do I have to go back out there?" her voice shook with fear, and he could hear the tears in her voice, "I know that this needs to be kept quiet for now, but we still need to find that *thing's* body. Do I have to go back out there?" She was in full tears by the time she had finished.

"You don't have to leave again until you are ready." John was giving her the most comforting smile that he could, "Daniel can handle the retrieval on his own once he wakes up. You have done more than I could have expected with what you experienced. You just worry about resting for now." This was supposed to be a simple mission for her. Her first experience in the field and she had to witness two men die, and she had to face a creature that would have left him shaken.

To experience this though and maintain enough composure to write the report she did, spoke levels to her tenacity. If she can overcome the fear she experienced, she is going to be able to go far. She wiped her tears as she finished packing her things. Before she left, she turned back to ask him, "Will Daniel be ok?" John nodded his head which seemed to be enough for her. She turned, and John was left alone with her report.

He quietly left through one of the back doors of the guild. As much as he loved carrying on, and talking with his guild, he needed to get this report to the church. Many of the streetlamps had already been lit as the evening twilight slowly faded away. John wore his usually hearty grin as he offered many pleasant greetings along the way. After crossing over the river, he came to the old plaza near the church; the Long Way Home had just put out the last of its lights as he passed.

Back when he was a kid, this was the center of town. Merely a packed down area of dirt where people would gather to trade and sell what they could. Now, stone-paved and surrounded by buildings, this placed had so much life to it that John struggled to remember how it once was. The road north would take him to the church, but his attention was pulled away from his path. Standing nearly in the center of the plaza was Elijah. With him, were two men. Two men that the sight of shook him to his core. Ben and Grant.

It can't be. John's head was pounding, and he had forgot to breath as he stood there staring at the two men who were supposed to be dead. Not only were they present, but neither seem to be injured in the slightest. The part that troubled John the most though is that they were speaking with Elijah. John did his best to maintain a stoic face, but he could feel the blood boiling in his cheeks as he approached the group.

Ben was the first to take notice of his approach. With a beaming smile, he waved at John as he approached, "Good evening master! We were just on our way to report in." The other two took notice of John now. Elijah's face was twisted as though he just had seen something that disgusted him.

"Yes master, we got separated and took a little longer to get home." Grant laughed, "I'm sure we have some sort of punishment coming, don't we?" He asked nervously as John looked from person to person. He had no idea what to make of this whole ordeal. The state of fear the others returned with didn't match how carefree these two seemed to be. Something felt very wrong with this.

"Well you are both here now, that's all that matters. Why don't you two head back to the guild. You can tell me everything after you've had some time to rest." John found his beaming smile once more, "I'm sure you two must be as tired as the others." Ben and Grant exchanged looks of joy. They quickly thanked John as they began to walk away. A sudden sharp voice made them stop in the tracks.

"I'm not finished with them *yet*." Although Elijah's voice was soft, it carried a chill that would make a child run home crying. The two adventurers were shaking as they turned to look back at Elijah, but it was John's face that captured their attention.

The usually cheerful guild master was now frowning. His furrowed brow and near blank expression gave the same eerie feeling that Elijah's voice had given. "If there is something you need to discuss with them *stranger* then it would be best to take it up with me." John's booming voice rang out loud enough that many people passing by, stopped to listen in. "Actually, I've been trying to locate you since you came into town *Let*. Or should I call you by your proper name." John gave a smile as he saw Elijah's face twist at his comment.

"I have no business with your *guild*, or whatever you call your sad attempt at a militia here." Elijah's words were short and struck John through his core. Elijah continued, "My business is with those two. There is something wrong with them." He was now pointing towards Ben and Grant. John kept his eyes focused on Elijah's left hand though. While pointing, Elijah had slid his arm behind his cloak as if to reach for a weapon.

John repositioned his body, placing his hand on the great sword he wore over his shoulder. "If there is something wrong with *my* men, then I will care for them." John took notice of the many people that were now gathering around. A fight here could put one of them in danger. "I know your true name Let." Elijah's turned his glance back to John. "Unless you want to talk about that here in the open, I suggest you follow me back to the guild hall so we can talk."

Elijah moved his hand back where John could see it. He looked between Ben, Grant, and John before glancing around at all the people who had gathered. John could tell that Elijah was aware of the situation he was currently in. He didn't know why Elijah was here, but John knew that he didn't want his identity exposed. As Elijah began to say something, he was interrupted by a shaky and soft voice.

"Now, isn't this an old sight?" The priest suddenly stepped out of the crowd. Elijah tensed at the sight of the old man, but John was relieved for him to be here. The priest continued, "I'm sure everyone has something that needs to be said, so why don't we all head back to the church and talk in private." Elijah was the only one who didn't appear ready to comply. "Now Let, I'm sure there are some people I can write to about your arrival. Yes, a good many people who are probably interested in your whereabouts. Why don't you come along so we can all talk?"

Elijah's hands were clenched. He lips were pressed tight together, but he appeared to agree as he took the lead and headed towards the church. John, Ben, and Grant took mind to keep pace with the old priest. The chapel was empty at this time of the evening. Elijah was pacing around the front of the room. John could tell that Elijah was trying hard to avoid being in the situation he was in, but now he could get some answers about him being here.

The priest was the first to speak up, "There seems to be a lot of excitement today. Let, it has been an awfully long time since you came to visit. What brings you here after all this time?" He smiled as he spoke. Leaning on his cane, the old man's exhaustion apparent.

"I'm here of my own accord, and my business is my own. I crossed these two, and if you truly are a priest of Esprit, you must understand what my business is with them." Elijah spoke with no less tact than he did earlier, "If you truly *are* a priest of the order."

These words hurt John more than they appeared to hurt the priest. "Now that you mention it, there does seem to be something different about these two," the priest spoke as he now approached Ben and Grant. Placing a hand on Grant's face, the priest smiled, "Yes, they are quite tired from their journey. That's it." He laughed, "Why don't you two head on home. John will meet with you should we need anything else." The two quickly thanked the priest and left the chapel. Elijah appeared to hold back some harsh words.

Once the two had left, and the door was firmly shut behind them, the priest turned back towards Elijah, "Now we can speak a bit more freely. I believe you are trying to hide your true name while you are here, Elijah?" He laughed as he spoke these last few words. "I am curious though, as I'm sure John is. Why are you back now after so long? I'm sure there are more important places you should be?"

"I'm not here to discuss my business. Least of all with *you*." He spit at the floor where the priest stood. John couldn't bite his tongue anymore. He quickly drew his sword and was now pointing it at Elijah. Elijah cocked one eyebrow as both his hands disappeared behind his cloak.

"I have had enough of this!" John was screaming, "You disappear without a word to anyone. For ten years, off doing whatever you pleased while everyone here struggled. Every day we struggled, some of us even died. You left behind people that cared about you without even a note to let them know you were alive." John's hands were shaking, and his face was now blood red, "Now you show up out of nowhere, insult the man who took us in, pick a fight with men whom I trust, and worse than any of that, seem to only care about deceiving the one person who was hurt the most by you leaving!"

Elijah was clearly shaken by that last comment. "See!" John spurted out, "Even you know how much it'll hurt Katie to know that you are deceiving her; so why? Why are you here, and why are you trying to hide who you are?" John's heavy breathing was the only that could be heard in the chapel.

Elijah slowly moved his hands out from behind his back. He let out a long breath before he spoke, "I figured you wouldn't have been told anything." He gave a small laugh before continuing, "Ten years ago, I didn't leave. I was taken. The rest of the details aren't important, but after ten years, how do I just tell everyone that I'm still alive?"

"Taken? What do you mean you were taken?"

"Exactly what I said. That night I disappeared was because some group took me in my sleep. Right here. Under *his* watch." Elijah was pointing to the priest as he spoke, "I didn't want to be here, but there is some information that I needed. I was told that the head of the library here was the only person I would be able to get that information. I had no idea it was Katie till I came here. Once I get what I need, I intend to leave. I know that everyone believes I'm dead. I'd rather keep it that way. Everyone has already come to terms with it, and I just feel it'll be easier on everyone to avoid bringing those emotions up."

John couldn't speak, not knowing what to say. His sword had already been lowered as Elijah spoke, but his grip was tighter than before. "I can't accept *that*." John straightened up again, "Why would the priest hide that you were taken? How would you have even gotten away? I just can't believe anything you are saying." John's words were shaking, "I want you out of my town. Tonight. If not, I will make sure Katie and the others know your real name."

Elijah reached his hands behind his back again, "I can't accept that." The tension was thick within the chapel. The candle's flickered around the hall, and John could hear the flames waver each time someone took a breath. He had been so focused on Elijah that he didn't even realize the priest had walked up to him. He placed a gentle hand on John's arm.

"What Elijah is saying is the truth." The priest's words sent a dagger through John's chest, "Ten years ago he was taken, and I was not able to do anything to stop it. You were all still dealing with so much, I didn't want you to be afraid of kidnappers as well." A cold sweat broke over John. He was so uncertain about everything.

He hesitantly sheathed his sword. "I don't think I can process any of this right now." He briskly rubbed his forehead, "Elijah, can I meet with you again once I've had a chance to think about all of this?"

"I don't think I'll be in town longer than the week. I'm at the Unicorn Inn. There are a lot of questions I won't have an answer for though." John simply nodded. "As I said before, I have somewhere to be." Elijah walked towards the door. He didn't look back nor did he say anything else. He was gone, and John was left to ponder what Elijah had just told him.

"There was something else you wished to discuss with me, John." The priest was at John once again.

"I...It had to do with Daniel's return." He handed the report to the priest who quickly began to read through the pages. "Some of it makes no sense to me now though. For the first time in a long time, I'm at a total loss."

"My, that is a first." The priest chortled at his comment as he continued to read. After a few moments of silent reading, the priest handed the papers back to John. "I see where your confusion would come from now." The priest seemed to be lost in a thought.

"I trust Daniel and Christine more than anyone else. If their report is correct, Ben and Grant shouldn't have been here just now." The priest merely nodded in his agreement. "Whatever is going on, I think you should write to the Citadel. I think we need someone with a little more knowledge to assist with this."

Taking a moment more, the priest finally answered, "You trust my judgement more than anyone else's?" John nodded, "Then I say we still wait. The kingdom is flooded with superstitious people. If we don't have concrete proof of what is going on, the Citadel won't take us seriously. It'll be even harder to request help if we get that proof later if we ask them now.

John attempted to protest, but the priest had cut him off, "Knowing Daniel, he'll be awake no more than a day, or two. When he does, why don't the two of you go and retrieve that thing's remains, and we can send the request then. One or two more night isn't going to make that much of a difference if it means we can ensure we get the help we need now will it?"

"I guess not." He stammered as he spoke now. John had given up trying to make sense of all of this. He decided that he would trust the priest as he always had. "I think I'm going to go home and get some sleep for now. Too much has happened today, I need some rest."

"I think that is a grand idea." The priest was patting John's shoulder, "I think I shall do the same." With that, the priest waved goodbye as John headed for the door. *Organize your thoughts!* John repeated to himself. He tried to make sense of everything, but it all felt unreal right now. He was now away from the church when Elijah's voice caught him off guard.

"Don't trust anything that old man says to you." Elijah had stepped out from behind a tree as John approached. "Since you know who I am now, and *he* knows that I'm here, I need to tell you more about everything. Can I meet you at your guild hall tomorrow?"

John needed answers, this could be it. "Yes. When will you come?"

"Around this time. Keep an eye on those two from earlier. They aren't your friends, not anymore."

"What do you mean by that?" John's voice was filled with doubt, but Elijah didn't answer. He was already walking away, "What do you mean by that!?" John repeated out towards Elijah, but he still found no answer. For a moment, Elijah had stopped before turning back to John.

"I'm afraid that some trouble may have followed me here. For that, I am truly sorry. I'll be sure that it follows me when I leave as well." John was left once again without answers.

CHAPTER NINE

THE ESCAPE

"That Bastard!" Katie yelled out as she paced her study. She had been waiting for Let several hours. He had said that he would be there in the evening, but the sun had been down for several hours. She normally wouldn't even meet with normal people late at night.

Looking across her desk, she had gathered every book, report, and artifact she could think of to help with the interpretation of that sphere. Piet was a bizarre language. Not only does it change from God to God, it also changes based on astrology. The same sentence can be translated in more than twelve different ways and they all be correct and incorrect.

Reviewing what information, she did have, she began to wonder if she would be able to figure this one out. She spent three months in the capital once before to work with some of the experts within the Citadel. She was able to get a rough understanding of how the language worked, but she questioned if the so called 'experts' really knew more than she did at this point.

The trick to this would be the Elvish holy language. This was a language derived directly from Piet, and the elves made it easy to interpret by adding in the God's crest with whom it was associated with. They also added in a great number of pictorial glyphs to offset the geometric glyphs. Their goal for the night would be to determine the God for which the glyphs associate.

As Katie continued to read through her books, she began to wonder if he even would show up. She took a break to pull her eyes from the candlelit pages. Her eyes were sore from reading in such dim lighting. As she stood, there came a soft rapping at the door to her study.

Outside the door stood James, appearing to be rather annoyed as he informed Katie that Let was waiting for her downstairs. "You can bring him up. Oh, and make sure to let him know that I've *been* ready for him."

"I—" James wanted to say something, but almost seemed too bothered to say it. "I figured you would be, but he refuses to step foot inside. He demands you meet him at the front door."

No matter how prepared she was, his offensiveness will never cease to amaze her. Annoyed, she followed James back downstairs. She thanked James and informed him that she wouldn't be needing his help any further this evening. Hesitantly, he nodded and proceeded towards the dorms.

When she opened the door, Let stood only a few yards away. His travel pack still on his shoulder, and it looked as though he hadn't bathed since he arrived in town. She felt uncomfortable to think how long it had been since he had bathed. Even so, when he had been here earlier, he hadn't smelled horrible. He mostly smelled of grass.

"What's the point in me coming down here, just for us to go back upstairs?" She asked him hastily before he would have a chance to say anything first.

"Because we aren't staying here. I haven't eaten so you are coming with me." His words were as sharp as normal. *Wait...dinner?* She stood there for a moment trying to gather her thoughts. Noticing that she hadn't moved, he grabbed her arm rather forcefully, "We aren't going to get much done on the artifact tonight. Instead, I'll tell you what I do know about the sphere."

Katie moved her feet to keep pace with him. She was confused by his sudden change. Just that morning, he attempted to keep as much information from her as possible. Instead...it seemed as though she was going to get all the answers she was wanting to get. She smiled as she quickened her pace so that they could get there, curiosity boiling up from within her.

She followed him for a while before they finally arrived at an inn located near the entrance of town. Off the main market road, the Unicorn was always busy. Katie figured this must be where he was staying. She realized that he had still been holding on to her arm, and it was starting to hurt. She shrugged her arm, and he took the cue to let her go.

She could already hear music coming from within the inn. Oeran, the innkeeper, was great at keeping the place lively. As soon as they were in the door, one of the tavern girls had approached them. "Welcome back!" She shouted excitedly, "Just the two of you tonight?"

"Yes, somewhere private if you don't mind." Let stated quickly as he slid the girl several coins.

"Well, at this time of night, a private area is kinda hard to get." She quickly slid the coins in her apron, counting as she did so, "But I think I know a place. Follow me!" She led the two through the main floor and back to the staircase. She led them to the second floor, and all the way towards the end of the hallway.

She tapped several times on the wall. Katie was confused what it was she was doing, but as she was about to ask, the wall suddenly opened to reveal a small staircase. They followed the lady down the stairs to a second tavern area. There were many tables, bar, and the backwall must have been right behind the stage since the music could still be heard in here.

Katie looked to Let, as stoned face as usual. In this hidden area, there were only eight other people, including the barkeep. They were guided to a table off to the side of the room where they took a seat on either side of the table. Before leaving, the tavern girl spoke up again, "You know, Katie, this is the first time I think anyone has seen you out with a man before. Even hidden back here, you'll be the talk of the town come the morning. You two have fun now!" She prodded as she quickly headed back out of the room.

Katie wanted to say something, but the girl was gone before she was able. Nervously she looked around at everyone here. They all seemed to keep to themselves. She was the only one not focused on her own table. "If you keep looking around like that, people will get upset." Let spoke up, "people come here to be left alone, not looked on by a nosy little girl."

"I am not a little girl!" She pouted, bringing her attention back to him.

"Then stop looking around like a kid visiting the Capital for the first time." He said, vexed. She held back the words she wanted to say although her frustration was written well across her face. "I think we finally had that talk about the artifact." Her face straightened up again as he spoke. *Finally, I'll get some answers.*

"Before that though, why have you agreed to tell me about it?" Katie asked quizzically. "Just this morning you wanted to keep as much to yourself as possible."

Let stared for a moment before answering, "I still don't want to tell you much, but some people I was trying to hide from figured out I'm here already. The sooner we figure out the artifact, the sooner I can leave." This wasn't rude, his words almost sounded kind, "As long as I am here, people are in danger. I didn't even want to bring this to you, but according to my master, this was the only place I can trust to bring it."

"Your master? Why did he tell you that I was the only you can trust, and what exactly are you a part of?"

"I think to answer that, I will need to give you a bit of a long story." She nodded her head as if she were ready to listen. As she did though, the tavern girl from earlier was back with some ale and food. She gave Katie a quick wink as she walked away. Let waited for her to be back out of the room before continuing.

"I can't tell you exactly what it is I do, or what I am a part of. What I can tell you is that my master and I have been tracking a dangerous cult. Their goal is to resurrect Quietus."

"Wait!" Katie suddenly interjected. Her eyes were wide and shaky, "you mean *The* Quietus? The God of Death?" Let nodded, "But...the other God's defeated him, right? The God's War was to stop him, wasn't it?"

"It's impossible to kill a God. Even all the other God's together couldn't do it. All they accomplished during the God's War was sealing him away. This cult I've been following thinks that this artifact is a clue to releasing him."

"If he were to come back, couldn't it mean the end of the world?" Katie was enthralled by the story.

"That is why my master stole this from the cult. They recovered it from some hidden part of the those ruins you claim to know so much about." Katie's eyes quickly glanced away before looking back. "My master believed that the cult may have contacts within the Citadel. He told me that the head of the library here was someone that I can trust. I didn't know who it was until I met you. Unfortunately, they know that I am here now and there is a chance that you could be in danger for it." He paused as he took a drink of ale. "I'm sorry that I made you a part of all this." His apology was sincere.

"You may not know much about me, but I crave for something exciting to happen." Katie exclaimed as she downed her ale in a single drink. "This place is too stuffy! I'm excited that your master sent this to me." Her face was glowing with excitement as the barkeep brought her another ale. "So, you think that if we can figure out what this artifact is that we may be able to stop this cult, right?"

Let seemed bewildered by her excitement for this. He nodded to her as he took a drink from his own ale. His eyes were looking behind her now. She began to turn her head, but he quickly stopped her by grabbing hold of her hand. "I believe that several of the cultists have found us." He said at nearly a whisper, "don't look their way. Let's just continue. I won't bring up anything they don't already know." She nodded.

"So, there is something very important you need to know about this cult which is why it is hard to find people that I can speak with." Let continued, slightly louder than he was before. "We don't know if it's just one person or several of them, but they have a certain skill that allows them to make their numbers as big or small as they choose."

"What is that?" Katie asked, trying to keep focused on Let. It felt as though eyes were burning into her back. The presence of those men changed the atmosphere of the room.

"They can use necromancy." Katie started laughing without thinking. Looking at the angry look on Let's face, she quickly regained her composure.

"Magic hasn't existed in the kingdom since the time of the elves. Even then, necromancy was a magic that people refused to mess with. It was hard to control and devoured many mages. There was an entire book that I recovered from the elves which talked about it as well as other dark magics." Katie was trying to stifle her laughter again, "Has all of this just been a joke? I'm starting to think this was all some sort of a prank now."

Let didn't appear surprised by her reaction. He reached into his pack and placed the sphere on the table with a loud thud. Katie's face turned with surprise, "Why did you pull that out here?"

"If this is all some sort of a joke, then why does it matter?" He sat there with his stone face, waiting for her response. As she stared confused for a moment, she began to push the sphere towards him again.

"Maybe it's not a joke," she seemed unsure of herself now, "but, if what you are saying is true," she hesitated, "why would you just pull this out. If there are people here from that cult, why would you flash this in front of them?" The more she spoke, the more concerned she grew. She began to wonder if this all might be true.

"I owe you one other apology." He said as he looked passed her. He downed what was left of his drink before speaking again, "I actually used you and the sphere tonight as bait to lure these two out." He was staring intently at the two men that he claimed were from this cult he talked about. Despite his warning, she turned to look their way.

When she saw the two men, she quickly ripped her hand away from his. "You have been lying to me, haven't you?" There was no laughter in her voice this time. "There is no cult, there is no one following you. You're just some crazed guy." She seemed to gather her thoughts for a moment. "I need to leave." She quickly got out of her seat and headed for the door.

The two men who had been sitting behind them were not strangers to Katie. Ben and Grant were two of the adventurers who traveled with Daniel often. They had even escorted her to the Capital several times. For Let to accuse those two of being part of some cult, made her feel sick to her stomach. As she quickly headed to the door, Ben grasped her wrist firmly. His grip was tight as her hand began to turn white, and his skin was cold as ice.

"I'm sorry Katie, we can't have you leaving just yet." *This isn't Ben's voice.* His voice was cold and lacked any sign of the kindhearted man that Ben was. Her mind raced as she tried to understand what was happening.

The barkeep shouted out towards the group as he took notice to the tension, "It'd be best if you let the girl go now. I won't warn you a second time." He was now brandishing a large club as to threaten. With a smile, Grant stood. His arm moved faster than she was able to watch. With a thud, the barkeep had a dagger buried in his throat. The man crumpled to the floor as the other patrons took notice of this.

Ben shoved Katie to the ground as he and grant quickly threw several more blades. After merely seconds, it was only the four of them still alive in this hidden room. All the while, Let sat at the table with his hand firmly placed on top of the sphere. Katie crawled away from the two men she once saw as friends as the bitter truth rolled over her.

"Now this simply won't do." Let began to stand as he spoke, "If everyone is dead, how will your golden boy guild master believe that I didn't do it?" His words were hollow.

"We tried so hard to stop you, but you were just a mad man." Ben spoke with fake sorrow in his voice, "We followed him since he seemed dangerous, but we just couldn't stop him! He even got poor Katie." Grant gave a devious smile at Katie who was still on the ground. She now had crawled back to where Let had been standing.

Grant's hand quickly moved as he stared at Katie. Time moved slow for her in this instant. She saw the sudden flash of metal as the blade left Grant's hand. A wooden mug fell before her, blocking the sight of the blade. With a thud, the mug flew off to the side with the dagger buried into it. Let was now past her. In each hand, he held a beautiful dagger. A ruby crested the base of each, and the handles were delicately carved in many patterns that were unfamiliar to her. The blades had a small curve towards their ends.

Let drove one of the blades deep within Grant's chest who quickly crumpled to the ground. Leaving the blade there, he turned his attention to Ben who had quickly jumped away from him. He had his dagger's in his hand now as he adjusted his balance to strike back at Let. Before he could though, Let had grabbed ahold of his hand. His moves weren't perfect as Gram's blade sliced Let's palm open, however Let took no notice of his wound.

Let drove his dagger into gram's shoulder and drove the man into the ground. Watching this, Katie noticed something unusual. Let's hand was bleeding, but neither Ben nor Grant were bleeding. Grant was lifeless, but Ben began to laugh. "You think that you can stop us? I'll let you have these puppets since you exposed them, but you haven't stopped a thing!" Let pulled the dagger from Ben's shoulder and drove it back into his chest. With a single exhalation, Ben too stopped moving.

Katie was struggling to gather her thoughts. *Ben, and Grant. They were friends, right?* Let withdrew his daggers from the bodies and returned them to their sheaths behind his back. Katie's vision began to blur, as tears filled her eyes. She had seen people die before, but she couldn't even think now. Let had reached out to offer her a hand up, but Katie was still in shock from everything. He was now kneeling next to one of the other bodies. His face was emotionless. Blank. Empty. There was no word she could find to describe it. It was as though killing those two meant nothing to him.

"It seems as though the cult really does intend to make its move here." Let examined the wounds of each person in the bar before he returned to Katie. "I brought you into more than I expected. After this, we are going to have to leave Pneu if we are going to solve this artifact."

Katie was finally able to find her words as she spoke quickly, "You just sat there. They killed everyone and you didn't even try to help." She sounded as confused as she was angry. "Why would I go anywhere with you?"

He didn't answer with words. He grabbed her shaking hands and pulled her to her feet. He led her to the nearest body and showed her the knife wound. Just like with Ben and Grant, there was no blood. "I can show you everyone in this room, but they are all the exact same."

"What does it mean?"

"It means that they knew I would be here. They set all of this up to try and show me the power they already hold over this town." He retrieved the sphere from their table and returned it to his bag. "The next time they attack will be to kill, and unfortunately you are a part of this now."

Katie could hear the remorse in his voice. "I'm...a part of what exactly? This cult, this artifact, whatever you are a part of, I don't get it."

"I can't explain it to you well, but what I can say is that we need to solve this artifact. We can't do that here anymore." Let thought for a moment before turning back to her with a snap, "We are going to the ruins where this was recovered. There we can hopefully figure this out and bring an end to this."

"What if I say no? What if I tell you that I refuse to leave here?" Katie was shaken from everything.

"At this point you don't have a choice. If you stay you will die. This is my fault, and I am sorry. Right now, though, I need you." Let reached his hand out to Katie, "Together we can solve this. Alone, I am useless."

Katie was thrown aback by his statement. She knew that line. She heard them so many times that they were engraved into her very dreams. He had to have read it from her book that she found him with that morning but hearing him say it reminded her once again of the familiarity she felt with him.

"If we are going to do this, I'm going to need a few things from the library." She reached out and took his hand. Although she was fearful of what will come, she couldn't help but shake the excitement which grew within her.

"I already have two horses ready in the stable, lets collect your things and be gone before anyone knows that we've left." With that, the two were off. Without telling anyone, without knowing what she would find, without even knowing what kind of danger she will face, Katie found herself at the start of an adventure.

ら

CHAPTER TEN
MISSING PERSONS

Daniel felt himself fading in and out of conscience for some time. Each time he was able make out undistinguishable voices, and occasionally he had been able to feel a soft hand holding his own. Pain surged through his body that would quickly force him back into his restless and endless sleep.

He didn't know how much time had passed since he had first fallen asleep, nor could he even remember how. *Christine!* Unable to remember why, he knew she was in danger. His drifting mind had begun to ask all the why's and what's, but he could not put any of it together. He felt himself slipping away further than just sleep. *What was happening to me?* The only clear question he could find for himself.

For the first time in what felt like an eternity, Daniel was able to open his eyes. The burning light that shone through a nearby window made it hard for him to see. He could feel the soft linens of an unfamiliar bed, as he listened for any signs that could help him understand where he was. He could hear muffled voices from somewhere far off, but from within the room, the sudden sound of a metallic object hitting the floor sent a sudden jolt through his entire body.

The surge of adrenaline which now fueled him, forced him upright within the bed. In an instant he was able to see, hear, and feel as though he had been awake long before he had. His now clear vision was able to see that he was in the infirmary of the guild hall. The muffled voices were coming from what was probably the main hall, and John's booming voice was the most notable of the bunch.

All the other sounds and sights were meaningless to him as he focused in on the source of the metallic clank that had forced him out of his haze. His eyes needed no time to recognize the pale-skinned girl standing nearby. With reddened eyes and a tear-soaked face, Christine stood there cupping her face as she watched Daniel. The startling sound had come from her dropping a pitcher of water which had spilled out around her feet.

Before he was able to say anything, she had leaped across the floor and threw her arms around him. Daniel did not hesitate to move his arms around her waist. For a moment, he enjoyed knowing that she was safe. As soon as he had thought this, all the memories of their encounter and what led him to this state flooded back to him. The fear that the creature had left in him, unconsciously forced his grip on Christine tighter as if to make sure she never left his grip again.

Ow! Christine's outcry of pain made him aware of just how tightly he had been gripping her. He loosened his grip on her as the two slowly separated. "How long was I here?" Seemed to be the first question he was able to ask.

"You've been asleep for three days now." Christine managed to say as she begun to quell her tears. "Honestly Daniel, I thought I was the one who's supposed to worry you!" Her voice had retained some of its vigor as she joked with him.

Daniel let out a small chuckle, "Honestly, this sort of treatment is nice every once in a while. Maybe I should get hurt more often if it means waking up to such care." He felt Christine break away from him as she brought her fist down on his head. She may have struck as hard as she could, but due to her frailness, the strike wasn't much. He looked up to her to find she was crying again.

"I don't want you to joke like that." She spoke through her tears, "If not for Madame Jolie you would have died." She had punched him several more times as she cried out, "You mean everything to me. I don't ever want to hear you joke about getting hurt again. Do you hear me? I will kill you myself if you try to go and die on me again."

Grabbing her wrists, Daniel had stopped the gentle bludgeoning long enough for him to steal a kiss from his distraught wife. "I promise not to joke about it again." Daniel reassured her after she had begun to calm down. "What all happened while I was asleep? Were you and Stephanie able to report everything when we got here?"

Christine seemed hesitant to answer. Her face read of something that would only lead to him becoming disconcerted, and she appeared to be searching for a way to tell him that wouldn't upset him. "I think you should take a bath and get something to eat first." She had chosen to deflect his question entirely.

"I would rather hear about what you don't want to tell me instead." His face now stern, Christine turned away from him, ashamed that she couldn't give him a decent answer. Before he could probe for answers any further, John's booming voice rang out loud enough for him to hear.

"I'm tired of listening to your excuses!" He sounded enraged by something he was told. It was very rare for John to be angered like this. "Katie is missing and should be more important than some stupid festival!"

Christine's sudden change in expression told Daniel that this was what she couldn't find words to tell him about. Katie, Christine, and John were Daniel's oldest friends. Something happening to any of them was more painful than the constant drifting of nothingness he had just experienced.

Christine had placed her hand on Daniel's shoulder after he had quickly risen to his feet. "Don't get too worked up yet! You haven't healed yet. Let John handle this, please." Her gentle plea fell on deaf ears as he gently pushed past her to head where John's voice was echoing from.

The infirmary was located at the top of a short stairwell at the westernmost corner of the guildhall. Once Daniel had stepped out of the door, he was able to see the hall in its entirety. The front door of the hall led in from the northern wall, and at the southern end of the hall was the head table where the city council, minus Katie, was currently meeting.

From what Daniel could see, John had been yelling at Bryant, which was not a surprise to him. Daniel had slammed open the infirmary door so loud that the council had stopped and were now staring up at him.

"Daniel!" John suddenly burst out as he ran across the hall to greet him. The greeting was both cheerful and sorrowful. "How are you feeling? It's unusual for any of us to have to worry about you for change!"

He tried to play off his tension and anger with a joke, but the strain in his voice was as apparent as the furrow in his brow.

"You no longer have to worry about me," he stated flatly, "What happened to Katie?" John could hear the frustration in his voice. Instead of protest, John invited Daniel to join the council for their discussion.

"*He* is not part of the council and has no place here." Bryant spat out as they approached the table. "The council has too many kids on it to begin with." He must have been arguing with John quite a bit to be as worked up as he was.

"It is my understanding that he is just as involved with all this as the rest of us." It was Hugo who spoke up this time, "He might be able to provide some valuable insight to the current events." He gave a wink to Daniel as Bryant simply huffed himself silent.

Daniel did not take a seat as he spoke, "I've been asleep for days and Katie is missing. Please tell me what has been happening." Silence followed as they all exchanged looks. John forced Daniel to sit before he started.

"It's Elijah." Seemed to be the only words John could find.

"Elijah?" Daniel was shocked to hear that name again after so long. "You mean—"

"Yes. The same Elijah. He came back the day before you did." John interjected.

Daniel's mind was spinning to the thought of him returning. After ten years with no sign, he had assumed Elijah had died. "So, did Katie just run off with him? I mean they used to talk about that a lot when we were kids." As soon as he asked this though, he knew there was more to it. John wouldn't be this upset if that was what occurred.

"*My* thoughts exactly!" Spouted Bryant, "Which is why we should just stay focused on the festival. She'll come back like she always does. That girl has no sense of responsibility. You all know this." Bryant was frustrated that everyone keeps forgetting how Katie repeatedly runs off without telling anyone.

John slammed his fist on the table as he spoke, "It's not just that!" His breathing was heavy as he spoke. "The same day that Elijah returned, twelve different people reported that they thought someone was following them. A shadow as they described it. Every one of those people went missing the same night that Katie and Elijah disappeared."

Daniel silently took this in as John continued.

"The night you returned, Daniel, I found him speaking with Ben and Grant which had just been reported killed, and even later that night a disturbance had been reported at the Unicorn Inn. Elijah and Katie had been spotted running from the Inn where several murders had occurred with Ben and Grant's bodies being found among the dead. This was the night they, as well as all the others, went missing. 14 people have been missing for three days now."

"I watched them die!" Daniel was on his feet again. His fists were clenched so tight that his nails drew several drops of blood. "There is no way that it was Ben and Grant!" His mind raced as he tried to process what he was being told. "Why would Elijah return after so long, and why would he be involved with all of this? How do we know it was actually him?"

"It was him." This time it was the priest who spoke up, "I'm sorry I never told you all before, but several years ago I was informed that he had arrived at the Eight-Faith's church in the Capital. Although he was offered shelter, he continued to travel on his own after this. The churches have all been tracking him since." He paused to take a shallow breath before continuing. "Every place he has been sighted; the same string of events follows. Disturbances are reported, people go missing, people being attacked as they travel. He is linked to them every time, and the occurrences always end when he leaves. The church believes that he is in league with a dangerous cult that has been traveling around."

Daniel processed this as fast as he was able, but there was so much that he didn't understand. "Even if Elijah has been involved with this, how can we just say that its him? I mean, as a kid he looked out for us more than anyone."

At Daniel's remark, John landed a strong punch in the middle of their table. It cracked and buckled under the force of his blow. Papers that had been on the table now littered the floor around the table, now split in two.

"This all seems like nonsense," Bryant was quick to jump in, "magic left the world with the elves, and it seems to me like John's hatred for Elijah runs deeper than current events. Just like a child, you are blinded by your own rage."

"So, in your opinion we are just making this all up?" John looked as though he was ready to strike Bryant.

"In *my* opinion. You are all fools jumping at bedtime stories. Katie met an old friend, and she ran off with him like she always does. All the *missing people* you mentioned, are from other villages. They just got spooked and went back home. The only danger anyone is in, is from the inexperience and childlike behavior of certain members of this council. Hugo, please. Help me talk some sense into these children and fools."

Hugo did not speak up initially after being addressed. He thought and chose his words carefully as he often did. The council was used to this and gave him time to speak. "I think there is too much uncertainty with everything that has occurred. There could be superstition playing on John and Father Bernard's mind that has caused them to read too much into these events." At this, John looked betrayed by Hugo's words. "However, to ignore all these events and writing them all off as coincidence would also be unwise. We should search for Katie, and we should send word to the Citadel if we haven't done so." Bryant huffed once more in place of words having no argument for the man.

"I have already sent word to the Citadel." Father Bernard spoke up, "I did so the morning after finding the bodies at the Unicorn. As I stated before, Elijah is already wanted by the Church."

"There we have it." Hugo's words were soft, "Speculating on everything will get us nowhere. For now, we stick to the plans that we have already made. Finding Katie and Elijah will be the only way we can get any truth behind the matter. Until then, there is no point in getting the people upset. Can we all agree to this?" One by one, each member of the council agreed to this plan.

Without another word being spoken, Father Bernard, Hugo, and Bryant gathered their scattered papers and left the guildhall. Christine, who had been silent the entire time, finally spoke up to the other two, "I didn't want to say this with everyone here, but when I had gone to the room Elijah was staying in, I was able to get his scent. Daniel, I can say without a doubt it is him. It has changed some, but his scent is still his."

Daniel stood and gently patted Christine on the head, "If nothing else, I can at least accept that. Thank you." He smiled to her as he began to place his thoughts in order. Elijah was back, and Katie was with him. As long as he knew that, he could figure out the rest when he found them. He looked to John who was still lost in his own thoughts.

Stoic, John stood there still enough to be believed as a statue. So much so, that when he spoke it had startled Christine, "These last few days, I can't seem to keep my anger in check." He stared at the table he had split, "I don't like being this way, and I am sorry you woke up to see this Daniel."

Daniel had moved to John's side and placed a hand on his shoulder, "I remember the promise you had made. Let's go and find Katie. Some answers would do us all good."

"Thank you." John was smiling again, "Where do you suggest we start?"

"Well, our guild network will be able to search faster than we can. Send a message out to every village we have a guild house in that Katie is missing. If they are still in the western providence, we'll have a location on her within a week." In agreement, the three of them solidified their plan, and their search began.

CHAPTER ELEVEN
THE ROAD TO KEND

Katie panted as she attempted to catch her breath. She didn't know how long she had been running, and in the pitch-black night she was completely lost. She rested with her back against a tree as she listened for any sign of her pursuer. As she rested there, she became painfully aware of the large gash in her arm.

She resisted the urge to cry out as she tried to put pressure on her wound but lacking any material which she could use as a bandage, the result was just more pain. An eerie silence swept across the forest. Even the sound of her own breathing had disappeared.

She began to run again as the chill of the soundless, darkened forest pierced her to her very soul. It felt as though someone had tripped her as her foot caught and she fell. She attempted to pull herself free, but whatever had caught her only seemed to squeeze her leg tighter. Her head began to feel dizzy from the blood loss, and she tried to scream out for help. She screamed as loud as she could, but this world had become a void where noise was not allowed to live.

Somewhere to her side, she thought she had seen movement. She tried to look for whatever had caught her eye, but the harder she stared, the darker the forest became. A sound finally crept out, but it was not from her. The soft crunching noise came from somewhere far off yet nearby. She looked every way that she was able, but the cracking echoed as though it was coming from all sides.

Along with the crunching, she was able to hear whispering. The words were indistinguishable. She felt as though something was staring at her as she laid in her panic. Laughing. A new sound had joined the others as a man was laughing. It was quiet but droning. Paired with the snapping and whispering she was now surrounded by mixed sounds that had no meaning while she laid on the ground. Crying, she covered her ears which only made the sounds even louder.

As suddenly as everything had started, the noises stopped, and she was once again sitting in a soundless void. Whatever had grabbed her leg was also gone, and the wound to her arm had disappeared. Thinking the worst of it was over, she raised her head. "Boo!"

Terror filled her soul as she was now staring into a black mask enveloped in purple flame. The voice was stabbing and comprised of thousands of voices. Her ears rang and bled as the many voices began to laugh, cry, scream, break, curse, whisper. She attempted to crawl away from cacophony of mad sounds, but as she did, hundreds of lesions covered her arms, and she collapsed in tears.

She could do nothing but watch as the mask, and voices crept towards her. No longer floating, the false face was on the ground so that she was forced to stare into a black abyss. She wanted to scream. She tried to scream but was still unable to make a sound. She closed her eyes as she gave up.

She felt the hands as they crept around her arms. They began to lift her body from the ground, terror set so deep in her that she didn't notice the sounds dissipate. The hands began to shake her back and forth, and a familiar voice forced her eyes to open again.

Katie realized that she was no longer in her dream, and it was Let who was shaking her. She could feel her eyes swollen from crying, and her arms felt numb as she remembered the pain she experienced. It was nothing more than a dream, but the terror which had filled her remained. Without thinking about it, she quickly threw her arms around Let, and she began to cry with her face buried in his dusty shoulder.

He didn't protest, and he allowed her to stay like this until she was able to calm down. In the three days they had now been traveling together, Katie has had a different nightmare each night. Each time it had always been Let who would bring her out of those horrid dreams. They changed each night, but the purple burning mask was always present. After calming down, she told Let the details of this dream to which he sat silently as he listened.

"How familiar are you with the church of Mesmu and the dream world?" Let sounded far away as he asked her.

"I know the same as anyone. Mesmu is the God of dreams, he resides in a world made just for him, and you pray to him for peaceful dreams." Katie was perplexed to be getting asked such a simple question, "I don't really believe in all of that though." Let remained silent as she spoke. "People have good dreams, and they have bad dreams. I don't believe there is some spiritual force behind it all. If you are going to try and tell me to pray to him and ask for peace, I'm not going to do it." This was a speech she has had to give countless times over. Father Bernard was always trying to push her to follow in the faith of the churches.

"Even if you don't believe, you should at least believe in the power of faith." Let began to search through his bag as he talked. "If you believe in something enough, there will be truth to it." He had found what he was searching for and withdrew a strange looking doll, and he handed it to Katie.

"What is this for?"

"If you believe that it does, it can keep nightmares away." He smiled as though he was making fun of her.

"I wake up terrified, and the most you can do is make jokes?" She threw the doll back to him before turning away.

"It's not a joke. I know you don't believe, but dreams work in a very special way." She looked back at him, and he was holding the doll as though it was sentimental to him. "Unlike the elves, a human's body was not created to be able to use spiritual energy. We still create it though, just like any other living creature. Therefore, Mesmu and the dream world are important. His creatures come to us in our sleep, when our consciousness touches the border of his world, and they absorb excess spiritual energy that is created. If for some reason though, we produce large amounts of it, stronger dreams are needed to absorb it all, and those are nightmares."

Katie had studied each of the churches, but the church of Mesmu had the least regarding literature. The story he was telling her, it is not one she had ever heard before. She was absorbed in his story as he spoke.

"Even if you don't believe it. You are producing a lot of spiritual energy for some reason. This doll is sort of like a summoning. If it is on your person when you sleep, it'll draw older creatures from the dream world. Ones that can absorb your energy without giving you nightmares."

"Even if I believed in all of this, why would I want some creature taking energy from me? Would it not be better if they just left us alone?"

"Your body can only hold so much. Since humans can't use spiritual energy, and we don't have tools to get rid of it, we need the dream creatures. Otherwise, our body would overflow, and our souls would perish."

"How is it you know so much about this? This isn't anything I learned in the few books I have about Mesmu and his church?"

"I found one of their church's while traveling. Me and my master had stayed there for a while, and I managed to learn quite a bit from them. That is where I got this doll. I needed it for a while, but I think you need it more now." He once again handed the doll to her.

Katie still refused to believe in fairytales, but there was something mesmerizing about the doll. "I've heard you mention your master a few times now. Where is he?" This was a question she had meant to ask a few times, but the moment never seemed right for her to ask.

"You should try and get some more sleep. We'll be in Kend tomorrow, and you will need some rest." He had completely avoided her question. She wanted to ask again, but he had already returned to his own bedroll and her time to ask was gone. The last few nights they have camped out away from the main road. Usually in what seemed like little dens made of foliage. Anyone passing by would have thought it was all a part of the tree line during the night.

She laid back down in her own bedroll, and she had stared at the doll for a while thinking about how strange all of this was. She looked back over to Let who appeared to be fast asleep.

"Let" her voice was a whisper, but he didn't answer back. "You probably are already back to sleep, but I needed to tell you something." She again waited for an answer that he didn't give. "I just wanted to say that you remind me of someone from my past. When we were kids something bad had happened to us all and…well, let's just say I owe him a lot." Katie could feel the tears welling up inside as she spoke about him.

"I hope one day I'll be able to see him again. The others were all angry that he had left us all, but I know that whatever his reasons were, they were important. I just want him to know that we all turned out okay, and if he ever feels guilty for leaving us, he shouldn't. We all depended on him too much anyway." She gave a small chuckle to her last remark.

"Ever since you showed up, I haven't been able to stop thinking about him again. You feel so familiar that it hurts sometimes." Katie trailed off on her last few words as she readied herself for the question she was leading up to. "Is it you, Elijah?" She waited, but no reply came from Let. She held the doll close as the pain of knowing Elijah was gone set itself again. "I'll just go to sleep then. It was stupid of me to think about it all again."

"If he is still out there," Let's voice made her jump, "I'm sure he has been thinking about you too. Now go to sleep."

It wasn't the answer she had wanted, and she began to feel embarrassed by what she had said. She laid there in silence until she was able to fall asleep again. The rest of the night was peaceful, and if she did dream, she was not aware of it.

She was awoken suddenly by Let. He had placed his hand over her mouth, and he was signaling for her to remain quiet. He removed his hand, and he had pointed towards the horses which he had already prepped to move. It was still night outside and earlier than they had left the prior mornings. Something seemed off and as she quickly tied her bedroll to the saddle, she heard voices coming from road.

"Are you sure they are here? I don't see anything!"

"Yes! Trust me, this one can find anyone. Must have been a hunter before turning."

"I think you are just full of yourself. Admit it! We lost them."

"And what do you think will happen if we go back and tell *him* that?"

"I...I guess you are right. Any idea where they went?"

"No. it's like they just disappeared when they got here. Maybe we should check the trees nearby."

Katie could hear the two men begin to shuffle their way towards their hiding place. Let pulled on her arm and motioned for her to climb on her horse. "Ride to Kend, I'll catch up before you get there." Let's voice was quieter than a whisper, but she began to worry for him. The moment she was in the saddle, Let slapped her horse on while shouting.

As soon as she broke through the den, she spotted the two men that had been speaking before. Neither of them looked exceptional, nor did they have any features that would make them stand out. They both wore black robes, and they had gold medallions around their necks.

They had been startled by her sudden appearance. As she was passing, a black creature seemingly appeared out of thin air. It was unlike anything she had ever seen before, and it let out a shriek that sent chills through her body. Focused on her, they didn't notice Let come out of hiding. With the sound of metal striking metal, Katie was too far away to see what had happened.

She did as she was told and continued to ride towards Kend. They were only a few hours from the village so she figured that she would be able to see it as the sun was rising. She hadn't heard anything for some time, and decided it was safe enough to slow her horse down to a trot. She was worried about him, but she kept her pace forward.

As the sun began to rise, her earlier prediction had been correct. She stopped for a moment as she looked over the town. It had been several years since she last visited, but it appeared as unchanged as always. She turned to look behind her in hope of spotting Let. Facing the rising sun though proved difficult to see.

"I thought I told you to keep riding?" Let's statement caught Katie by surprise. She turned her horse back towards Kend as he somewhat overtook her.

"How did you—"

"I rode through the forest, I got ahead of you before realizing you slowed down." He appeared amused that he had caught her off guard. "Come, we are almost to the city. The sooner we can figure this out, the sooner we can get those guys off our back." Watching the gleeful way he trotted ahead, her question from the night before burned deeper in her mind.

Ϙ

Chapter Twelve

KEND

K end, locally known as the textile capital of the west, was busy as usual as the pair made their way into the city. Katie loved being able to visit. Partly due to her celebrity status within the city, but also because she loved the culture of the people here. A constant flow of traders and shops selling their variants of fabrics, clothing, dyes, gave the main street so much color that merchants would swear it could be seen from clouds. Nowhere else in the country could replicate the craftmanship of Kend fabric, which made them coveted even in the Capital.

Despite the cheery nature of the city and its people, Katie found her travel partner to be in rather poor spirits. He tended to be off-putting, *but how can he still be his usual gloomy self in such a beautiful town?* Every so often, someone would approach the two in exuberant spirits as many people within the city recognized Katie offering out greetings and presents. The more this went on, the worse Let seemed to be.

"If you keep glooming around like that," Katie spoke sharply, "people are going to start questioning my company!" Her status in this town was something that she held very dearly. She had quite an experience here several years back when she had first discovered the elvish ruins.

"We were supposed to keep as low a profile as we can while we're here." His response was short, "Both the guild and our *friends* will find us in a day with all the attention you draw." Now that they were in a city again, all the coldness returned to his voice.

"I think I can take care of the guild for us if it'll lighten your mood some!" she stated matter of fact. She puffed out her chest as if waiting for him to praise her.

"Good. You aren't completely useless then." His sarcastic response succeeded in upsetting Katie, "I have some business to take care of with the church then while you get that settled. Meet me at the Silk Fur Inn when you are done." Like that, he rode off ignoring the angry remarks she shot off to him for his insolent comment.

She managed to quell her anger rather quickly once he was no longer in sight. After all, it was mostly to get a rise out of him for a change. Returning to her prior good spirits, she rode off to the local guild hall. Substantially smaller than the main hall, it was still large in comparison to the buildings surrounding it. The buildings of Kend tended to match its populace. Brightly colored roofs and each one built in a different style. The local guild hall though stood out in its own right.

Towards the northern most part of town, stuffed between a domed house colored in a variety of pastels and a squat blue building stood a large two-floor log cabin. This cabin had no paint to cover the natural wood of its structure, and the tin roof shone brightly as the sun beat down over top of it. The hall had grown since her last visit, but it still had the same feel to it.

There was a constant flow of people going through the front doors, even more so than usual. "With the recent events," a loud voice boomed out from behind her making Katie nearly fall from her horse, "we've been ordered to restrict any unescorted travel." Katie turned and was met by a familiar face with a rather frustrated look. "Something about a missing girl and strange man as I recall."

"Rufus!" Katie was more than excited to see her old friend. Although, the look on his face informed her that he was not equally excited to see her, "I was on my way to see you!"

"Katie," His voice was stern as he prepared to lecture her, "every guild hall in the west has been put on high alert. The word is that you have been kidnapped by a dangerous man, and that your life is in peril danger." Katie knew that John would be upset with her just leaving, but this is not the first time she had done so. She did not understand why he was making this time a big deal. "More importantly, he ordered us to take you into immediate custody regardless of what you say!"

Katie couldn't believe how strict John was being about this. He was treating her like a child who's run away from home. Even if the latter is true, she is still an adult capable of taking care of herself. Rufus continued before she could interrupt though, "Despite what John says though," his voice softened, "I've never known you to be the one needing rescue." His smile gave her some reassurance that he wasn't quite ready to give in to John's order. "I am glad that you are safe, but before I let you go on about your way, I need to know what is going on. John's letter made it sound as though some really bad things are happening." Relief turned to concern as Rufus raised his question.

"It's hard to really answer that." Katie was struggling to find a way to explain things to him. She barely believed the truth even having seen what she had. As she attempted to find words to put to her thoughts, she could see Rufus tense up as he looked past her. Approaching, was Let.

"I thought you said that you would take care of things on this end?" Let's frustration was apparent in his voice. By now, Rufus understood that this was the man from John's letter and drew his sword. He trusted Katie, but he wasn't about to take chances on a stranger.

"If you are the traveler by the name of Let, we have been ordered to place you under immediate arrest." His words were calm but sharp. "I would prefer to avoid violence so would you kindly come with me?"

For a moment, the two men stared one another down. The tension of their two strong wills made Katie's skin crawl. She knew she needed to intervene before they collided any further. "Rufus, please! This man hired me to assist him with the ruins." Katie had dismounted and placed a hand on his raised arm. "I know that I shouldn't have ran off like I did, but I need you to trust me."

Let refused to back down from his glare. Rufus felt uneasy staring at this man, "Katie, I trust you, you know that I do. This man though, his eyes tell me that he is followed by trouble." Katie was worried. She had known Rufus since he moved here from the Capital two years ago. Nothing shook this man. However, he was here now with a shaken voice. "We have been given strict orders to take you into immediate custody." He managed to put his voice together enough to issue a formal order to Let.

Katie quickly turned her attention to Let hoping that he would back down enough for them to speak. She didn't notice before, but his eyes had hardened over. Stiff and focused, he appeared ready to fight as though his life depended on it. Sitting high upon his horse still, he looked larger and more awe-inspiring than Rufus's natural large frame. She didn't understand where his apparent anger came from. Instead of words, she grasped his leg.

Let was shaken from his murderous trance with a sharp pull on his pants. With a click of his tongue, he broke his glare with Rufus. Katie felt a flood of relief spread through her body sensing the immediate danger was gone. *What made him tense up the way he did?* She began to wonder. At the same time, Rufus too lowered his guard.

"I have a letter to present to you which should clear some things up." Let's response was callous as he tossed a sealed envelope to Rufus. Rufus quickly grabbed the letter. Breaking the seal, he quickly read through the contents several times, each time murmuring quietly to himself.

"I'm sorry to have doubted you," Rufus's entire demeanor had changed after returning the letter. Sword sheathed, he offered a quick bow to Let and offered quick apologies. "Anything you need from us; we will gladly oblige." Suddenly turning his attention to Katie, "You appear to have made a very unusual friend Katie. I never should have doubted your safety." Katie was dumbfounded by how quickly events had played out. The questions she had just continued to pile up. Before she could ask her first one, Let began ordering out demands.

"I'm glad we came to such a quick understanding. All we need is for you to hold off on informing John that we are here. Once we leave, you can send the letter."

"Is that really all you need?" Rufus sounded unsure as he spoke.

"Yes, Katie and I's business is rather short, and I planned to speak with John after this anyway so it will work out well for me to meet him on the road." With a bow, Rufus quickly acknowledged the request and set off towards the guild hall. Katie stared dumbfounded towards Let. "His look tells me that he was born in the capital. Probably served in the army as well. I have some old favors from the Capital I never cashed in. That's all the letter was." Let spoke as though he could hear the thoughts pouring from Katie's mind. "How long have you known that man though?"

His question had thrown off Katie's train of thought. *Why does it matter how long I have known him?* "Around two years." She answered quickly. "why?"

"Just…curious is all. Does he seem any different today than usual?"

"No, other than the fact that he seemed extremely nervous about you for some reason." This was true. Katie had never once seen him that scared. Of anyone. "Did John really make you out to be that dangerous?"

"No." He spoke calmly for the first time since arriving in the city. "The two are unrelated. I'll explain more when we are out of the streets. We need to head for the inn."

"If it is alright, there is a family I would like to see first." Katie's request had come quite suddenly as she had already planned to see them before meeting up again. "They are the oldest friends I have here in town. They'd be heartbroken if they heard I came through without seeing them." She didn't expect much from her request with what she knew of Let thus far.

"I don't see the harm," Her eyes grew wide in shock, "We aren't heading for the ruins just yet. Until then we don't have anything else to do. Lead the way." Katie was ready to put up a fight till she was able to go. This was the first time he had ever agreed to something this easily. She almost forgot that she needed to move her legs to walk. "Well? Are we going or not?"

"Right. It's this way." She stammered.

The family lived slightly outside the city towards the South. Thanks to the main road, it was a short trot to their home. The cottage was styled as elaborate as the others around the city with a brilliant pink roof, and the walls were a dark blue with a multitude of murals painted around the entire home. The home was followed by a large field with sheep and woolied boar that appeared to be herded. Woolied boar were a unique breed whose wool would naturally grow in various shades to match the boar's skin pigment. This particular flock grew the same dark blue color that the home was painted in.

As the pair approached the home, a young girl roughly eight years old came running out to greet them. "Miss Katie, Miss Katie!" The young girl was exuberant at the sight of Katie. Equally as excited, Katie quickly dismounted and ran over to the girl. Embracing the girl, she swung around in a quick circle with the girl's small legs swinging freely behind.

"Abbie!" Katie shouted as she put the girl down again, "You have grown too much. I don't think I'll be able to do that much longer." The two girls laughed excitedly at their reunion. Meanwhile, Let had also dismounted and was guiding in the horses as he watched without complaint. The girl, Abbie, had finally taken notice to the stranger, and quickly hid behind Katie's leg.

"It's ok, Abbie," Katie stated as she placed a hand on the girls back, "He's a friend."

"His eyes are scary though." Abbie wasted no time cutting to the point.

"That's a rude thing to say, Abbie." Katie scolded the girl, "Apologize to him."

"No, Katie. It's alright." Let's voice was softer than it had been since meeting him, "hi! My name is Let. Can I ask you for your name?"

"Abigail McKenna." She stuttered.

"Well Abigail, have you ever heard of magic?" the girl quizzically looked to Katie to see what to do. Katie understood that Let probably knew some sleight of hand tricks which he was going to show and nodded the girl on. Slowly, the girl walked towards Let who was now holding both his hands open.

"As you can see," Let flipped his hands to either side, "I have nothing in my hands." Making a fist with his left hand, he laid it on the palm of his right. "Now I want you to think of a flower. Any flower you like! You got it?" She gently nodded her head. "Good! Now, one, two, three." On his third count, splashes of gold light began to shine from between his two hands. Waves sputtered out as if a small explosion was released from his fist. As the lights continued, he flattened out his fist and separated his hands. The lights faded and lying flat in his palm was a silver tulip bud with a small stem.

Katie was awestruck by his trick. She had seen a great number of sleights but nothing like this. He handed the small flower to Abigail who graciously accepted. The trick played its role in soothing the girl's hesitation to him. "It's so pretty! Thank you!"

"See? I'm not so scary."

"No, you still are scary, but I think you might be okay." She turned her attention back to Katie, "I'll go and get momma' now! She's going to be so happy to see you!" Hurriedly the girl had taken off for the house.

"What was that trick you just did?" No matter how much Katie thought about it, she couldn't think of how he had done that.

"It's just a simple hand trick. I know some kids her age, and they all love that one."

"I've seen hand tricks before, but nothing like that. How did the you make the lights? And where did you get a tulip that looks like that?" Her questions were flowing as fast as she was thinking them.

"Now Katie. I figured you were grown up enough not be fooled by simple tricks anymore." The sarcastic tone reflected his enjoyment out of teasing her. "I don't think I need to remind you that magic has been gone since the elves. With that in mind, how could it have been anything but a simple trick?" His trickster smile said more than his words did to Katie. She knew there was more to what he said but knew he wouldn't tell her. The pair continued to walk towards the house as a plump, homely woman came out to meet them.

"Ms. Katie! What an absolute surprise to see you here!" Mrs. McKenna delightfully hung to Katie just as Abigail had. After greeting the pair, the over-zealous housewife quickly ushered them into the house. Now sitting at the table, Mrs. McKenna struck back up the conversation while the young girl clung to Katie's side.

"You should have told me that you would be coming, I would have prepared things better for you! As is, we are in the middle of getting packed up for the festival, oh, and you even brought a gentleman with you, my this *is* a first for you dear."

"No, no, Maggie! It's perfectly fine. I didn't expect to be this way myself. The man here, he hired me to take him into the ruins. That's all."

"That's all there is? Well, if you insist then I'll take you at your word and no more. Now young man, Katie here is someone very dear to our family. I love her as though she were another child to me. You better keep her safe or you'll have my husband to answer to."

"Have you ever met this girl!? I should be asking you to help *me* out!" Let and Mrs. McKenna bantered back and forth at Katie's expense. Through puffy red cheeks and her countless attempts to butt-in talked over, she realized that Let had never been this open during the time they've been together. She felt as though he was an entirely different person here with this small family than anywhere else they had been. She felt at home.

Afternoon passed into evening and Mr. McKenna had joined them inside. The evening passed with Katie and the family talking about different topics, with Let butting in to add a comment intermittently. Abigail clung to every story Katie told. No one could describe the events better than a daughter come home to visit.

"Throughout this whole night, I don't think we've had the chance to hear much about you Let!" Mr. McKenna spoke out as he turned his attention away from Katie. "How is it you came to seek out this wonderful young woman here?" Even Katie was drawn into this question as she hoped to get some new answers from him.

"An old friend of mine recommended her to me. She's an expert regarding the elves. Knowledge I needed for this project I'm on. That's really all there is."

"Now do you really expect me to believe that's all there is to it?" The way he worded his question made Let straighten in his seat, "The first thing I saw when I looked at you were your eyes. Like stones and ice, even when speaking kindly.

"When you look at Katie though, your eyes change. Soft and familiar as though you are looking at someone you have known your whole life. I'm not going to ask if you don't wish to talk about it, but I can tell you right now that you know her a far more than you let on, I guarantee that!"

The entire room fell silent for several moments. Katie too knew there was more than what Let was saying, but she was still shocked to hear him get called out by someone who just met him. Let was lost in his own mind after this. No words to refute what had just been said, he remained in silence. It was Mrs. McKenna who broke the silence first.

"Why'd you have to go and sour the mood like that? Besides, if anyone should be called out like that, it's Katie. The girl's eyes have gone inward from staring at him so long."

Katie's cheeks went bright red as she quickly stood from her chair. "We've already taken up too much of your time." Katie's voice shook with embarrassment as she spoke. "We need to be getting back to the inn now. I'm sorry to have taken up so much of your time!" She was trying to exit before the couple could say anymore.

"Now you hold on for just a moment." Mrs. McKenna was quick to say, "you've never came here and not stayed with us! We already had planned to put you up with Abbie, and the boy can have the spare room you usually keep."

"We really couldn't intrude like that—" Katie was interrupted.

"Nonsense! You might as well be our daughter too, and I'll be damned to lose any time with you while you are here." Mrs. McKenna's words were final.

"Sorry to intrude on you," It was Let who spoke up next, "Thank you for housing us." And just like that, Katie lost any argument she had once the awkwardness of the moment was gone. The night had carried on until Abigail began to nod off in Katie's lap. As the girls began to head off to bed, Mr. McKenna invited Let out for a walk.

They walked in the cold night for a while in silence. After they had walked to the edge of the family's field, Mr. McKenna was the one to break the silence, "I meant what I had said earlier. Your eyes truly harbor some terrible things. If not for Katie, I would have thrown you out in an instant."

"Well, to be fair if it wasn't for Katie, I never would have darkened your doorstep. I'm guessing your invite to stay was more for your distrust in me than the other way, correct?"

"An observant one you are." Mr. McKenna gave a small chuckle. "I served in the army before I met my wife. I was discharged for an injury I received." He lifted the side of his shirt to show what looked like a burn that never healed. "Only one kind of beast leaves a burn that won't heal. Because of it, I met some interesting men. The type of men I can tell you are." For a moment, he only stared down at Let.

"If you understand that, all the more reason you should have made me leave your home." Let carried his gaze to the ground.

"Maybe, but whatever business you have with Katie, I hope you finish it quick and leave her alone. I can tell from her look that she is ready to run off with you into whatever mess you are in. She doesn't understand but I do. Leave that girl out of your mess!"

"I know." Let turned away from his gaze, "I didn't want her involved to begin with. You were right when you said that I knew her. I was told to find the head of the library in Pneu. when I saw it was her, I wanted to leave right then. Once I get the answers I need in the morning, I plan to go my separate way from her. That is a promise I can make you."

"Good. I'm glad we agree then. With that, I can truly welcome you into our home, and you better keep Katie safe until you do that." By the time the pair had returned to the house, the girls had already gone to bed, and Mr. McKenna showed Let to their spare room.

Several hours had passed since everyone had gone to bed, and Katie had laid awake thinking about what Mr. McKenna had said earlier. It kept pounding away in her mind that even he was able to see that there was some familiarity between the two of them. No matter how hard she tried to bring her mind away from it, she could only think about Elijah. Let was nothing like him, and yet he felt like Elijah.

Her mind wandered on the side of curiosity so much, she didn't even realize that she was sneaking off to the room where he was sleeping. Not fully understanding what she was doing there, she tapped on the door quietly. She decided that if he did not answer, she would return to her room, but after only a single quiet knock, he opened the door.

"Let," she was at a loss for words. She hadn't thought of what she would say. She stared at him for a moment as she struggled to come up with something, and she spoke what was on her mind, "Can I stay with you?" *Stupid! Why would I ask him that?*

"Banshees in your sleep again?" As soon as he said that he froze in place. The way he quickly looked away from her showed that he realized he had slipped up. Katie felt as though her heart had stopped, and her breath caught in her throat.

"Why did you say that?" Her eyes began to glaze over as she felt the tears begin to swell. "Only one person has ever said that to me." Her voice was choked up as she tried to speak. As a child, she asked that question many nights over, and Elijah had always answered the same way.

He quickly turned away from her, "Even if I was who you are thinking, it doesn't change the fact that I will leave when we are done here." He regained the stiff cold voice he had when the first met, "Don't you think that—" before he could finish his thought, Katie had leaped forward and was now clinging to his back.

"I told you yesterday, didn't I?" Katie's voice was muffled from burying her face into his back, "I'm not mad that you left. Nor am I mad that you stayed away for so long. I'm just happy that you are safe."

He was silent.

"Even if you have to leave again. At least let me just have you back until you do go." Katie had fallen into full tears as she clung to him even tighter. "And give me a proper goodbye this time!"

Elijah seemed to be at a loss for words. It felt like hours passed before he gently placed his hand over hers. Katie didn't realize it till now, but he had taken his gloves off. She could feel the callused palms of his hands; she could even feel the deep scars on his wrists. "If you stay in here," his voice was cracked as he attempted to keep his cold tone, "you sleep on the floor." And with that he pulled her hands off him and walked back into the room.

Katie felt both relief and tension as she watched his back. When the time came for him to leave, she resolved herself to finding any excuse she could to go with him. She refused to give him up ever again now that he was back in her life.

§

Chapter Thirteen

RUINS

"And here I was thinking you were still a little girl, Miss Katie," Mrs. McKenna's voice rang out as Katie entered the kitchen of the little farm home, "It's a good thing the husband headed out early. Even Esprit wouldn't have kept that boy safe if he saw you coming from his room this morning!"

"No!" Katie's voice grew flustered as she tried to explain herself, "it was nothing like that, we just got caught up studying for today. That's all, I promise!" Her face had grown bright red as Mrs. McKenna stared her down with disbelief in her eyes.

"No need to get all upset! After all, you are a woman now, I suppose." Her voice now sounded rather prodding as though her mind was already made up on what she believed. Katie's face hung low as knowing that Mrs. McKenna would not believe any excuse she tried to give. She was soon given an escape from the uncomfortable topic as Abigail soon came bounding into the room.

"Katie! Why did you leave my room last night?" The girl seemed as though she was trying to make herself sound more upset than she was. "I don't see you much, so I want to spend as much time with you when you do come!"

"I'm sorry Abby." Katie gently patted her head as she spoke, "I promise to spend as much time with you as I can when you come to the festival, okay?"

"If that's a promise, then ok!" The girl was now beaming as her mom made the girls some breakfast.

"Actually, I wanted to talk to you two girls about the festival." Mrs. McKenna sounded serious as she moved onto the subject as well.

"We're still going aren't we mama'?"

"Oh, yes dear! We wouldn't miss it for anything!" She was rather cheerful as she spoke, "Me and your father spoke about it the other day and have been waiting for a good time to tell you." The air seemed rather stiff as both Katie and Abigail waited to hear what Mrs. McKenna was going to say. "Your father is out now finishing up all the paperwork. After the festival, we are going to have you get an education at the library in Pneu. You'll get to see Ms. Katie quite a bit now!"

Both girls were jubilant to hear the news. Abigail shouted a multitude of thank you to her mom as she leapt into her arms. "You hear that Katie? I'm going to get to see you all the time now! Thank you, mama, thank you! I still have more to pack! I'll be in my room."

"Wait your breakfast!" Mrs. McKenna's shout came too late. The girl had already bounded off into some other room of the house. "Oh well. That girl has been asking for this since last year."

"I thought her dad was against it though?" Katie was more than ecstatic to hear the news, but Mr. McKenna shut her down immediately the year before when she had brought it up.

"He was. After he came back in from his talk with your young friend, he suddenly brought it up saying that it would be good for both of you." Mrs. McKenna seemed to be equally confused as Katie was, "I think that man is just growing softer as he ages." The two girls laughed as Elijah soon joined them in the room.

"We'll have to leave as soon as we can, Katie," his voice seemed calmer than it was the night before, "we have a lot of work to do today."

"Let, I know when you're young you feel things have to be rushed, but you really should do things in proper order, and patience is worth plenty." He seemed slightly confused by Mrs. McKenna's statement, but Katie's face grew red as she knew what her meaning was. "Before you two head off, let me pack you some food for the road."

"Mrs. McKenna, thank you for your hospitality. It has made this trip rather enjoyable for me."

"Now why would you go saying such sweet things to an old married woman when you have such a pretty young one right there next to you?"

Mrs. McKenna winked as she joked with Elijah. The trio spent some time around breakfast talking about various things as the old housewife prepped the food she had promised.

Katie and Elijah began to wrap up their things to head out for the ruins as Abigail came running out of the house to say her goodbyes. "Katie! I can't wait to come see you at the library. You better see me every day when I'm there!

"Of course, I will! You need to remember though, at the library I will be your teacher, and I'm not going to be easy on you just because I love you." Katie teased the girl as she hugged the girl.

"I love you too Katie! I'm so excited to see you more!" The girl turned to Elijah next, "You seemed really scary, but I know that you are nice. You better not let anything happen to Katie, or my daddy will hurt you!" The girl punched him in the leg with a feigned pout on her face.

"I very much believe he would." Elijah smiled as he pat the girl's head goodbye, "I'll take care of her till we get back to the Kend. After that she will be all yours." Elijah had smiled more in the last day than Katie had seen since he came to her. She was grateful to get to see little flashes of who he was as a kid. Before long, the two were mounted on their horses, and waving goodbye to the McKenna's.

As they worked their way back through town, there seemed to be a lot more commotion than there had been the day before. Katie didn't put much thought to it initially, but as they went further through town, the smell of something burning seared into her nose. Soon, she was able to see smoke rising from the remains of the Silk Fur Inn. People were still running back and forth to put out the last of the embers. Nothing remained of the inn.

Even the priest was helping when he caught sight of Elijah and Katie. He came bounding over to speak with Elijah. "It was just as you had thought, sir." He was speaking strangely formal with Elijah. "I made sure everyone was out of there before it caught fire."

"Watch the formalities in public." Elijah's voice was stern, "I'm just a traveler. Remember that."

"Sorry. I'll do my best."

"Any news from the Citadel yet?" Elijah's voice had lowered as he spoke.

"Still no. Just a letter from Kend wanting me to keep a lookout for you. Should I send the letter?"

"Yes. Even as is, we won't have enough time if they change up their plan any. For now, I'll head back to Pneu and take care of what I can."

"If you are right, a lot of people can be in danger."

Elijah paused before he spoke again. "I know. I'll make my trip here as quick as I can and get back. Keep the faith strong, and don't you dare let anything through."

"My faith is always strong! Safe travels and may Esprit go with you."

"You too." With that, the priest returned to the inn to help. Without a word, Elijah turned his horse and headed towards the ruins.

Katie had picked up that the city was not a good place for questions. She waited till they had already passed into the woods for some time before raising her question, "I've never seen a priest speak to anyone with formalities. What have you been doing these last ten years, and how did you know the inn would burn down?"

"I can't say, just trust that I'll make sure you know what you need to." His voice lost the easiness he had that morning.

"You aren't telling me anything though!"

"I know." From his voice, Katie knew the conversation was over. He wouldn't speak anymore. She felt the frustration she had from when they first met. She hated not knowing especially when the answers were right there. They rode in silence as they continued their march towards the ruins.

From the center of what looked like a small town rose a tall monument that stood above every tree in the forest. It shone bright like gold as the sun reflected from the surface. It was made of different metals that would change color based on how much light reflected from it. Another one of the strange designs that the elves had which Katie still hadn't figured out.

Around the ancient village were buildings in various shapes of disrepair and overgrowth from the local plant life. It seemed to be nothing more than just another abandoned city. To Katie though, she knew every entrance that ran underground into an amazing system of tunnels where the elves had hidden much knowledge that she worked frivolously to understand.

"Well here it is. What could be here though to help us solve that puzzle box?" Katie wanted to take the chance and test Elijah on how much he knew about the ruins.

"All of these entrances won't take us where we need. Where is the hidden one that you caved in?"

She froze in place. It was not a tunnel she wished to ever visit again. "How do you even know about that one?" She was worried how anyone else could have heard about it.

"The cult that's following me uncovered it. That's where the sphere came from. My master stole it from them after they had excavated it, but I never saw where it was. It should be unburied now."

"Follow me. I need to see this myself." The tunnel she had left buried held secrets she couldn't let anyone find. She gripped the artifact she wore around her neck as she quickly urged her horse past the city to the north. There was a large hill that blended into the forest floor at first, but after riding around to the other side, a huge tunnel was seen. The shocked look on Katie's face was enough for Elijah to realize that she honestly believed it would still be collapsed. She quickly dismounted and ran to the entrance.

"Whatever it was you were trying to hide down there, they thought it was important." Elijah had placed his hand on her shoulder, "What were you hiding here?"

"I wasn't really hiding anything. Two people I traveled with died there, and this place became their tomb. I just didn't want anyone digging around their graves."

"I think we should head in then and see if they dug anything else up." He grabbed her arm and began to walk towards the tunnel. "Hopefully there will be a clue down here to figure out the sphere." The two descended in silence led only by the light of a single torch they carried.

The tunnel continued to descend for a while with only dirt walls. However, they soon left the dirt cave and entered a hall made of stone and lined with glowstones to illuminate the pathway. The walls were lined with hieroglyphs in all three languages of the Elves. Brilliant pictures and scripts ran as far as the lights could reach, and all the writing and pictorials were organized in geometrical patterns that Katie had read thoroughly the last time she had been here.

She thought back to the first time she had found this place. She spent a week straight never even leaving this tunnel trying to read and understand what it all meant. To the right, the tunnels led into an endless maze that she couldn't navigate without a map. The bridge which led from that maze to the tunnel they were in was now collapsed. To the left, the tunnel would lead into a chamber where she had found the necklace she now wore, and the same place one of her friends met their end.

"Go left." She whispered to him, "nothing is worth seeing the other way." Without questioning, he followed her directions. They continued to follow the illustrations along the walls. When she had first seen these, it was overwhelming to try and decipher. Now, she could read it as fast as they walked. The stories told of the secrets that the Gods had shared with the Elves. It told the story of special knowledge and history which they hid within the stars, and it told of the story of when Angeli had first come here to bless the chamber in the name of all eight Gods.

She suddenly stopped though forcing Elijah to quickly turn back towards her. She was running her hands along the wall as she read the same part over and over again. "Do you see something there?" Elijah gave her the time she needed to read this part thoroughly.

"It was something I misread my first time here." She ran her fingers along the wall as she read. "I thought this read that Angeli blessed this place in the name of all the Gods, but—" She tapped her finger over the same text several times. "This place is only blessed in the name of Esprit. A holy place that only Esprit and her anointed could enter. That doesn't make sense though."

"Why not? We have people now that only worship one or two of the Gods."

"Because this place was built after the God's War. Esprit was already in resting by the time this place was built. None of the Elves would be able to enter since she was no longer around to Anoint anyone." The God's War was chaotic and took a heavy toll on the world. Esprit, the Goddess assigned to protect the living, was placed in a slumber during the war which she still had not returned from. "Why would Angeli create something none of the elves could enter?"

"Maybe because something was here that she needed to make sure the elves could never find. Like the sphere."

"No." She pulled the necklace out from her shirt so that Elijah could now see it. The charm on it was nearly three inches in length with a diverse flow of shapes and patterns on it. "This relic I've kept hidden on me. I don't even know the details of it, but it is some form of a key that was hidden down here. I was even told that this was the hidden secret here so how could the sphere have been hidden here as well? Also, why are both the key and the sphere written in the Piot of Esprit?"

"Told by who?" Elijah was standing taller than before and he spoke sternly, "And how do you know that this is the Piot of Esprit?" Katie hadn't meant to reveal that she had met someone here that taught her about the elves. There was too much going on though to hid it anymore.

"When I first came here, the chamber ahead was guarded by an Elf. She had been here all this time to protect this place, and she is the one who taught me enough to learn everything I know now. She is the one who told me to protect this key." She was shaking as she spoke. The anger was visible as she began to spoke faster. "She had lied to me about these writings here, and now that you show up with the sphere, I can't help but wonder if this key is a fake too. If that sphere was the real artifact that was hidden here, then how much was I lied to?"

"Why would she have bothered to teach you as much as she did if she was only going to lie about it?" Elijah had grabbed her hands to stop them from shaking anymore. "Elves had little to no love for humans. If she were going to lie to you, she would have just as soon killed you and kept her place a secret. If that key is fake, I don't think the elf knew. Perhaps though, both artifacts are real. Who knows where exactly in here the cult found the sphere? It may not have even came from here. This is just where my master had stolen it from them."

Katie had calmed down and her hands were no longer shaking, "You are probably right. Thank you. My research is everything to me, and it all started here. I would hate to find out that it all started with a lie."

They started walking again towards the main chamber while Katie continued to silently read the walls. The chamber was massive however there were still several places that weren't fully excavated by the cult. Towards the middle of the room though, was the remnants of a pedestal with light coming in from several places to light up that one area. There were several scraps of torn cloth that rested near the pedestal as well.

Katie had already made her way here to pick up the cloth. "Now I can give you a real burial. Even if it's just this." She smiled as she stashed the clothe in her bag. "This is where the key I have was placed. I was never allowed to touch it nor examine it. I spent over a week here with that elf learning so much. I've missed this place." Katie moved fast as she walked from one side of the room to the other.

This continued for several hours as Katie searched every inch of the room for some sort of clue. Elijah knew that he was out of his element and quietly sat near the center of the room as she worked. He pulled out the sphere and began to spin the dials in various ways and orders, but he just couldn't make sense of it. The light coming through the ceiling began to turn red as the sun was starting to set.

Katie laid on the ground next to Elijah looking defeated. "Nothing," her voice was exasperated, "there isn't a single clue in here. It's all just songs and prayers, and none of them mention anything that would be important to us." She was looking to the ceiling as she noticed the setting sun. "You're going to love this place when the sun sets. Glowstones are placed into the ceiling that light up like the stars at night. This seems to be the only part that didn't cave in so I'm thankful for that."

"Katie," he was looking over to her as she was dazing off with the sun, "What happened here? How did this place cave in?" Her face went pale as she appeared to recall painful memories.

"If I tell you, will you answer one question I have?"

"I can agree to that."

Yes! She was excited to get him to agree to something. "While I was working here, someone came. Someone dangerous. I never saw their face, but he wore a mask that glowed a dark purple." Elijah's face changed color as she mentioned this. "The elf knew he was dangerous and triggered the collapse to try and trap him. She refused to leave and was crushed under the rubble. One of my companions with me stayed behind in that main part of the tunnel to try and hold that evil man back so I could get out."

"Have you seen that man since then?" A slight anger was in his voice.

"Once. I was trying to dig the rocks out by hand to try and save my friend, and the man stood behind me laughing." She was squeezing the necklace again. "My friends died to stop him, and he still got out just to mock their death. He told me that he would come back for the key one day and to keep it safe. He always threatened me to stay quiet. I have until now."

He offered no words.

"You really know how to comfort a girl, don't you?" She said as she curled her knees up to hide her face.

"I know the man who threatened you."

Her face shot up to look at Elijah eyes still red and puffy. "Who?"

"Have you ever heard of the Arken-Faith?"

"Once. In an old story book that talked about the demons. Are you going to tell me they are real too?"

"Would It surprise you?"

"No."

"Although I am not sure exactly who, but those masks are worn by the Arken-Sons. Their version of a saint." Katie was silent as she watched him talk. "I can't explain a lot, but this guy leading the cult is an Arken-Son. He might be the one who attacked you. I should have known you would be more connected than just my librarian." He began to laugh as he laid on the ground to stare up to the ceiling. He was able to see some of the stone begin to light up just as Katie had said.

"You owe me an answer now," Katie spoke forcefully, "you aren't going to like this one either."

"Then I'm not answering."

"You promised!" Katie's voice cracked as she tried to push for him to uphold his part. Elijah was silent as he gently waved a hand to tell her to ask. "What happened to your hands and arms?" He didn't realize that his sleeve had fallen back. The heavy scars on his wrists were visible as well as many other burns and scars that went along his forearm.

He quickly sat up to pull his sleeve down, hiding them again. He didn't answer, and he turned his head away from her. "I can't answer that one." His voice was broken. "Ask me anything else, but I can't answer that one."

"That *is* the question I asked, and that *is* the answer I want." She was firm as she pressed for this one answer.

"I spent several years in chains." He was now rubbing his wrists. Katie was able to infer that he meant he was locked in shackles as either a criminal or slave for a while. "Please, let me leave it at that." Suddenly, Katie started to laugh. It kept going before Elijah cut in angrily, "What? You think this is funny?"

"No." She stammered, "It's not that." She was still chuckling, "When you first came to me, you would have stormed off swearing instead of saying please. I knew your shell would come down with me." She grinned eagerly toward him, "Even if I didn't know it was you at the time, I know you too well for you to stay defensive around me." At first, he tried to hold his anger, but he too began to laugh.

"I don't like being around people anymore, and I really didn't want you to be involved with this. That's the only reason I was so angry with you. I'm still going to be leaving though. It'll be easier if—" his voice drifted off. The sun had now set fully and the glowstones lit up the chamber brighter than a full moon night. Just as Katie described, they looked like the nighttime stars. "What did the walls in the hall say about the stars again? What did it say exactly?"

Katie didn't understand the question at first. Following his request, she began to recite what she could remember from the wall. "To summarize, it said that Esprit hid the secrets she held with the elves within the—" It suddenly clicked to her. As she was staring at the ceiling, she realized that Elijah had seen it too. The glowstones weren't organized to look *like* the stars, they were organized to *match* the stars.

"Can you rearrange the sphere to match those glyphs?"

"Yes...it'll take some time though." She quickly moved to her bag and pulled out paper and a pen. "It'll be easier to copy the ceiling as is and try to solve the sphere back home. Just give me a few minutes to write it down." A slow clapping was suddenly heard from the entrance of the cavern. Elijah was already on his feet with his blades in hand.

Their vision moved to where the clapping was heard from, but having limited light now, they couldn't make out its face. "I'm really thankful for the two of you for figuring that out." Elijah and Katie both recognized the voice, "Now it's time to take the artifact back and explain to the Son and how to open it. Truly, thank you both!"

The man began to step forward until the glow from the stones made him visible enough to see. Elijah didn't seem shocked by his identity, but Katie was struggling to understand why Rufus was here with them.

Chapter Fourteen
ROAD TO HARRINGTON

Rufus stood before the pair with his arm extended as if greeting an old friend. He had his other hand resting on the hilt of a great sword on his back. "I was pretty upset when I found out you weren't at the inn to receive my gift last night. I worked so hard to keep it a secret too." He feigned sorrow as he spoke callously about burning down the inn.

"Fortunately, I had a hunch about that." Elijah's voice was as cold as it was the night they were attacked in Pneu, "I really would appreciate it if you let us through."

"As if, I have direct orders to make sure neither of you make it back to Kend." Rufus began to draw his sword as Katie felt the breath catch her throat. "If you surrender though, I can bring you to the Son before you die."

"It'll be your own death if you choose to stay." Elijah sounded excited as he spoke, "I think it's fair to assume you are an Arken-Priest?"

"How very observant of you! We aren't too happy though that you had to go and drag Katie into all of this. We still planned to get so much more out of her before we took care of her too." He was gazing towards Katie now, "I really do hate this part you know." Rufus was shaking his head as he gave his half-hearted remorse.

The tension was thick in the room as everyone waited for who would make the first move. Rufus was steadfast in the entry way as he rested his hands on the hilt of his sword. Elijah gripped both daggers firmly in hand as he looked for a way to move past the man. Katie was dumbfounded as she stared at the man, she considered a friend for so long. She reached out as if to say something to Rufus, but she was blocked off by Elijah's extended arm to hold her back.

"Katie, I'm sure you are confused by a lot of things, and when we are on the road, I will tell you as much as I can." Elijah's eyes never broke from Rufus as he spoke, "Right now, the most important thing is for you to copy down those constellations you see on the ceiling. When you have that, we run." Katie realized something new in his voice as he spoke. Fear.

With a simple nod of her head, she returned to her paper and began to trace the stars as fast as accuracy would allow. The small glimpse of fear she heard in Elijah's voice urged her to start moving. She didn't have time to think about things right now. From her years of duplicating and scribing the voluminous number of artifacts and documents she has handled, her hands moved with exceptional accuracy as she traced. There were many placed on the ceiling though, and from the cave-in of her first visit to these ruins, several of the constellations were no longer there.

As Katie diligently worked, Rufus merely stood sentry as he watched the pair within the chamber. His crooked smile made it clear that he intended to let Katie finish before he made a move. This gave Elijah time to start planning their escape from the ruins. Studiously he watched as Elijah sheathed his daggers and began to search through his bag. He kept his hands hidden as he hid several small objects on his person. Maybe due to his overconfidence, Rufus merely chuckled as he stood statuesque in the doorway.

"As long as she is working," Rufus' voice was brimming with sureness, "I don't plan on doing anything. After all, her work is the root of the Arken-Father's knowledge. She was more important than you could have realized." he clicked his tongue, "Why did you have to bring her in this early, *apprentice*?" Katie took a mental note of the comment which marked Elijah as an apprentice.

"On another day, in different company, I would have already put you in your grave, *false priest*." Malice filled Elijah's voice as he spoke. Rufus replied with nothing more than a pensive glare. The room was filled with the sound of the scratching of Katie's pen. No one spoke a word as the tension grew thick enough to press the stone walls into a groan. Katie's document was the hourglass which counted down to the break in the stagnant air, ripe with hostility.

Nearly an hour had passed when the sound of her pen had silenced. She was still as she reviewed her work to check for errors. Her work was accurate though, and despite her desire to drag out the project longer, she had no reason to subsist. Each formation on the ceiling above was copied perfectly. Using the center of the page as the center of the room, the document traced each formation to circle around that center, and she even left the spaces where the ceiling was missing.

As she rolled her parchment, it was Rufus who broke the silence first. "I really would like Katie to remained unharmed until we are finished with her, but if you try to fight me, I won't hold back on either of you." He changed his pose to take an offensive stance.

"Hold on to my arm, and when you see the spark, guard your eyes." Elijah's voice was barely a whisper as she quickly slipped the document into her own travel bag. She noticed that he had not drawn his daggers again. She could tell that he had a plan, and she decided to put her trust in him. As she closed her grip around his arm, he made his move.

He started moving towards the doorway, keeping Katie slightly behind him. Rufus raised his sword to strike. In a single motion, a small spark lit something that Elijah had been holding in his hand. A sparkling light was seen from the object, and Katie shut her eyes as Elijah had instructed her to do. She could feel him toss the object towards Rufus who managed to utter a quick, "Huh" before a bright light filled the entire room. The light was so bright that even through her closed eyes she could see it. Rufus let out a loud cry as Katie felt Elijah shove his way past and through the door.

"You can open your eyes now," Elijah shouted out as they ran through the hallway. Although her eyes were closed, she still had spots in her vision from whatever had made the bright light. If Rufus didn't have a chance to close his eyes, she wondered how long it would take for him to see again. She could hear him shouting in anger from behind them as he attempted to follow without his sight.

They sprinted through the small tunnel leading out of the ruins when Elijah had stopped. "Keep going, get the horses, and get them as far away as you can. They won't like the noise." As he pushed her forward through the exit, he withdrew a couple objects from his pockets that were slightly longer than the length of his hand. She had never seen anything like these, but he wasn't giving her the time to ask about them. Trusting in him, she turned and followed the direction he had given her.

She wasted no time in mounting her horse and taking the reins of Elijah's. As she galloped away, she finally allowed herself a moment to think about her situation. Rufus, someone she trusted for years, attempted to kill her. Her thoughts ran circles as she tried to make sense of it.

Before long though, her thoughts were brought back to her as a thunderous boom reverberated from the direction of the tunnel. She had never heard any sound like it before, and it terrified both her and the horses. *Elijah!* She turned the horses back. She knew he told her to get away, but she refused to flee if he needed her.

When she arrived back at the entrance, a large dust cloud was being blown away by the light breeze that night. After a moment, her eyes finally adjusted enough to take in the aftermath. The hill which served as a guidepost for the ruins was gone, the entrance itself, disintegrated, was either in the air around her, or piled high over the old passage. She witnessed something similar several years prior when the elf used the last of her magic to close the entrance, but this was something far different.

Scanning the collapsed tunnel and surrounding tree line, she looked for him. Scanning back and forth, she could see no movement. She began to fear that he may have been caught up in the blast. *No! Not him. I just got him back.* She desperately searched for him as she made a full loop around the now collapsed hill. "Elijah!" She shouted his names several times, but she received no answer.

She stopped in front of the old entrance, "Please no. Not. Him. I just got him back." She repeated to herself as her eyes began to tear up as she thought about him being under all of the rubble. She didn't understand what had happened. As she dug through the refuse, a hand suddenly grabbed hold of her shoulder. She screamed as she jumped away from its grasp. Turning around, she was greeted by the face she feared to mourn. "Where were you!?" She shouted as she jumped to her feet, "I was calling out for you and you didn't answer!" She started to cry as she jabbed her fist into his chest several times. "You promised to tell me about everything, how could you go missing again!"

"I'm sorry," he was nearly screaming as he spoke, "I didn't know it would be that loud! I can't really hear much!" From the tone of his voice,

Katie could tell that he was struggling to hear his own voice. "We need to get going, I didn't expect things to be like this! We don't have a lot of time! I'll explain better when I can hear myself think!"

Not noticing her visible upset in his debilitated state, he quickly mounted up on his own horse and motioned for her to follow. She wiped the tears from her eyes and quickly followed his lead. Silently he led them out of the forest, and back to the main road. He didn't lead them east to Kend like she had thought he would. He was taking her further Northwest.

They traveled most of the night in silence, mostly due to Elijah trying to recover his hearing. The silence began to bother her, and an unsettling feeling began to rise from the pit of her stomach. Looking around, she realized it wasn't just them that was quiet. Then entire forest seemed to be muted. The only sound that seemed to exist in the world at that moment, were the sound of the horse's hoofs as they stepped upon the earth.

"The forest is scared," Elijah seemed to be talking in a normal tone again, "This cult has creatures at their disposal that exude terror among the forest and its animals. They are trying to find us, and their movement puts the forest to silence."

Katie felt a chill run through her body. She couldn't think of any creature she knew of that could terrorize an entire forest. Even the wolves were probably in hiding if it was as bad as Elijah meant. She began to wonder what exactly she was dragged in to. *Rufus!* She remembered that he claimed they already had her involved. "Can you hear again?"

"For the most part. A faint ringing sound, but I can talk at least. I did promise you that." She was thankful that he remembered that much of it. "First, I have to ask though. Did you know they've been stealing your research?"

"No!" Her voice raised, "I knew that man might come back for me one day, but I had no idea he had people watching me." She never thought that the events during her first visit within the ruins would be wrapped up in some sort of underground world, and she never imagined that this is what would lead to her finding Elijah again. "I don't even know if any of my research is even of any value. I refused to look into anything that may have led back to this key or that chamber." She was gripping her necklace as she spoke.

"It's probably best you never said anything." His voice trailed off for a moment, "There is a lot that I can't tell you. I will tell you everything I can though. I'll start by asking what you do know of the Arken-Faith."

"That's the religion that was founded during the God's War, correct? They were the followers of the fallen Quietus."

"Yes. Well, the faith never died. That man in the mask you encountered, Rufus, the cult I'm chasing, all of them are linked to the Arken-Faith." He withdrew a small book from his pack and handed it to her, "That is a Gospel of the Fallen. As you can see, the faith is still very much alive."

Katie took the book in her hands and traced her fingers over the elegant work on the cover of the small tome. The crest embroidered in the center was that of the reaching hand of Quietus. The Gospel of the Fallen was the second Gospel that the God named Quietus gave to Earth when he attempted to rebel against the other Gods. This word was preached as though it was designed to lead people to the truth that the Gods' withheld. The Common Faith teaches that this Gospel was destroyed as well as its followers. Holding a copy in her hands, Katie realized that it was a lie.

"The Arken-Faith, is organized very closely to the Eight-Faith's church only smaller." He continued, "They have the Arken-Father who serves like the pope. Five Arken-Sons who serve like the saints, and each Arken-Son has two Arken-Priests. Each Arken-Son can have as many members as they see fit, but they can only have those two priests."

"Is that the cult you are following?"

"Related, but not the same. This Arken-Son decided to organize his followers into a cult. They focus purely on the destruction of the world, and they have little desire to learn the *truth* that is preached in their Gospel. This is the only Arken-Son we have been able to find though. Rufus, I believe, is one of his Arken-Priests which is why I was hesitant to fight him."

"He was always so nice though. Are you sure he isn't a puppet like Ben and Grant?"

"No. They were dead, and their bodies were being used as puppets. He was very much alive. When we first met him, I knew he wasn't someone to trust."

"How?"

"He claimed that John made the order to take you by any means. John may be an idiot, but do you really think he would let someone besides himself or Daniel come rescue you if he truly thought you were in danger?"

Katie didn't answer. She didn't need to. He was right about John. At most, he would have issued an order to report her sighting so that he can ride out to find her. That is exactly what John would have done. Now that she thought about it, being confronted the way they were made no sense if John was worried about her.

"That's also why I was willing to let us stay with the McKenna's. Rufus knew where we were staying. That's why he burned down the inn we were supposed to be at. I had a feeling that we would be attacked. The priest there in Kend is an old acquaintance of my master and I have him writing some people to get assistance with a few things. My job here was to confirm the location of the Arken-Son and it is done. This artifact though, it stays a secret. No one besides you and I can know about it."

He had an intense fire in his eyes as he looked to Katie on the last statement. She knew what he was wanting from her and she answered intently that she would keep it that way. They rode on again in silence as Katie processed everything she had been told. After some time, a question finally came to her though. "Why aren't we heading back to Kend, or Pneu? My library may be able to help us decipher these clues we got."

"If we go back, we risk getting more people involved. Besides, do you recognize those constellations?"

"I never spent a lot of time studying the stars. That was the one subject I kept putting off." Katie shook her head as though she was upset that she missed the opportunity.

"Those are all constellations that have to do with stories related to Esprit. Only one city here in the west ever documented the stars well enough to fill in those holes we have on your page." Elijah hesitated as though the city was some place he didn't want to go. Katie studied his face for a moment before she understood which direction they were heading.

Katie felt her heart stop as she realized where they were heading. "Harrington!?" Harrington was the home of the former lord that served over this region. He was a horrible man that worked as a roadblock to Pneu's initial growth. He felt threatened by the attention she and John were receiving by the capital, and for a while, he raised taxes so high and placed so many soldiers in the city that the king himself had to intervene.

Tensions were so high that there was fear of the civil war reviving here in the west. One day though, no one received any word from the city. Messengers never returned, and letters were left unanswered. Hesitantly, the king sent a full envoy to the city only to find every citizen had been wiped out. The city with a population of 186,000 people were all just dead. No one had appeared to be murdered, and it looked as though most of the citizens had just laid down and stopped breathing.

The envoy sent a report back to the capital, and by the time more soldiers arrived, the initial envoy was found dead where they had camped within the city. Several more times it happened with no explanation as to why people would die here. It was ordered that any attempts to clear out the dead were to be abandoned. By order of the king, no one was allowed to enter the city.

Katie felt her heart racing as she worried about their destination. "No one has ever survived going into the city!" Her voice cracked with her fear obvious, "Even if we did find something, how are we supposed to leave?"

"Information you probably never received; you only die if you are in the city after sunset. We just need to be out of the city before nightfall."

"How could you possible know that."

"I just do. Besides. I have an idea about solving that artifact, but we need the full map. We have no choice but to go." He stated, making no attempt to hide his own hesitation.

"I'll put my trust in you, but if we die, I will kill you!" Elijah began to laugh at her remark. Seeing him laugh like this made her smile. It didn't seem as though he'd been able to laugh much these last few years. Another question came to her, "I almost forgot about this. What was that flash in the ruins, and what brought down the tunnel?"

"They were tools made by the alchemists in the far East. I'll probably never get more, but it seemed to be the best way to get us out of there."

"I've never seen an alchemist with things like that! They all use herbs or powders to do things like heal and mend small objects."

"There are a lot of secrets hidden in the Alchem Empire. I've been once, and I saw things that you wouldn't understand even if I explained it." Katie didn't press any further. For the time, she would keep her thoughts on their task in Harrington.

§

CHAPTER FIFTEEN

HARRINGTON

The once great city of Harrington stood tall as a stone tomb for the many inhabitants and travelers that never found their way out of the city. Before the city could be seen, the stench of death and rot had overtaken the senses of any who ventured too close to the city. The remnants of a major highway that ran through the city were overgrown, and several of the taller buildings in the city were now collapsed.

Katie used a cloth soaked in lavender and lemon oil to cover her mouth and nose however the decayed smell coming from the city still managed to reach her. The two had left the horses tied up far enough from the city that they wouldn't be at risk of exposure. A city filled with unburied corpses left a person exposed to a variety of diseases, even if they could survive whatever had taken everyone.

The hike into the city felt as though they were marching to the summit of Zosen's Gate. A city so close to the border of the afterlife, made you feel as though you were walking to your own demise. After their encounter with the Arken-Priest, Elijah determined that they had extraordinarily little time to figure out what they needed to. Although it was already noon, they decided to attempt their trek into the city rather than waiting for the next day for fear of not knowing how far out of the city was dangerous.

Conversation was kept to a minimum to avoid excess breath in a city full of so much decay. As if to reaffirm their concern for this, the first remains they encountered were those of some animals that had believed they found easy prey within the city.

The city was surrounded by a large stone wall that had begun to break down in several places. The former gate had been torn down by the first group of soldiers that had come to investigate the city. Entering the city was as easy as crossing the broken threshold. Leaving would be a matter of luck, as very few have ever returned from this living crucible of death.

Most of the bodies near the gate had been removed during the prior attempts to cleanse the city. As they traveled further, a multitude of corpses presented varying states of decomposition. Despite the king's orders, people still attempted to loot the city, only to be met with the same fate as the former denizens meaning a constant influx of new cadavers that would remain uncollected.

Harrington was built on a large hill. From the entrance, you could see the large mound rise to where Lord Briarholt built his ostentatious home. Even after all these years without a living habitant, the image of the Briarholt estate dredged up unpleasant memories for Katie. She personally experienced the hardships many people had to suffer while collecting the taxes he needed to build that atrocious thing. Fortunately, they would have no need to go anywhere near it. The place they were looking for was the Church of Astrology which was located at the Northernmost edge of the city.

Looking towards the sky, Katie could tell they still had roughly six hours of daylight left. That gave them less than four hours to find what she needed. The plan was to look through as many of the astrological records as they could to find the matches for the constellations, they discovered in the ruins near Kend. If they ran out of time, they would bring as many of the records out as they could. In the event they still didn't have enough time, Elijah would venture into the city alone the following day and bring as many as he could back to her. Katie opposed this of course, but he won the argument stating that if he were to get sick, she can still read the records. It would not work the other way.

She kept her eyes focused ahead, avoiding any sights she wished to limit. Most of their journey into the city proved uneventful. Her eyes began to wonder as she took in the sights around her. From the corner of her eye, a shadow went by. She jolted her head only to find a home with the door ripped from its hinges.

The longer she stared into the darkened doorway, the more she felt it pull her toward it. Without realizing, she began to walk towards the open doorway. *Why are you here? You don't belong! Get out! It's not time!* So many voices whispered in her ears that she struggled to understand even the few she could make out. She crept closer; Elijah's voice drowned out by the whispers of the voices.

She stumbled steadily, in her trance. Losing all sense of self as the cries and hushed voices of thousands paraded into her mind, becoming so muddled as to create a constant droning. The droning turned to a roar as she crossed the threshold of the doorway, simultaneously enveloping her in shadow, and abandoning the radiance of the sun. The roar all at once became a bellow, then ceased altogether. Absolute silence.

Before her was a sight she wished she could have avoided. A table, long since forgotten that once had held food for the family who lived here. Around the table were four chairs, one still cradled a corpse. The body looked as though it had found its way here not but a few weeks prior. The clothes were worn down and her head rested on the table.

On the floor were several more deceased in nearly the same state. Their slow rate of decay filled the room with such a putrid odor that Katie felt her stomach wretch. Even with the voices gone, her body felt so inflexible that she couldn't even turn away.

"Katie! Katie!" Elijah's voice brought her back to her senses enough to turn away. Not realizing how close he was standing, she turned straight into his chest. She buried her face there for a moment to force out the stench that filled the home. He wasted no time pulling her from the home, leaving the family to the eternal dinner that would never be consumed.

Elijah didn't rush her as she regained her composure. After a short break, her breath was steady again, and she was able to stand on her own. He stared at her with concern which she waved off with her hand and started their pace once more towards the church. The image of the family still as strong in her mind as the smell in her nose. She didn't have the luxury for them to preoccupy her thoughts though. If they wanted to avoid joining them, they had to hurry.

It took little time for them to reach the church, as the two were met with the sight of a cathedral that could compare to the Grand Church in the capital. Its twin spires stood above all in the city, save the Lord's home, and elaborate stained glass windows still shone brightly into the chapel. Solid oak doors remained untouched as they barred the interior of the cathedral from the plague living outside its walls.

Elijah struggled as he forced one of the two doors open, assaulting them with stagnant, dusty air. Once they were inside, Katie felt relieved to find the air within the church easier to breath than outside. "It seems as though the air is still clean here in the church." Katie was happy to be rid of the stench that lingered throughout the city.

"True." Elijah stopped Katie's hand as she attempted to remove her mask. "I still wouldn't take a chance though. Even in here, let's keep talking to a minimum." He looked to the back of the chapel, and then his gazed moved to a stairwell rising to the higher levels of the church. "The most important records are always kept in the study of the priest, but there's a chance that what we need are in their observatories in those spires."

"Which one should we search first?"

"I'll handle the study; you should check the Northern spire first." He handed her an old arm piece which had fallen from a nearby pew. "If you find anything, drop this down the stairwell and I'll come to you." She nodded to him as she took the debris.

As she headed for the stairs, he shouted back to her, "Even if you don't see me, when the sky turns red, you run for the horses. Don't you dare turn back or wait for me! I promise I will meet you there." She hesitated as she looked back at him. She was worried that he was expecting something to happen while they were there. "It's time to get to work Katie. I'll see you back at the horses." And with a flick of his hand, he headed for the chapel offices.

I can't find them anywhere! Katie slouched in the office chair as she felt defeated. The Northern spire had nothing to offer other than old family records and a few scandals that seemed to be kept on retention solely for black mail. Katie thought this city really was a despicable place, but she couldn't bring herself to think they deserved what happened to them.

She had been searching the room for nearly an hour with no luck. Time was running out, and she maybe had an hour to search. She decided to try the Southern spire. As she left the office, she took a moment to appreciate the architecture of the building.

The bottom floor was built the same as any other church. The front doors led into the chapel where the priest would deliver his sermons. Behind the pulpit was two doors that held two offices and a bedroom where the priest could study and sleep. The top floor however didn't house spare bedrooms like most churches did.

Being built in the Northern-most end of town, the front doors opened to the south with a spire directly above it, and the second spire was built to point north. Each one of these spires housed astronomy tools and were connected by a hallway which housed all the offices the astronomers would work from.

As she moved through the hall, she noticed that one of the offices just before the southern spire had been broken into. As she moved closer to the door, the scent of death had reached its nasty hands through her cloth mask once again as she felt her gut wrench. She decided it would be worth a quick look before heading into the spire.

The room wasn't very large, but it was decorated with several bookcases, a desk, several candle mounts around the walls, a single bed, and a dresser. Lying on the bed, neatly tucked into the sheets, was the body of what she could only assume was one of the astronomers. The body was in a similar state to the ones she had seen before only this one appeared to have died in his sleep. Held in his hands was an unmarked leather book.

Katie was drawn to the book although she hesitated to pull it from his cold hands. She knew that she didn't have time to be sidetracked yet her natural curiosity was driving her to see what this person couldn't separate from even as he slept. Finally, her curiosity won the best of her. Those fingers gripped tight to the book as if it were fighting to keep it even in death.

Finally, she had freed the book. Bringing it to the light of the window, she skimmed through its pages. It appeared to be the journal of an apprentice astronomer. In it, were many paragraphs and study notes over his teachers, personal doubts, and other such things. Nearly halfway through the journal, self-drawn constellations were present. Reading through the entries just before, he was struggling with remembering them all, and decided to try to recreate them here. The earlier ones were hard to tell, but he seemed to quickly pick up on his drawing technique. Eight, nine, ten pages and more of star systems. She turned a page and froze.

The first one he had drawn on this page matched one of the constellations she had been looking for. Quickly she had pulled her own star map from her travel bag and one by one she was able to identify all the patterns she had over the next three pages. Unfortunately, he had not drawn them in the same order they appeared on her star map but did have the ones she needed. She hurriedly packed away her map, but in her rush, she dropped the journal. It fell open to a spot where several pages had been torn out. On a little scrap near the corner of one of the torn pages, a single word was left. *Astero.*

That single word pulled all of Katie's attention. She failed to notice that the sky was turning red as she began to read the entries leading up to those pages.

XX Spring, 807 A.D.

A strange man showed up today. He spent quite a while speaking with the priest too. Apparently, he came from the capital to assist with some of our research. The citadel must be tired of us sending dull reports with nothing new. He seems stiff, but we were all told to report directly to him. When I met him, something seemed off...? I don't know what it is, but I have no choice in it. Hopefully, things go well.

XX Spring, 807 A.D.

Since that man showed up, four people have gone missing. We keep getting told that they are helping with private matters, but the rest of us know something is wrong. That man, his eyes are like stones and his words feel like venom. I hate his very presence. Even now, in my own room it feels like he is watching me. Today he declared that he made a discovery that will change things. I'm not sure what is going on, but I don't trust that he found anything good.

XX Summer, 807 A.D.

There are only three of us left in the church now besides the priest and him. Last night, I even heard screams coming from beneath the church. I'm terrified for what will happen over the next few days. I sleep with my journal now out of fear that the man will see what I'm writing. Even as I sleep, I'm terrified that I won't wake up one day. Whatever project he is working on is supposed to end this week. I don't know what will become of everyone, but I have a bad feeling about what this end will bring. I don't have family to write to, and I have no possessions to leave anyone. If I do die, no one will even notice. This isn't existence. I'm tired.

That was the last passage before the torn pages. *Astero* was a name everyone in the common faith knew. He was a being who rivaled the Gods during the early days of creation. In the Book of Astero, it is said that his body was destroyed, and used to make the stars we see at night so it isn't hard to believe that an astrologist would mention his name. It still struck Katie as odd though that it would have been mentioned in pages torn out of a personal journal.

She began to read through the pages again when the lack of light suddenly caught her attention. Not only was it past time for her to leave, she waited so long that she wasn't sure if she could make it out of the city before the sunset now. Panic set in as she stuffed the journal away and sprinted out of the door.

She took the stairs two or three steps at a time. The chapel came into view as she hit the bottom of the stairs; shadows began to dance among the pews as she turned to the front door. As she neared the exit, someone stepped into the building that made her stop in her tracks. Standing before her was a man that made her heart stop. Rufus.

He stood there with an estranged grin on his face. His clothes had been torn in several places and he was appropriately dirty for someone who had been buried in rubble. "Katie, Katie, Katie..." He repeated her name as he chuckled. "This was a pretty reckless place to visit. *and* to be here so late. Tsk...tsk."

"And it was pretty reckless of you to follow us here *priest*." Elijah's voice from behind made Katie jump, "and I thought I told you to be out of here already!" This remark was thrown at Katie with detest that she was still in the building. "If you don't want us all to die tonight, I suggest you move too. We'll barely make it as is." Elijah and Rufus were once more locked in a staring match.

"I think you misunderstand what my orders are." Rufus was now laughing again, "I am here to make sure the two of you die. If I go as well then it will be for the glory of the Arken-Son and the holy Quietus!"

"I avoided fighting you last time, I hope you don't think the same will happen now." Elijah had drawn his daggers and readied himself to attack. "Katie, stay behind me and as soon as you're clear, run." His direction was clear, and he refused to let Katie attempt an argument. They both knew that the goal is to get her out of here and for him to follow.

"I don't think you'll have a chance to fight me if you are too busy fighting my pets!" With a smirk, Rufus pulled a medallion from beneath his shirt. It was solid gold and formed in the shape of a warped face screaming. The eyes were blood-red rubies that began to glow as he brought it into the open. It hung freely from his neck as the mouth opened and a dark smoke poured out onto the ground around him. Three deformed creatures began to crawl their way out of the medallion. They pulled and pushed against one another until they had touched the floor of the church.

Shrieks rang out from their open maws that made Katie fall to the floor in tears. She covered her ears in an attempt to drown out the same cries that she had heard for years within her dreams. Looking back to the source, she witnessed as the three horrors appeared to be melting as they struggled to stand. Rufus looked horrified as if this wasn't what he had expected. The screams continued as these creatures slowly liquified into ash stains on the floor of the church.

"I restored the seal beneath the church." Elijah was smirking as he spoke. "Your little *pets* won't help you in here." He grabbed Katie by the arm and forced her to her feet. His eyes stayed locked with Rufus' who now looked ready to scream.

"I don't need them to stop two little kids! Argh!" He rushed towards the pair; his patience gone. The man was large, and his powerful legs carried him as quick as a snake striking its prey. The medallion swung freely from a chain around the man's neck with screaming face and crimson eyes demanding blood for the demons it had lost.

Elijah took advantage of the man's advance. A larger man can't change his direction fast, and he pushed himself and Katie out of the distressed man's charge. Rufus swiped his arms wide in an attempt to catch the pair, but he only managed to grab the stagnant air which had begun to mix with the acrid odor air from outside.

Elijah still held fast to Katie's arm, and he forced her into a run as he charged for the door of the building. His hand gripped her arm so tight that she could feel it bruising in his grip. Rufus was shouting in anger behind them as he chased after the two.

Harrington was built so that the sun would set behind the Lord's manor. It was a message to the people that even the sun bowed to this man. It was a fact that disgusted most people. For anyone who dared enter the city now, that setting sun was an omen that death was approaching. Katie watched as the sun disappeared behind the manor, feeling pincered by death as both the city and Rufus were shouting out for her life.

Elijah forced the pair forward paying just enough mind to Katie to make sure she didn't trip. Shadows began to dance around every building and street as though the trio of living beings were a parade being ushered in to soon join them in death. Katie spared a moment to look at several shadows standing behind building as they passed. The shadows opened their eyes to stare back at her. She felt her heart stop and her foot trip.

Time seemed to slow down as she fell to the ground. Watching as the stone road approached her face, she couldn't even seem to move her arms fast enough to brace her fall. With her trip, she knew they lost the time they had. Those ghostly dark eyes of the shadows seemed to pierce her very soul. Whispers found their way into her head again. *You shouldn't be here. It isn't time. Leave! Kill the large one. It's over! LEAVE! LEAVE! LEAVE!*

She lifted her head to see a figure standing above her. "Why did you come here?" The shadow's voice was as soft as a child's. Her eyes were locked with its own as it stood patiently waiting for her answer. From the corner of her eye, she could see Elijah had turned to face against Rufus. She managed to look over enough to see that both he and Rufus weren't moving. They seemed frozen where they stood.

"Please, Katie, tell me why you came to the city so soon?" The shadow's voice had changed to sound like a gentle mother speaking to a child that was caught somewhere they shouldn't be. "Don't you know that you weren't supposed to come here yet?"

"How—" Katie was staring into the eyes of the being again. She couldn't find the right question to ask nor could she think of a way to answer its question.

"I see." It seemed to have found its answer without her, "Please come back when it is time. I'll take you and your friend to the gate now. The big one will be handled here. I won't be able to keep you safe if you show up early again! After all, they are all very hungry." The shadow had changed its voice again to a father-like voice offering his child a gentle scolding.

Katie followed its gaze towards the center of town. Down every alley and around every building were dozens of figures staring at her. Even as shadows, she could feel their bloodlust in the gaze as they looked down upon a fresh meal. Katie looked back to the figure only now, she was staring at the gate which they had come through. Both her and Elijah were now standing outside of the city. The shades and Rufus were gone.

"Argh!" Elijah shouted as he lunged at the Rufus who was no longer there. "What?" He quickly looked around as he skidded to a stop. Even though he could see they were out of the city, he couldn't seem to grasp the idea of where they were. His eyes finally stopped when he looked down to see Katie who was still laying on the ground just as she had fallen in the city street.

"I—" Katie didn't know what to ask, or how to ask it. They both stayed as they were in the confusion of how they managed to appear outside of the city. Katie was the first to move as she stood and began to walk towards the horses. "Something happened. I'll explain on the way, but we need to move for now." It felt good to Katie to turn that line back on him for a change.

CHAPTER SIXTEEN
ROAD TO LAKE TOWN

"Daniel! I'm surprised to see you here. How can I help you?" James's voice was as soft as ever. The boy looked sickly pale, as he smiled the best he could towards Daniel, who was reading through a report Katie had left on her desk. "If you are hoping to find something here, I think you would have the last several times you checked."

Daniel felt a chill run down his spine as the boy spoke. Something had always seemed off about the kid. He was an orphan who came from lake town, but during his last trip there no one seemed to remember the kid. Lately, Daniel had been trying to pay more attention to his instincts and everything about this kid made Daniel feel uneasy.

"I don't mind you looking around but do keep in mind that Katie will be greatly upset with us both if you mess up her work." The kid laughed as he made his attempt at humor. Daniel merely stood there as he stared down the boy. "I hope this doesn't seem rude, but it makes me uncomfortable with you looking at me that long." He gave a nervous chuckle, breaking eye contact.

"Are you sure you haven't heard anything from them? It's been a week now and no one in any of the cities seems to have heard from her. It isn't like her to go this long without at least sending a letter." Daniel made no attempt to quell his anger. He knew that James' was hiding something, and he intended to find out what it was.

"I promise!" James' straightened up at being questioned, "I'm worried about her too. I—I heard some guy took off with her. Someone even rumored that it was by force." His eyes drifted off as he gently scratched his cheek. "Daniel, is there something you aren't telling me? I would very much like to know if Katie is in danger." His concern seemed genuine. Even if Daniel doubted him, he didn't doubt that the boy was worried.

"We don't even know ourselves." Daniel answered in earnest. "That is why it is important you let us know if she does happen to reach out. We are going to go get her, but we can't afford to run around aimlessly. Please be diligent on informing us if she even sends a clue."

"I will make sure to do that." James said bowing politely. "Is there anything else I can help you with since you are here? All the Library's knowledge is at your disposal."

"Thank you, but I think it's time for me to leave." Daniel placed the report back on Katie's desk as he had found it and followed James back to the entrance. As they prepared to say their goodbyes, a mail courier jogged up to meet them with a letter addressed to James. Daniel had seen Katie's handwriting enough to recognize it. "From Katie?"

James had opened the letter quickly as Daniel impatiently waited for the boy to finish reading over its contents. "Oh, what a blessing!" James' thrust the letter towards Daniel as he sang his joy to whatever news he read.

Daniel wasted no time reading the letter several times over. It was her handwriting, but it didn't feel like the message was truly from her. The letter claimed that they had been traveling for a while, and she didn't have time to write sooner. It claimed that they are in Lake Town and planned to be there for a while, and it said to tell John not to worry so much.

"It seems all of our worry has been for naught." James was beaming as he spoke, "It seems Katie is just being her usual self!" He spoke with relief, but Daniel felt more concerned than ever. His suspicion of James made Daniel decide to play along until he could consult with John. James agreed to let him take the letter, they said brief goodbyes, and Daniel hurried off to the guildhall.

The guild was as lively as ever. People lined the reception hall to request help tasks ranging from moving supplies to armed escorts for travel. After Daniel's encounter, John ordered that all travel is to be escorted with zero exception. No one was more upset about his order than Bryant who was supposed to support these escorts from the city treasury. He felt the risks were unfounded and that the funding should be focused on the festival.

Daniel managed to overhear someone from Lake Town mention that the mayor has been acting strange lately and hasn't been seen around the town as much as he used to. He only caught that little bit in passing as he walked further into the hall where only members were allowed.

The hall was filled with tables and booths for members to eat, drink, plan out jobs, and sometimes you would even find them sleeping. The hall never closed so the members could come and go as they need to at any time of the day. A large bar was set up on either side of the hall for members to drink, and the second floor had plenty of rooms to rent for anyone that happened to drink too much. John's office was at the furthest back end of the hall, behind the large table for when John hosted big events.

Thomas had managed to work his way inside again and was currently arguing with Harden as he attempted to get the kid out of the hall. Daniel remember when Harden was no different than Thomas, and it was Daniel who had to go chasing him out of the guild hall. He reveled in how much the guild has grown since those days. He and John had worked hard to bring the place so far.

He finally had reached the large wooden door that led to John's office. He gave a brief knock before entering the room where John had been working on some report. He donned his large radiant face that drove Daniel crazy. *You don't have to always strain yourself to look so cheery* Daniel thought to himself as he closed the door behind him.

"Daniel!" John's voice was always so loud, "what brings you here?"

"A letter from Katie." He tossed the letter onto John's desk. The large man broke character at the news of Katie, and his eyes skimmed the letter several times. Each time he started the letter over, his face grew more and more grim.

"This isn't her." His voice was flat, "She's wrote me enough times to know that this isn't from her...but the writing looks just like hers."

"I felt the same. I don't know if Katie really is there, but I'm worried about Lake Town." John was silent as he thought about it for a moment. He handed the letter back to Daniel before he nodded to him. John knew that Daniel had intended to head to Lake Town to investigate, he just wanted to confirm with John about the letter.

"I'll get ready to leave as well. I don't think it'll be smart for you to go on your own this time." John began to rise as he headed to the wardrobe he kept his travel gear in.

"I don't think you should." Daniel's interjection made John stop in his tracks, "If this isn't from Katie, someone may still send information about her. One of us needs to stay in case it comes in."

"The last time you went to Lake Town," John's fist was shaking as he spoke, "You came back half dead. I will *not* let you go alone again this time." His face turning red as he spoke. Daniel loved John like a brother, but he hated how easy it was for him to get worked up.

"I'm going alone." Daniel stood his ground, "Of everyone who has traveled to or from Lake Town, no one else has been attacked." John took a step back, "It's likely that was the only one, and if there is another one of those things out there and it attacks, we will at least know who it was after."

"I won't let you go and be bait for some creature we can't even find!" John pounded his fist into his desk, "I don't want to willingly send anyone to death, so I am going with you." John moved back to his wardrobe.

"And what if there is another one, and what if it does attack me? It took a straight hit by my bow twice before it finally went down." Daniel was crushing the letter in his hand, "What do you think you and your sword will do to it?" The two were silent. John had been gripping the handle of his wardrobe so tight that he had accidently splintered the wooden handle.

"I don't think I've lost my temper like this in a long time." John sounded as though he had calmed down some. "Can you promise me you will return?"

"I refuse to leave Christine a widow. You can count on that as your promise." Hearing Daniel use his wife's name like that brought a grin to John's face. The only thing Daniel would never do, is use his wife's name in a promise unless he truly meant it.

"Daniel, I don't think I told you about this yet," John was smiling as he stared at the wood pieces in his hand, "I got engaged during my last trip to the capital." Daniel was startled by this sudden revelation. "I promise to tell you all about her when you get back so make sure you do."

"If nothing else, I'll make it back just to warn the poor girl to run while she still can."

"I already tried to warn her. She was the one who proposed to me."

"This woman knows you and still she proposed? I don't know if you will survive a marriage like that." Daniel bowed as if paying his condolences, "I've decided you should go on this trip. I will write a beautiful eulogy for you."

John let out a thunderous roar of laughter, "You think that creature can save me?"

"The eulogy was meant for my wedding speech. I know you'd come back. That's why I'll mourn for you." The two bursts into a fit a laughter for a while. Having the tension finally lifted from the room allowed the two to share a few jokes before Daniel took his leave. "So, who is this woman?"

"I will tell you when you get back." John had returned to his chair, "Now go. You'll probably need the rest of the day to convince your own wife to let you go back there. That'll be a harder fight than what we had here."

"I intend to leave without telling her." Daniel looked as though he was starting to sweat, "If she knew I was going back, she'd close the city and put the entire guild on guard duty to stop me." Even John felt tense as he thought about how strong such a sickly woman could be.

"If you are going without her knowing, I'll have *your* eulogy ready for your return." This time, their laughter was nervous. She would kill both of them when she finds out that John knew he was leaving. "You better getting going soon then. Christine is visiting with Madame Jolie. You might want to get out of here before she finishes her appointment."

As Daniel turned to leave, John called out to him again, "How has Stephanie been doing by the way? I haven't heard from her since you all returned." Daniel remained silent for a moment. Struggling to gather his thoughts around the girl, he finally found the right words.

"She's locked herself up in her room. We can't seem to get her to eat anything, and I don't think she is sleeping either. Christine has been staying with her the last few nights to try and help her, but I don't think it's doing much."

"Maybe if she had worked up some more experience before she ran into that, it wouldn't have been so bad." John seemed to shuffle some papers around on his desk haphazardly. "It was awful luck you ran into that thing on her first mission."

"If she doesn't get better by the festival, we're going to take her home. She doesn't need to stay here the way she is now."

"That's probably for the best. I'll get the paperwork started in case Katie doesn't come home in time." John sighed, "Doesn't she understand all her paperwork falls on me when she takes off like this? If nothing has happened to her, I'm going to scold her for real this time."

On that, Daniel quickly said his goodbye and headed out of the office. As he left, he thought about Stephanie more. He felt responsible for how she was handling things, and she was partly the reason he wanted to go alone. He knew that he was most likely going to encounter another, and he didn't want to get anyone else involved with whatever these creatures were. He quickly left the Guild Hall and made his way to the stable.

The road to Lake Town ran mostly through the Vaieli. This road was always silent, but today the deafness of the forest was ominously piercing. Daniel would normally travel with his wooden bow in reach and his elvish bow strapped to the saddle. He reversed that for this trip. He was tense as he recalled the last time he had traveled here. The silence around him was unsettling as even the birds and insects seemed to have disappeared.

As he traveled, he traced the writings along his bow. Each one had been a different enchantment placed on the bow by the elves. Katie had done her best to interpret them before. One enchantment made the bow resistant to weathering and age so that it would maintain its quality, another, influenced the wind which is what creates the arrows it fires. There were several that even though Katie could read them, she couldn't understand them. Something that has to do with spirit and energy, but none of it made since to either of them.

As he traveled wrapped in his thoughts, the sight of a covered wagon caught him off guard. He looked around the carriage as he came from behind, but he couldn't see any guards on escort. "Excuse me!" he called out to the driver, "It's dangerous on this road. Where is your escort?"

"I was waiting for him to catch up!" The voice that called back chilled him to his core. He felt as though his heart stopped when the familiar voice continued, "John's worst trait is that he talks to loud. And *your* worst trait is not understanding how much a wife can know about her husband."

As he approached the side of the wagon, the driver bore an icy glare that made Daniel nearly fall over. Not only did his wife figure out he was leaving. She managed to get a wagon ready and leave fast enough to have gotten this far ahead. "Why did you come? It's too dangerous for you even without chancing another run in with that thing." Daniel was scared about her confronting him, but he was equally upset for putting herself in danger by traveling at all.

"*You're* worried about *me* when you were going to run off and not even tell me where you were going?" She had stopped the carriage so that she could stand as she shouted, "Did you not think how it would have affected me anyway to have to sit around and hope that you come back? What would have happened if you used your bow again? It nearly killed you last time, and you are going to run off and do that again? I'm so angry right now that I—" Unable to think of what to say, she took off her shoe and hurled it at Daniel as hard as she could.

"Don't be too upset with him," another familiar voice came from the back of the wagon, "He just wants to make sure you are safe, I'm sure." Stephanie's head popped out from behind Christine. Her skin was paler than before, and her cheeks seemed to sink in. Just seeing her face made Daniel's heart sink.

"Don't get me started on you right now!" Christine had turned her attention to the girl, "I brought you here because you wanted to try and get out of your slump, not stick up for my good-for-nothing husband!" Daniel took a moment to catch his breath now that she had turned her attention away from him. A question suddenly came to him.

"Why didn't you just stop me?" It didn't make sense to him why she would have come this far. If she were worried, she would have tried to keep him home. "Knowing you, every gate would have been shut down if you had gone to them."

She hesitated before speaking, "I'm worried about Lake Town as well," her motives became clear to him, "I knew you wouldn't have let me come along. I made sure to get as far ahead as I could, so you couldn't send me back." Daniel finally took notice to how winded her horses sounded. She must have had them galloping to get the lead on him. "Come on. We need to hurry. It's a three-day ride to Lake Town, and I really don't want to be on this road longer than we have to."

Daniel motioned back to Stephanie as though asking why she was brought along. It was Stephanie who answered in her place. "I came to Pneu so that I could become something other than a fisherman. I'm not ready to give up on that yet. I'm scared, but I can't stop yet." Without a word, Christine smiled as she ushered on the horses.

"Hurry and bring me my shoe back so we can get moving," she called out to Daniel without looking his way. The group remained silent for the rest of their trip to Lake Town.

§

CHAPTER SEVENTEEN
LAKE TOWN

The town looked as though it was nearly abandoned. The group had been in the same town not even two weeks prior, but the city was nearly unrecognizable. During their last trip, the town had been so busy that they had to board their horses near the edge of town. Now, there were so few people that they would have been able to ride straight into the city square.

The sight was enough to put Daniel on edge. He reached for his bow when a quick look from Christine told him not to. They looked over the people who were in the streets and each one looked to be in a hurry to get home. No one even bothered to give the pair a second glace as they hurried about in a near panic state.

"Christine? Daniel?" A familiar voice rang out from beside their wagon. "The two of you really shouldn't be here!" Elizabeth's normally cheerful voice was filled with fear as she shared her concern with the pair. Normally, the town's source of rumors and scandals, she appeared to be terrorized from a lack of sleep and overwhelming fear. "Please! Come with me. Quickly!" She didn't wait to see if the pair were following before she started to shuffle off towards her home.

It was only a short walk before they were sitting inside the woman's home. Elizabeth usually kept a very warm and welcoming home. Now... the only lights were from the few candles that she kept lit in the kitchen. Christine and Stephanie were documenting as much as they could recall of the city when they arrived as Elizabeth wandered from window to window searching frantically for anyone watching. The eerie presence

Daniel felt when he first arrived grew stronger as he realized something crucial about the woman's home.

"Elizabeth," his voice was like a weight crashing through thin ice. The woman jumped at the sound of his voice causing a vase to crash into the floor. "Where are your husband and kids? Usually we would see one of them hanging from your arm." Christine must have been wary of this as well as she was now staring intently at Elizabeth.

"Um. Well, you see—" She struggled to find the words. Tears welled in the corners of her eyes as she tried to find a place to start. "Gone. They were just gone."

Daniel heard a gasp escape Stephanie's lips as one had made it past his as well.

"What do you mean gone?" Christine's voice was nearly at a shout, "Where did they go?"

"I don't know. I wish I did, but they were just, gone." She was in tears now as she spoke, "I came back from Pnue and no one seemed to be able to tell me where they went. People I used to be close to were suddenly bitter and cold towards me, and even the mayor refuses to speak with me now. It's like, people aren't the same anymore, and everyone else is too scared to say anything."

"We were here not even two weeks ago!" Daniel had raised his voice as he spoke, "What's happening here?"

"I don't know." Elizabeth voice cracked, "I wish I did. I want to know where my kids are. They are probably scared and alone and no one here seems to know or even care for that matter!"

The room was silent except for the sound of Elizabeth's sobbing. Christine made her way over to comfort her. "We are here now, so let us look into what is going on. We'll find out what's going on around her." Her attempt to soothe the woman seemed to go unnoticed as Elizabeth remained inconsolable.

After a few hours, Elizabeth managed to fall asleep. After Christine managed to put the woman to bed, she returned to the kitchen where Stephanie was still scribbling away in her journal. Daniel had been staring out the same window Elizabeth had been at. The window gave a clear view of the town square, and Daniel had been staring at the same building for some time before speaking.

"I think someone has been watching us since we got here." He didn't look away from the window as he spoke, "I can't shake the feeling that the shadows around that building are watching." Christine looked however she was unable to see anything. She was ready to dismiss Daniel's paranoia when, for just a brief moment, a shadow moved… or to her it seemed like it moved. Nothing had actually changed. "You saw that too then?" Daniel's voice was nearly a whisper when he spoke.

"I think we are just a little jumpy." Christine said, attempting to dismiss what they had seen. "Maybe we should call it a night too and regroup in the morning." She placed her arm on his shoulder when she noticed something in the window of the building where the shadow had moved. In the front window, near the door of the building, very faintly were two eyes staring at them. Unblinking, not moving, dark black eyes staring.

Christine quickly dropped to her knees to look away from the home as Daniel continued to stare. She grabbed one of his legs as she covered her mouth with her other hand. She felt frozen in that moment as those eyes seared their way into her mind. Stephanie's attention was drawn to the pair when this occurred.

"The last time I looked away from those eyes they vanished." Daniel placed his hand on her head as he spoke, "I plan to keep an eye on whatever that thing is. Go get some sleep. I don't plan on losing sight of whatever the hell that thing is. If I shout for you to move though, grab the others and get out of here."

Christine could hear the fear in his voice as he spoke. He had seen the same eyes that she did, yet he refused to look away from it. She remembered how strong he could be as she hugged his leg. "As long as you are up, I'm going to stay here. I don't think it would be smart for either of us to fall asleep here in the city."

"Thank you." Daniel gave no argument to her statement. This showed Christine how scared he was as well, and how hard he was trying to hide it. As Christine took a moment to appreciate him, something moved from one of the bedrooms. Daniel must have sensed it as well as he quickly jerked away from the window with a dagger drawn.

Staring towards the doorway where they thought someone was standing, was only darkness. No person was visible, but the couple could feel a presence there that made their blood run cold. Stephanie too seemed to be aware of whatever that presence was as her eyes were glued to the same doorway. Her hands were shaking as tears welled up in the corner of her eyes.

She had slipped off the back of her chair as she had attempted to distance herself from the empty doorway. Daniel managed to shake himself of his fear and pulled Stephanie towards them. "Stephanie, you and Christine get things wrapped up. We need to leave soon." His voice was layered with fear as he turned back to the window in hopes of finding what was staring at them again.

"Steph," This time it was Christine to speak, "it's time to get moving. We can't stay here any longer." She too tried to keep her voice as calm as she could, but she was as shaken as Daniel.

Stephanie nodded as she got to her feet and retrieved her journal from the table. The two women stared at one another for a moment. Finally, Stephanie slowly nodded her head. "Good! Let's get moving!" Christine looked to Daniel, "Do you want me to wake Elizabeth too?"

"I don't think we should," Daniel's voice faded off as slight tapping sound was heard from one of the other rooms. Stephanie froze stiff as Christine quickly pushed herself between the girl and the sound. Daniel had his dagger drawn again as he slowly walked towards the girls.

A thump from a different room was heard as something was dropped to the floor. Daniel pulled the girls behind him so that they were between him and a corner of the kitchen. A door in a different room slammed shut which brought out a sudden squeal from Stephanie. Heavy footsteps could be heard from the room where Elizabeth had been sleeping; too heavy to have been from the woman who had been sleeping in there.

Christine moved to try and go to her, but she was blocked by Daniel. She looked to him in concern for the woman; he shook his head telling her that they shouldn't go to her. The window where Daniel had been standing before suddenly shattered as glass sprayed across the kitchen. Stephanie screamed out. A loud scratching noise was heard dragging from the window and across the outside wall of the home. A moment later, another window shattered, followed by another, and another. Slowly, the scratching noise worked its way around to the front door of the home where it stopped.

Several moments passed before a sudden *boom!* Over and over again something heavy pounded on the door. The hinges screamed as they barely held to the door. The sound of wood splintering was heard on the last hit. Daniel could hear Stephanie sniffling as she had broken into tears. He knew the door would break apart on the next hit. He waited, waited, waited, but the next hit never came.

"What's going on?" Elizabeth's draggy voice was like an explosion to the trio too scared to even breath. "Were you three really going to just leave me here?" The woman was smiling at the trio who wore confused expressions. "This is my house after all. I tend to hear everything that goes on in here. I can even hear your thoughts." Speaking through the beginnings of laughter which quickly turned to a cackle as Daniel and Christine felt the hostility rising from the woman.

"Yes, I can even hear your thoughts in here, Daniel." She was pointing her finger towards him. "You did indeed make a mistake following me home."

"Who are—"

"Who am I?" She laughed again, "I'm Elizabeth! Lonely housewife who seeks out scandals to fill the lonely void my husband leaves." She placed an arm across her forehead as she pretended to sniffle. Another window suddenly smashed in making Christine jump along with Stephanie. Elizabeth glared at Daniel through her arm. "You were an unexpected character in all this, Daniel! We didn't even consider you worth looking at until you killed our demon out in the forest." Her voice was filled with malice as she lashed out at Daniel.

"What do you know about the demon?" Daniel wanted to keep her talking until her could come up with a plan to get them out of this house. From his peripheral vision, he eyed his elvish bow which was resting on the table. He could only assume that the creature outside of the home was another demon. This one seemed larger than the one he encountered before. He was also concerned about the footsteps he had heard before in the home. He continued to wait and watch.

"That demon took me some time to develop!" she screamed out, "He was such a good pet and you went and killed it! How dare you try and destroy what I have been working so hard to build!" The woman was hysterical as her face seemed to shift. She looked as though she was aging before his eyes. "How did you do it!? How did you kill my pet when it was so strong?"

Daniel was relieved to hear that she didn't know about his bow. He planned to grab for it once he saw an opening. Suddenly though as though she really could read his mind, "Ah! That bow is the source then." Her sight shifted to the table. He needed to make his move before she did. "Don't you move from your spot!" She spit as she screamed to him.

She slowly moved to the table. Eyes locked with Daniel, she reached down and grabbed the bow with one hand. Her fingers touched the bow when she shrieked, recoiling in pain as the skin on her hand peeled and burned as though a fire was put to it. Things seemed to move slowly in the next few moments.

As the woman screamed, the front door was smashed to pieces. Standing taller than the doorway was a dark creature. Those deep black eyes they had been staring into from before were now there staring at them again. It stood several feet taller than any person in the room. Its skin was like burnt flesh still dripping from infection. Long claws protruded from each finger, and the creature's teeth, fangs ready to shred any flesh it could bite into.

Daniel threw the dagger towards the woman as the demon moved into the home. Hand free from the blade, he moved for his bow. The creature was now several steps closer to them. After a few steps, Daniel watched as his dagger bore its way into the woman's skull. Still too far from his bow, that *thing* moved unnaturally.

Although the world seemed to move slowly, the monster moved as though he existed outside of time. Each step it took, it moved the pace of a step and a half. Christine was now standing guard to Stephanie as Daniel finally grabbed hold of his bow; the creature was now standing in the entrance of the kitchen. Elizabeth still hadn't hit the floor as she fell from the wound that Daniel had inflicted.

He ignored the danger and drew the string of his bow. The demon who was now close enough to touch, and Daniel felt the unnatural presence of death as the thing raised its claws to strike him down. His hand released the powerful tempest which tore deep into the chest of the demon before him.

The shot was so powerful that it left the demon in pieces as the furniture, glass, windows, roof, the entire home was blown away with Daniel being the center of the blast. Stephanie and Christine were shoved away from the incredible blast that left the home in ruins. Daniel was thrown to the ground where he had stood, and Elizabeth's body thrown several feet away, lying motionless on a piece of the table.

The pieces of the disintegrated demon slowly turned to ash and crumbled away to nothingness. The only sign of its presence were the ash stains left from the pieces that had found the ground. Amidst the debris, only one person remained standing. A man that none of them had seen before was now standing in the room where the woman had been sleeping before. His fiery red hair burned as brightly as his eyes.

He appeared to be amused as he softly clapped his hands. Daniel moved to aim his bow at the man before falling ill and dropping to a knee again. The man quickly raised his hands as if to tell Daniel not to move. "There is no need for any more fighting!" The man's voiced sounded as though he were singing his words, "I merely wanted to learn how it is you killed our demon before, and now I know!" He gave a quick bow.

"This was a very helpful experience!" This time, it was the woman who spoke out. It wasn't her voice though. It was the voice of the man that came from her mouth, "That bow apparently has an enchantment which protects it from the undead. This puppet was useless the moment it's hand began to melt!" The woman who was once Elizabeth began to crumble to ash just as the demon had before.

"You have given us a lot to plan for, and I appreciate you coming all this way for us to see! I look forward to seeing you soon!" The man gave an enthusiastic wave as he began to walk away. Daniel struggled to get up again before falling back to his knees.

The man waved eccentrically as he rubbed a gold medallion that hung around his neck. A demon crawled its way from the mouth of the medallion that appeared grotesque. It crawled on all fours with bits of burning flesh dripping from its body. Its face was something crossed between a horse and a dog with strips of flesh missing that exposed bright red bones beneath. The man mounted the creature and disappeared into the forest.

Daniel quickly scanned the debris until he had found where Christine and Stephanie had fallen. He stumbled his way to the pair; Christine having been knocked unconscious however Stephanie had been quickly writing and drawing away in her notebook. Tears filled her eyes, but she had fought through her fear to do what they had needed from her. She seemed to tune out everything else around her, so much so that when Daniel put his hand on her shoulder, she didn't even seem aware of him there.

He moved his attention to Christine as Stephanie continued to work. She was out, but she was breathing and didn't appear to have any injuries. Her fever had returned though, and Daniel began to curse himself for letting her come along with him again. Her illness was severe, and he knew how dangerous it is for her. Despite this, she continues to go along as though nothing was wrong. He knew he would have to talk with her some more about settling down again, but for now, he needed to evacuate the town and let John know what had happened.

A shaking hand reached out to grab his arm. Still holding her pen, Stephanie had finally realized he was there, and she began to break down into tears as she gripped his arm. "I can't" *sniffle* "I can't do this anymore." *sniffle* "I want to go home." She buried her face in his arm as she broke down into tears and couldn't speak anymore.

"I promise to take you home after this." He placed his hand on hers, "I won't ask you to do this again. I'm sorry." He got the girls loaded into the wagon and headed back into the town. People were wandering back and forth looking for others. Around the same time that the man had disappeared into the forest, many people to include the mayor had suddenly fallen, and rendered to nothing but ash.

Daniel moved from building to building to evacuate the town. No one seemed to argue, and some didn't even wait for others before taking off. The only place Daniel had stopped for long was at the building where he had seen the demon staring at him. Hidden within the shadows beside the building, he felt a presence. He could feel the eyes of something watching him. Whatever was there, it made no move to interfere. It simply observed. Daniel decided that getting everyone out of here was more important than chasing shadows and led the evacuation of the city.

§

Chapter Eighteen
Scars of the Past

Daniel, Christine, Stephanie, Katie, *Elijah.* They all continued to mount upon John's mind as he attempted to work his way through the seemingly endless pile of paperwork he needed to get through for the day. So much had happened over the last several weeks, that John began to wonder if he was really qualified enough to handle this position.

His mind wandered even further back to when Master Lockharte was still here. As the former swords master to the king, he had more experience and skill with a sword than John could ever hope to achieve. He was a good friend, and the man that helped John bring the guild to fruition. The day he had left, he spoke with the city council that was still new and had named John his successor before returning to his family in the capital.

John still doubted that he was the right choice, but he didn't want to disrespect his master by turning the position away. He's looked for Master Lockharte several times during his visits to the capital, but no one seems to have seen him or his family since he left Pneu. Even his fiancé with her influence had attempted to find him, but no one could find any information on the family.

He put away his pen as his thoughts lingered on *her* for a while. After the festival, and after things are wrapped up with Elijah, he decided that he would travel to see her. After all of this stress, he could use some time with her. He always found it hard to describe, but she always held a portion of his thoughts no matter what else was going on.

She was the most beautiful woman he had ever known, and the thought of her ever returning his feelings were still unfathomable even after she had proposed. He couldn't wait till their marriage. All he wanted, was to see her smiling face every day. This was the one wish he had that stood above all others. He only wished that Amelia were still around to have met her.

The thoughts of his late sister made him decide to wrap up his work for the day. Nothing would let him focus again after she came into his thoughts. A knock on his door pulled him from his thoughts as he was packing up for the day. He took a moment to fix his face to what he felt was most suitable for a leader before calling out for the visitor to enter.

"Good evening, Master." Harden's voice was awkward as he attempted to speak. Usually Harden only ever met with Daniel so having to come here made him double check every word he spoke, "I wanted to inform you that Christine and Stephanie were reported to have left from the North Gate without an escort." His voice was shaking, scared at how John would react to the news.

Instead of being upset, John started to laugh to himself which brought about a curious stare from the young adventurer. "I'm glad to hear it. I was worried about Daniel being on his own," he trailed off for a moment, "anyway, thank you for the good news. You should head on out for the night." He was beaming as he tried to dismiss the young man.

"But what about her being sick?" Harden seemed genuinely concerned, "Isn't it dangerous for her to be out?"

"That girl is tougher than Daniel gives her credit for. I've known them both since we were kids. Those two do their best when they are together so try not to think too hard on it." Harden still seemed to be worried, but he accepted John's words and dismissed himself. John didn't waste much time before he too left for the day.

John loved to walk through the city in the evening. He always stopped on the bridge on his way home to watch as the sunset lit up the entire river like thousands of tiny lights reflected back into the world. This city meant everything to him. The city, the people, and all the friends he had made here. Daniel, Christine, Katie, Adam, Kimberly, and Amelia. Even Elijah was with them all before he had gone missing.

They were all each other had for so long, and all he wished for was to protect the ones he still had.

As he stood there, from the corner of his eye, something like a specter seemed to draw his attention. When he looked, it was just the normal business on the street as people were moved about at the end of their day. He began to wonder how tired he was when staring at him from behind a corner that led into an alleyway was a pair of eyes that he knew. Those two dark brown eyes pierced him to his core as he felt his heart freeze in place and tears filled his eyes.

With a quick blink, the eyes were gone as pain built within his chest and panic set into his mind. He couldn't think about how impossible it was for those eyes to have been staring at him. He simply ran towards the alley they had been peering from. He ignored as a few passerby's attempted to call out to him and continued until he was finally there. Glancing down the alley, a small figure ran around another corner. Her curled blonde hair danced as the girl quickly ran out of sight.

His eyes were swelling as tears ran down his cheeks. He was lost in the emotion of seeing the impossible girl and took off after her. The quick glimpses and shadows of her led him from alley to alley. He crossed into an older part of town and out to another courtyard that was busy with people hustling about their evening as he desperately looked around for where she had gone. "John!" The soft voice called out his name so softly he had nearly missed it.

As he turned around, he spotted the blonde curls disappearing down a new alley. He gave chase once again. His mind was filled with the images of those brown eyes and blonde hair. He knew them so well that he didn't need to waste any thought on figuring out who the individual was. Instead, his mind focused on trying to understand how she was here. eight years it had been since he had last stared into those eyes.

Towards the end of one of the alley ways, a door stood open to what looked like an old storeroom. The windows had been long boarded up, and without any lights, he struggled to see if anything was inside. The alley way had hit a dead end meaning that this was the only room she had to have gone in. Finally, he had taken a moment to think about the situation.

As he pondered the meaning of seeing her and the impossibility of her being here, he began to wonder if all he was doing was chasing a delusion of his longing mind. "John!" Hearing that voice and the playful ring it was carried on, all doubt left his mind, and he charged headlong into the empty storeroom. The darkness swallowed him as the door closed with a bang as soon as he had cleared the entryway.

He tried the handle several times, but no matter how hard he pulled on the door, he couldn't get it to budge. Silence surrounded him, and a sudden chill ran through to his core as he felt a presence within the room. He knew the presence he felt, and he could feel the hostility it bore down on him. He reached for his sword, but, nothing. He had left his sword back in the guild hall.

He stood with his back against the door as he stared towards the presence that he had sensed. As his eyes adjusted, a figure came into view. *Sniffle.* He could hear what sounded like someone crying as the figure which was crouched in another corner was crying. *Sniffle.* It continued to cry as those blonde curls began to shine like a light through the darkness. John ignored the feeling of hostility when he was able to make out the girls' hair. He moved quickly to where she was crouched on the floor and embraced her tightly.

He knew the impossibility. He knew she was dead. He was the one who buried her. But she was here. In his arms. He knew his sister too well to mistake her for anyone else. She was gone yet here, and his mind couldn't process it. He simply embraced her in fear that if he were to let go that she would disappear once more. Her small arms had wrapped around Johns arm, and the gentle bells of her voice were the first to break the silence. "It was so dark. Why did you leave me alone for so long?"

"How are you here now?" He pulled away from her so that he could look her over again. Staring into her dark brown eyes filled with tears belonged only to that one girl whom he had given up ever seeing again. His sister long dead stood there before him with her head cocked slightly to the side. His mind had no time to think before she spoke again.

"Did you not want me anymore? Is that why you put me in the ground?" Her voice shook with fear as though she were scared what he might say, "I even came back to you, but do you even want me here?"

He worked his mind as fast as he could. He didn't know how to respond to her questions.

"You had died—" These were all the words he could get out before she cut in again

"So, you didn't keep me safe? I thought you were supposed to keep me safe!" She forced his arms away as she broke down into tears. "You promised to take care of me! Why didn't you save me? You're such a horrible brother! I was so scared and alone! You were even going to start your own family! I hate you John! I hate you!"

His mind was reeling as he listened to his late sister scream at him. He tried putting words to how he felt, but the sound of his sister crying put knots in his throat that made it hard for him to speak. Before he could find any words for her, another familiar voice rang out through the darkness.

"I can't believe *this* is what became of the useless kid I left behind." The deep voice resounded its way to John's core. "I never should have left things to a such a pathetic child."

"My Baby!" Another voice came from where Amelia had been sitting, "how could you leave my little girl like this!?" A woman now sat embracing the girl. Both crying, the woman looked towards John in anger. All of John's strength now meant nothing beneath the gaze of his mother's scorn.

"Useless boy!" He felt the strong hand of his father strike him hard against the back of his head, "You couldn't even keep your own sister alive! How foolish we were to leave her to you!"

"It's all your fault our baby died!"

"I loved you so much and you just left me!"

"Don't you dare call yourself my son!"

"You should have died! Not her!"

"Brother, why didn't you love me? Why didn't you save me?" The voice bore into him like knives. With nowhere to run, John crumpled to the ground covering his ears. Even as he did though, the voices continued to grow louder.

"Useless!"

"Despicable!"

"I hate you!"

Then, for a brief moment it was silent. When he looked from the floor. The faces of his family stared at him, unblinking. His father stepped forward. As he did, blood oozed from a slit that ran across the man's throat. Despite the cut being deep enough to have stopped him from speaking, his father's voice was calm as he spoke. "I'm glad I died before seeing how useless of a man you had become."

His mother whose face was now broken and bruised spoke next. "We died to keep you both alive. You couldn't even protect the one person we truly cared about!"

"I loved you more than anything!" Amelia's voice was hollow and dry, "You left me alone in such a dark place for so long. I'm glad you are alone now. You deserve to be alone." John wanted to argue. He wanted to tell them they were wrong. He tried. He tried as hard as he could to keep her safe. He wanted to shout out that it wasn't his fault, but he couldn't bring himself to say it. He blamed himself as much as they did.

He accepted their words as he collapsed to the floor at their feet. "I'm sorry." These few words he spoke through muffled tears was all he could say.

"SORRY!?"

"THAT'S THE BEST YOU CAN DO!?"

"DON'T MAKE ME GO BACK INTO THE DARK! PLEASE NO!" Amelia began to panic as though something was reaching out to her. Eyes wide as she pressed herself hard into her mother's arms. John watched unsure of what was happening. As he reached his hand out to her, the three of them began to melt away. They screamed out as their skin and muscles turned to ash. In only a moment, John was suddenly left alone in the dark room with nothing more than his own fear and regret.

It seemed as though hours had passed as the words of his family replayed in his mind repeatedly. John was now resting with his back against a wall as his eyes burned from the tears, he could not produce any longer. He felt his mind drifting back to where it had been many times before as he questioned his own life. Why should he be here when *her* life was so short? His parents would have been better at taking care of her, and she may not have had to die if he had passed in his parent's place.

Amelia. John knew that he had done his best for her, and he knew that there was no way to have saved her. Knowing these things though did not stop the guilt from knotting within his chest. His deepest wish and regret were not getting to see her grow up.

The door to the abandoned storehouse suddenly opened. The moonlight seemed too bright after spending so long in the dark room. The light shone in to right where he had been sitting. Closing his right eye, John attempted to make out the person who had opened the door. It was the individual's voice though which gave the priest away to John.

"John? What—" The priest sounded shocked to find John as he did, "How long have you been here? Someone told me they saw you running like a madman! We've all been looking for you." As he approached, he was able to get a full look at John. "Now John. I don't think I have seen you this troubled in some time. Come. We can talk later. Right now, you need some rest."

John did not respond to the priest other than to follow him as he guided John back to his feet. Leading him by the arm, the priest led John out of the storehouse. With his mind still in a haze, John was not paying attention to where they were heading until they were already standing in front of the Pneu Church.

He sat quietly as the priest busily worked his way around boiling a pot of water and steeping some tea. John's eyes wandered around the desk before him. Several letters both open and sealed were strewn about. Reading the best he could from the wrong side of the table, a letter had been addressed from the priest in Kend. He had been writing about some fire that recently burned down the inn. He had also been asking for follow up on a prior matter that was not specified in this letter.

"Here you are, John." His voice brought John back to his senses as the priest placed a steaming cup of milky tea in front of him. "Drink some tea and rest your mind some. We can't have our town leader running around as wildly as you are." He gave a slight chuckle as to try and ease the tension.

"I'm no leader." John thumbed the rim of his cup, "I couldn't even keep one little girl safe." His eyes drifted off as he stared into the dark brown liquid reflected his sad face back to him. "Is it possible to bring someone back from the dead?" John placed his cup down with such little tact that some of the drink had spilled onto the desk.

"John," Father Bernard seemed to be searching for the right words. "It's ok to want someone to still be here with you. But there is nothing good in our world that can bring your sister back. If you search for it, you will only find a dark fate for yourself."

"I'm sorry, I think you misunderstood." John tried to regain his thoughts as he tried his best at cleaning up the mess he made. He had pulled down his shirt sleeve and was hastily dabbing away at the table when the priest placed his hands over John's to stop his erratic movements. Without saying a word, John understood that he was being asked to slow down and speak his mind.

"When I was leaving the guild earlier, I thought I had seen Amelia. Not just then though. When I first met Elijah the other day, he was standing with Ben and Grant who were reported to be dead." John paused a moment. "In the storeroom, my parents and Amelia were there. I heard them, I touched them!" John's voice began to rise as anger bubbled up within him, "They were there, and if someone is using them as puppets somehow, I swear I'll tear them apart!"

John had slammed his fists into the desk, papers and glass spread everywhere as the contents of the desk scattered frantically to escape the powerful fists which had only just shattered their home. Without even a wince, the priest sat quietly as John's breath raged in a fury.

"I'm sorry, John." The priest placed his hand once again over John's. Feeling the older man's shaky grip was enough for John to unclench his fists some. "There is nothing in this world that can bring someone back from the dead. I'm worried about you John." His voice was sincere and sad as he spoke, "I think you need to speak with Madame Jolie. Having such vivid hallucinations is not something to take lightly."

"They weren't halluc—" John attempted to say but was abruptly cut off.

"Jonathan Lemieux!" The priest was nearly shouting as he spoke, "I will not sit here and let your mind tear you apart!" His grip was uncharacteristically tight as he squeezed John's hand, "Out of all the kids I have cared for here, you are the closest to one that I can call a son. I won't see you fall apart like this." He had tears forming in the corners of his eyes as he spoke. "Please. Go see Madame Jolie. For me."

John felt a wave of guilt rush through him once more. He thought on what the priest had said for a few moments. "I'm sorry about your desk."

"If the cost of being here for you is a mess to clean up, then feel free to come and scatter all the paper you need." The priest laughed as he felt John calming down. Without warning, John hugged the man. It was a strong hug, and John began to worry if he would break the old man.

"You are a father to me. Thank you." John left it at that as he attempted to help the priest clean up the mess. He was quickly pushed away as the priest urged him to go home and sleep. The exhaustion of everything had finally began to set in on John. He did as the priest asked, and that night, John dreamt of Amelia.

§

CHAPTER Nineteen

TRAVELING ROADS AND DEMON ATTACKS

"I'm still confused as to why you act so differently around them than when you are with me?" Katie's voice rang with annoyance as her and Elijah stared at the empty home of the McKenna's. They had left for the festival in Pneu already as they discovered right before leaving. Along with an escort and three others from the city, the family had left the day before. "You don't have to keep up some façade now that I know who you are. You can try and be a *little* nicer to me, you know?"

"Come on. No point in staying in town. We may even catch up to them on the road." Elijah had ignored Katie's remark as he pushed his horse to continue out of the city.

"At this point, I think you enjoy ignoring me! When are you going to finally start answering me?" Katie followed in line with him however she refused to back off her questioning this time. She wanted one good answer from him while they were still on the road. "Can't you answer me just once? What was it about the McKenna's that made you so friendly?"

"It seemed like you found a family again." Elijah continued to look ahead as he walked. "It was nice to see you smiling that much again."

Katie found herself at a loss for words. She had been asking for a straightforward answer, but hearing one tied in with a sweet remark made her feel anxious. She had unknowingly slowed down and started to fall behind. As Elijah moved ahead, she stared at him. She took in just how much he had grown in the last ten years. Nothing about him was the same, not even the way he talked, and yet, he still seemed to be the same person. Even though he was back, he still seemed so far away as he continued to ride ahead of her. She knew that she had to keep him around this time. Even if that meant following him when he left.

"Let!" The priest of Kend was running to try and catch the pair. As Elijah heard the man call out, he quickly pulled his horse around to meet the man. Katie was still too far to hear, but the man handed a letter to Elijah urgently. She had just managed to hear some of what he was saying. "It's just as you feared, Let! None of them are safe are there. Some others are being sent, but it will still be some time before they arrive!"

"Thank you, my friend," Elijah's voice seemed to crack as he spoke, "I'll do what I can in the meantime." He pulled his horse around as the priest offered a brief prayer. "Katie! We need to hurry." Without another word, he sped off towards Pneu. Katie hesitated for only a moment before hurrying after him. His cold exterior seemed to crack from whatever news he had been given. She knew he wouldn't speak on this one, and so the two ran on in silence as they made their trip back to Pneu.

The evacuation from Lake Town back to Pneu went without incident. Christine was still unconscious in the back of the wagon, and Stephanie sat quietly next to Daniel. She would jump at every sound that came from the forest around them. Daniel promised he would take her back home to Round Rock when this was over. The poor girl wished to find adventure when she left home, but instead all she found was a reason to never leave home again. Whatever she was going through, it would be hard on her, but he needed to worry about Christine first.

Every so often, she would groan in her sleep. He had left Stephanie to handle driving to check on her. Her fever had returned, and it was worse than it had been in years. As he dabbed her forehead with a damp cloth, he thought back to that man he had seen, fear creeping back within him. That man would return again, but *who* was he?

"Daniel," Stephanie's voice was shaking, "we're nearing the gate. We'll be back in the city soon." At her remark, he left Christine once more to take the reins again. The evacuees were met at the gate by Hugo and Bryant who appeared to be in the heat of an argument. Daniel had a sinking feeling that something was wrong as they approached.

"What is the meaning of this *Daniel*?" It was Bryant who spoke first, "Why have you shown up with so many people? The city doesn't have space for this many! And besides, there are plenty of issues to deal with here without you dropping more on us."

"What's wrong?" Daniel spoke as he climbed down from the wagon. He waved for Stephanie to bring it in with the other evacuee's close behind, "Hugo, even you seem white as a ghost. What's going on?" Daniel could see the fear on the two men.

"Yesterday, around nightfall, a number of people seemed to have just vanished." Hugo was staring through Daniel as he spoke, "There are nearly fifty people who can't be found right now."

"*and* Katie was confirmed to pass through Kend nearly two days ago. Elijah was in her company. They are heading this way!"

"People are scared, and many people have started to notice something is wrong. We don't even seem to know what it is though, but there seems to be fear that is setting across the entire town. Even John…" Hugo was struggling to find the right words to say.

"What about John?" Daniel's voice rose as he spoke, "He is here right?"

"Maybe it would be better if he wasn't." Bryant spit as he spoke. Daniel reached for a knife at hearing his friend be insulted so vulgarly. Hugo raised his hand and moved slightly to stand between the pair.

"I think it will be best if you come and see. Father Bernard is with him now, but, well he is scaring people." Daniel followed quickly as Hugo led him to the guild hall. In the courtyard, Daniel could already hear John from the training yard behind the building. He was laughing and grunting as though he was fighting a rather amusing fight. Daniel took off ahead of the other two.

Arriving in the training yard, a massive crowd was surrounding a section of the yard. Looking around, people seemed a mix of fear, amusement, anxiety, and a multitude of others. Madame Jolie was standing with Father Bernard, and the two looked horrified. In the middle of the courtyard stood John. He was wearing his training armor, but he was wielding his great sword. His face looked as though he hadn't slept in several days. His hair was disheveled, and his beard a mess. What was most troubling though was his smile. His face was twisted into a look more like a man being tortured than smiling on others.

He was shouting and laughing as he exchanged blows with a couple of guild members who looked as though they would rather be anywhere else. "Come on you two! You said you wanted to be better! Well this sword is sharp enough to chop you two in half with one swing! If you want to live, you must do better!" He cackled. The exchange was horrifying to watch. Daniel pushed his way to where Father Bernard was standing.

"What happened to John?" Daniel continued to watch the fight.

"We aren't entirely sure." It was Madame Jolie who answered. "He was supposed to come and see me several days ago. Instead, he stayed locked in his room until this morning, and came out here to start this. Please Daniel, you must stop this before he hurts someone!"

"I'll step in now." Daniel seemed to flatten his voice as he prepared to step into the yard. "Christine fell out again, and her fever is bad. Stephanie should have already brought her to a bed. Can you please check in on her while I handle this?" Madame Jolie nodded and quickly scampered off.

"Daniel," Father Bernard seemed worried as he spoke, "Please help John. It hurts to see him like this." He grasped Daniel's arm tight to which he placed his own hand over. John landed a hard blow on one of the others, throwing the man to the ground. Without wasting another moment, Daniel drew his own short sword and stepped onto the field.

"Daniel!" John stopped just short of bringing his sword down on the poor man who had fallen. With John's attention pulled away, the two men made a dash back to the guild. "It has been a long time since the two of us sparred! Last I checked though, I was on another level of swordsmanship than you. Are you sure you want to be here?" John's voice seemed broken and scared. Daniel retrieved a discarded shield and faced John once more. Whatever was going on with him, this would be the only way of bringing John to his sense.

The two merely stared each other down. John's great sword was lined in elvish writings which granted it enchantments that never allowed the blade to dull. It also would adjust its weight to suit the wielder which made it light enough that even a child could hold it. In his hands though, the blade was heavier than any sword Daniel had ever seen. One blow would shatter bones, and in John's state of mind, would shear him in two with one strike. He truly was a formidable opponent to face down.

It was John who moved first. Charging Daniel with a forward strike, which he was able to easily step away from, but this was John who knew that Daniel would step left. Slamming his heavy foot into the ground, John was able to adjust his position and bring the sword heavily into Daniel's shield. The loss of momentum stopped his arm from breaking, but the strain was still heavy. John wasted no time to begin moving his body towards Daniel as he brought his knee up to meet Daniel's gut. He felt a crack of one of his ribs breaking as the wind was forced out of him. John took several steps back before speaking, "Come on Daniel, I know you are better than that. How can my number two man fall so quick? It's almost embarrassing!"

Daniel managed to stand again, struggling for his breath as he looked for an opening, but John was an impenetrable fortress. This man had trained heavily to be unbeatable, and he was the size of an ox. He could think of no way to get through John's defense. Daniel had an idea, but he hated the thought. Knowing he had no other option though, he spoke. "John, look at how disgusting you are right now. Amelia would be appalled. I'm glad she isn't here to see this. She would hate you as you are right now."

"She already is." He wasn't enraged like Daniel was aiming for. Instead, John only seemed to twist more. His face no longer gave a broken smile. Now, his face twisted in such horror that Daniel had never seen. "She is disgusted, she hates me, and she despises having a brother like me. I am disgusted with myself, and it is time for it all to end," John seemed to resolve something within himself, "So come at me! Come at me ready to take my life! Come on! Take my life!"

At this remark, Daniel started to make sense of what John was thinking. He had resolved himself to die. John didn't give him time to think any more before charging once again. This time, John thrusted himself with the resolve that this would be the last fight of his life. Daniel couldn't stand seeing John like this. He didn't evade John's thrust. Using his shield, he took the blow from John's sword. His arm felt as though he had been struck with a massive boulder that would crush him. Through the pain though, he could tell his arm hadn't broke. He took the opening to slam the butt of his sword into John's knuckles which forced him to drop it.

John took a few steps back, but Daniel was already moving again. He slammed his shield into John's breastplate, but it failed to cause John to stumble. Before Daniel could withdraw, John wrapped his arms around Daniel and began to crush him. Daniel pulled his head back and slammed his forehead hard into the bridge of John's nose. He could hear it crack from the impact, and John's nose began to bleed. The impact caused John to loosen his grip enough that Daniel was able to pull away.

As John reached for his nose, Daniel moved behind him fast and slammed his shield into the back of John's head. He fell to the ground hard, and Daniel jumped onto John with his knife drawn. He brought it to John's throat who finally stopped and laid there beneath Daniel. "I yield." John's voice shook as water filled his eyes. He had accepted his defeat, meeting the end he was not hoping for.

John, Father Bernard, and Madame Jolie all sat together in the infirmary. Christine was sleeping in a nearby bed. John was pressing cloth to his nose which had finally stopped the bleeding. "Do you mind telling us all what that was about?" Daniel spoke, irritation evident in his voice. Jolie was wrapping herbs on Daniel's broken rib with bandages.

"I'm sorry." John sounded broken, "Things happened while you were out. My mind is breaking, and I'm not sure how to stop it."

"What happened?"

"Amelia," he muttered, "she was here."

"John thought he encountered his sister the day you left for Lake Town." The priest sounded fearful as he spoke, "He was supposed to come see Madame Jolie about this."

"But he never came to me." Madame Jolie was working with various liquids that had a pungent odor as they spoke. "I could have fixed this issue in a single day, but no, instead he locked himself away."

"No." John wasn't talking to anyone specific, "Amelia came to my room that night. I spent the last few days with her. Some moments she was kind and needed to be comforted. Other times she was insulting and cold to me. But she was here and alive. Then last night she told me I never deserved her and disappeared. When she was still gone this morning, I snapped."

"John," Daniel was there the day Amelia had died. He knew she couldn't have been there.

"I just need some sleep. Madame, if it is okay, I would like to stay here for the night."

"You are going to be staying here for the next *several* nights! There are no ghosts here. Only healing."

"Thank you." With that, Madame Jolie walked to him with an elixir that looked as acrid as it smelled. John managed to drink the entire mixture in a single gulp. "Daniel," John turned to face him, "what happened in Lake Town? You had to evacuate everyone?"

"I can confirm that there are demons attacking us, and Lake Town seemed to be where they came from. There seems to be somebody controlling them. For now, I think it best we close off travel between the villages."

"What are we going to do about the festival?" John brought up the question.

"I think that will be best left to the city council. I feel though that it should be—" Daniel was interrupted by Thomas bursting into the room and out of breath.

"By the west gate! Some travelers were attacked coming from Kend!" The boy panted as he tried to give his report as fast as he could, "It doesn't look like anyone survived!" John and Daniel both jumped to their feet as they rushed to the door.

"John! You stay and rest!"

"Sorry father, but I've stayed behind too many times. I will not stay behind again." His resolve was firm, and Daniel made no attempt to stop him. The pair moved quick as they ran for the west gate.

"Elijah!" Katie yelled as the pair pushed their horses as fast as they could, "What's wrong!? What aren't you telling me!?"

"Just keep pushing! I don't know, but I have a bad feeling! We need to get there fast!" Katie could hear the worry in his voice as he made no effort to hide it. He seemed genuinely scared, but she couldn't tell why. As they kept pushing, the city finally came into view as they crossed over a hill. Nearly halfway between, she could make out the wreckage of a cart and the bodies of the horses that had pulled it.

Katie felt like a pit was growing in her stomach as she made out several bodies near the wreckage, and she knew who had been ahead of them. She wiped the tears from her eyes and hardened her heart so that she can make sense of things better. They were finally close enough for her to make out the bodies of Mr. and Mrs. Mckenna laying near the back of the wagon, and Katie's heart lost any mettle it once had.

Dismounting, she immediately ran to their bodies in hope that there might still be a chance to save them, but one look at the holes in their chests shattered that dream. Elijah was looking through the wreckage, desperately looking for something. He looked around for a moment before turning back to Katie, "Abigail isn't here." Like a stone shattering glass, Katie felt weight pass through her. Elijah seemed to pray for a moment before jumping from the cart and running towards the Vaieli. "The tulip! She still has it so I can find her! Let's go!" Katie ran after him as she tried to dry her eyes.

As they crossed into the forest, thorns cut heavy into her legs. She thought she had seen John and Daniel running towards them as well. As soon as she had crossed into the forest though, a veil of foliage blocked out any sign of the outside world. Elijah had suddenly clasped her arm, and the two continued to run deeper into the forest.

They continued to run until Katie felt like her lungs were burning. She refused to stop though. Abigail was lost somewhere in the forest, and whatever did that to her parents was still chasing her. They needed to find her first. Trusting in Elijah, she stayed right on his heels until he had suddenly stopped. Before she could speak, he placed a hand over her mouth and was pointing into the forest.

Following his finger, she witnessed a sight that made her shudder. It was in this moment that she took notice to the absolute silence that existed around her. No birds, insects or small critters made a sound, and all around the forest floor where she was looking was a pack of wolves that had been ripped to pieces. There was a hill that rose over a small river and sitting atop this hill with viscera still hanging from its mouth was a creature that made Katie's heart stop. She felt chills course through her entire body, and her blood turned to ice. She felt the sweat begin dripping from every pore in her body as she stared at this horrendous beast.

The creature stood nearly eight feet tall. Its skin was as black as coal and had fire burning where its hair should have been. The creature had sharp fangs which stuck out past its lips, and each of its hands had claws nearly six inches long. The creature was crouched over as it continued to feast on the wolf as bits of its flesh would melt off sporadically and turn to ash before touching the ground. A small glint of light though caught her eye from within the roots of a tree growing next to the small hill.

Looking closer, she could see that the light belonged to the silver tulip that Elijah had given Abigail. It appeared to have been braided into her hair before they had left Kend, and she had been covered in so much mud that Katie almost didn't see her. She laid there entirely motionless and fear set in that the girl may not be alive.

"She is still alive." Elijah whispered quietly to her, "I'll distract the demon, you run and grab her. As long as she keeps the flower, I will be able to find you two so just run." Katie agreed to his plan without argue, and soon, she watched as Elijah slipped away into the forest. There was absolute silence as Katie watched Abigail laying there.

A sudden pop from the direction Elijah had ran made her nearly scream. The creature heard the sound as well. Dropping the wolf carcass, the creature suddenly let out a screech so loud that Katie had to cover her ears. The creature leapt off into the woods to follow the pop it heard.

Katie wasted no time in letting her feet run free. Her legs burned from running so hard, but she refused to slow down as she neared Abigail. The girl had her eyes closed tight with her hands covering her ears. Katie reached out to grab her, and once the girl felt the hand touch her, she let out a scream so loud that Katie felt her eardrums tremble in pain.

She quickly put a hand over the girl's mouth, "Abby! It's me, Katie! You're okay now!" she pleaded with the girl who had finally opened her eyes. Once she recognized Katie, she quickly threw her arms around Katie's neck and began to sob heavily into her shoulder. She took a moment to comfort the girl.

A sudden screech from the creature made the two girls jump. Katie scooped the girl up in her arms and began to run away from the sound as fast as her legs could carry her. After only a moment though, she could hear the crunching of branches behind her followed by another screech. The creature was upon them, and Katie knew she was out of time.

She refused to stop as she heard the creature run after them. She could tell it was pointless though. It moved so fast that it would be only seconds before it overtook them. *Step. Step. Step.* She could hear it getting closer. *Step. Step. Step.* It was so close that she could feel heat coming from the creature. She kept running, but a root snagged her foot and the pair fell. She held Abigail tight as she heard the creature step right behind them.

She hadn't realized that Abigail's head was high enough to see the thing as it approached. As they sat there on the ground with Katie holding her tight, Abigail watched as the demon drew back its arm to bring its sharp claws down on them just as it had done to her parents. The arm began to descend, but it seemed to move slow. Unblinking, she watched as the arm continued to swing towards them.

As she accepted what was coming, she clung to Katie tight. Suddenly, a shadow seemed to leap in from the side. It was a man she had seen with Katie before. Let. In his hands, he was holding a spear that looked as though it was made of solid gold. He held the spear up and blocked the hand before it was able to reach her. She felt so many things rush through her in that moment, but she could say nothing as she continued to watch. Let managed to force the thing's hand back, and it stumbled several steps.

He twirled the spear several times as he now positioned it by his side. He thrust it forward twice which the creature managed to push away both times. It stepped back before charging towards Let. The spear in his hands however, had now turned into two pieces with one looking like a hooked sword. The creature hurled its hand towards him with the claws aimed right at Let's face. He didn't seem scared. Using his hooked sword, he caught the creature's wrist, and in a single movement the creature's hand had separated from its arm.

As the hand fell, it turned to ash and was dust before hitting the ground. The creature let out a massive shriek as it held onto its arm. The other half of Let's spear was a short spear with a long blade which he had thrust into the creature's side causing it to shriek even louder. As it stumbled away, Let repositioned his foot. He moved quick as he charged the creature. It held out its remaining hand in attempt to block his attack. Let caught its hand with the spear, driving it deep into the creature's arm. He twisted the spear which pulled its arm out of the way as Let brought his sword through the creature's neck. Its head fell, and it turned to dust just as the hand had. Not just the head, but the body as well. Nothing was left of the creature now besides a pile of ash littering the forest floor. The relief she felt in being safe allowed her to relax as the exhaustion overtook her body, and she fell asleep there on Katie's shoulder.

John and Daniel arrived at the scene to find Katie holding an unconscious girl, and Elijah holding what appeared to be a golden sickle and short spear. He was covered in soot, and the ground around him was littered in ash. Elijah seemed to notice their arrival and the golden weapons in his hands seemed to vanish.

He turned to face the newcomers, but as he did, a clapping was heard from behind a tree. A man with flaming red hair and eyes stepped into view who appeared to be amused by something, "These last few days have been so much fun! How have you been Daniel? I hope you haven't forgotten me since our last meeting." The man's smug face was blazing with joy as he looked from person to person, finally stopping his gaze on Elijah. "I am a little upset with what you did to my priest! Rufus deserved a better death than to the shadows." He clicked his tongue as he wagged his finger at him.

"I'm to guess you are his Arken-Son?" Elijah was visibly shaking as he stared down the man. He was now holding two jewel emblazed black daggers in his hands. John suddenly realized that Daniel was shaking like a child as he looked at the man. John squeezed the sword tight in his hands as he felt a chill run through his body.

"Why is everyone so tense? Look, this was all just a test run! I've been needing to see what makes you all tick." The man laughed as though he told a good joke. "I must say that each one of you surprised me though. I never expected to lose so many demons. Let, your master managed to cut down several before I finally got to him. He *was* a good man. You must mourn him greatly." He gave a wry smile as he could see Elijah's anger boil over.

With a scream, Elijah charged the man who gracefully dodged each strike from the daggers. Each step was beautiful and coordinated as though he were dancing an intricate number of much practiced steps. Humming a tune, the man seemed amused by Elijah's attacks. A sudden woosh of air and sound struck at John that nearly knocked him off his feet. An arrow of wind fired straight and struck the ground near the man.

With a small sound, the man was misbalanced, and Elijah managed to find a soft place in the man's chest for his dagger to land. Driving the second dagger into his chest as well, he forced the man back against a tree.

"Ah, it seems I've been had!" the man coughed in amusement as he slumped to the ground. "You tried so hard, but you should know that I control death itself." He laughed hysterically as he looked across the horrified faces of everyone. "This has been fun, but the next time we all meet, it will be all of you bleeding beneath my feet." He began to cough up blood as he spoke. "I'll be seeing you around!" The man spoke his last words as his body slumped over, lifeless. The group finally relaxed as the immediate threats were finally resolved.

CHAPTER TWENTY
CONFRONTATION

John stared Elijah down harshly. The two were so tense that Daniel worried a new fight would break out. "What did you bring down on all of us?" John thrust his hand into Elijah's chest as he spoke. "What the hell is going on?"

"John! Please back off!" Katie pleaded to the man, "Elijah stand down. This isn't going to help anyone." She was still kneeling on the ground with the girl sleeping in her arms. "We need to figure a way out of here before you two start trying to kill each other again."

"Katie is right," Daniel began to look around as he was coming to terms with their situation, "no one manages to find their way out of here. We need to come up with a plan."

"Plan?" John turned sharply to Daniel, "All of this happened because *he* decided to show up and bring all of these problems on us." He spun back on Elijah, "These *things* came here following you! People are dead because of you! We are lost here now because of you! I knew you were going to cause something when I had seen you back. I should have handled you then!"

"I followed this here!" Elijah shot back, "It would have happened with or without me. You are the one who is too much of a golden boy to realize that a lot of this is being caused by people around you!"

"What would you know of people around here? You were the one who took off and left us to handle everything! Why are you even here? It's not as though you care! You wouldn't have left if you did! Don't show up now trying to be some hero just to try and show off how you left us all behind!"

"Your just as empty headed as you always were John. It's your fault everyone keeps dying! How does Amelia put up with someone like you?" A fire ignited within John's eyes that even sent a chill through Elijah. He brought a fist to Elijah's jaw hard. The punch was strong enough that Daniel was sure Elijah would have been knocked unconscious.

Elijah though merely adjusted his feet, so he didn't fall over. He brought his fist to John's gut hard who stumbled back several steps as he caught his breath. Wasting no time though, he brought his fist back around and narrowly missing Elijah's chin. Elijah then brought his fist around to meet John's jaw. The two went back and forth exchanging blows as Katie and Daniel watched on.

John drew his sword finally and brought it around to strike Elijah. Daniel ran to try and stop the fight but wouldn't make it in time. As the sword neared Elijah's chest, it was met by a spear made of golden light. Elijah forced back the sword with such force that John was thrown to the ground. The spear tip was now pointed at John's throat, and Daniel placed his hand on Elijah's wrist.

"This fight needs to stop." Daniel's voice was flat as he spoke. "You've been gone for a long time, and there are things you don't know. For now, though, can you please calm down? Both of you." Daniel looked between the two.

"Please, let's stop this." Katie sounded near tears as she spoke. "Abby just lost her family, and we are lost in *this* forest. Can you please stop, Elijah?" He looked at her for a moment, and just as suddenly as it appeared, the spear vanished. He walked towards the girls, and gently lifted Abigail so Katie would be able to stand.

"Please, Katie." John was pleading as he was still on the ground. "Trust me when I tell you that Elijah is dangerous! Don't stay near him."

"I know he is. But I also trust him." Katie had walked over to John and was offering him a hand up. "Can you please trust *me* on this one." He stared at her for a moment before taking her hand and rising to his feet. "So, Elijah, what is the plan. You have one, right?"

"I don't." He was staring into the forest intently as though he were looking at something. "But he seems like he is wanting to help." The group all turned their heads sharply to where Elijah was standing. They didn't see anything at first, but then a great elk began to step into view.

As it grew closer, they were in awe at the size of it. As it approached, it walked calmly to Elijah and placed its nose to the girl's head.

The party watched as the pair seemed to speak without words. Soon the elk turned and began to walk slowly back into the forest. "He wants us to follow him. He will lead us out of here as thanks for killing the demon that had been plaguing his forest." He started to follow the elk. "Don't fall too far behind. He will only help us this once."

In silence, the party followed the elk. They hit a part of the forest that felt as though the undergrowth was closing around them and trying to pull them away, but as they pulled in closer to the elk, walking became easier. It didn't take them long to reach the edge of the forest and were standing near the wreckage of the cart. Elijah took a moment to say goodbye to the elk, and then they turned to return to the city.

Once they had returned to the guildhall, Abigail was placed in one of the infirmary beds. Elijah was very adamant about not letting anyone besides Katie and Madame Jolie in the room with her. Katie had decided to stay while the others went to take care of her family.

I'm sorry you had to go through this Abby. You have always been such a sweet girl, and you don't deserve all this. As she looked at the girl sleeping peacefully, she gently brushed the dirt clumps from the girl's hair. *She probably feels like all this was a bad dream that'll end soon. When she wakes, she going to have to relive everything.* Katie began to cry as she thought about how much this girl will be hurting.

Abigail's parents were much like her own which is why she loved their family so much. Thinking of what the girl would have to face, brought back her own memories of the night she had lost her own parents. Katie was five at the time. Her mom pulled her from bed that night without the chance to change or grab anything from her room. They didn't even put shoes on their feet. Katie was carried from their home as fast as her mom could run.

Leaving their home, her eyes were filled with the bright, yellow light of buildings on fire. Her ears filled with the screaming of people as they ran around the village. Her nose was filled with a foul smell that she didn't know. All these things that flooded her senses didn't compare to what her eyes locked onto as they ran from their home. Next to their home, lying in a mangled lump on the ground, illumined by a nearby flame, was her father. As they ran further away, her eyes never left this sight. Each step she begged for him to stand. That was the last time she would ever see her father's body.

Her mom held her tight as they charged along the banks of one of the rivers. They reached a small cove along its bank where they had finally stopped. Her mom sat near the river holding on to her as she cried. She had never heard her mother cry. They stayed there for seconds, minutes, hours. She didn't know how much time passed. Her mom had heard something that made her panic. After looking around for several minutes, she forced Katie to hide in a little hole near the river. Katie didn't want to part from her mom, but her mom didn't relent. She told Katie not to move until she came back for her. Her mom promised repeatedly that she would return for her.

Her mom looked around again and began to run. Katie laid in the mud as water and dirt splashed against her face. She repeated her mom's words in her head as she listened to the water splashing off the mud. Screams. Nearby, her mom began to cry out in pain. She didn't know why her mom was screaming, but she promised her mom she wouldn't move. She was scared and wanted to run to her mom, but her mom promised that she would come back. Her mom's screaming became so loud and piercing that it felt like she was listening to a *banshee* scream. Finally, the screaming had stopped, and Katie heard nothing except the sound of the water.

She laid in the mud until the sun rose. Hours passed, footsteps passed her several times that day however no one found her, and her mom didn't return. The sun set and rose again. She didn't remember sleeping or waking. All she remembers is the sound of water. She was starving, scared, cold, chapped, but her mom was coming back. During the next day, she was lying their watching shadows move around the ground as the sun passed overhead. The sight of her father and the sound of her mother burned her senses. At about this time, she would have been playing near the river close enough to the farm that she would have seen her dad waving to her from the field. She would have needed to go home soon since her mom would have lunch ready for her. It probably would have been something she didn't like again since her mom seemed to enjoy making her eat nasty food.

An unusual shadow was passing by her as she laid there in the mud. She pressed her hands against her mouth. She hoped it was her mom, but she was terrified that someone else would find her. The shadow grew closer and she clenched her eyes shut. She had felt a hand grab her. Although it was firm, it didn't hurt her.

She knew this wasn't her mom, but this person wasn't trying to hurt her. When she opened her eyes, she had seen that it was one of the older kids. It looked as though he had been crying, but he was fighting back his tears now. It was Elijah who had come for her. He was only eight years old at this time, but to her he seemed like someone much older. He had kept his hand on her as he told her that he was going to take care of her for her mom.

She still never figured out how he knew she was there or that it was her mom that hid her there, but he knew. Four years he did take care of her too. He fed her, clothed her, kept her moving when she didn't want to. When she was too scared to be alone, he would stay next to her. She would have so many nightmares that he had let her sleep with him most nights since that was the only way she was able to sleep at all. Those four years, he was the only reason she was able to live.

Katie was brought from her thoughts as she felt Abigail stirring beneath her. She knew Abigail will need her just as she had needed Elijah all those years ago. *I guess I still haven't forgiven him completely for leaving me. I still needed him, but he left me. He promised he wouldn't leave but he did.* Katie felt her eyes begin to swell as she tried her best not to cry.

Katie laid her head down on the bed as she waited for the others to come back. *Tired.* She didn't want to fall asleep. Despite her best efforts though, she silently drifted off to sleep.

Everyone was silent as they returned to the infirmary. Abigail's family was being prepped for their funeral now, and all their belongings were brought to the guild hall. The others involved with their traveling party would have to be handled as well.

John didn't fully understand, but in his travels, Elijah had learned most of the prayers of the church. He took it upon himself to hold the funeral service for Abigail's family when it was time. In the infirmary, Katie had fallen asleep in the chair next to Abigail. Seeing Katie sleep was the first comfort he had all day. He knew they would need to wake her soon, but until everyone had arrived, he wanted her to sleep. The group was only waiting for Daniel to return who had gone to fetch Father Bernard. Elijah had told them that he needed to speak with everyone, but for some reason he needed the priest there too.

He watched as Elijah stood near the window looking out across the town. Christine was still asleep in another bed nearby. John took Madame Jolie's chair, and began to think about what it was Elijah needed to tell everyone. The room was silent, and the setting sun left the room illuminated only by candlelight. Christine suddenly began to stir and look around the room.

As she seemed to be trying to figure out where she was, her eyes landed on Elijah who was looking back towards her. "Elijah? If you are here, then I must still be dreaming." She joked. "Why do you all seem to be so stressed and anxious? This isn't the first time I have fallen like this. Even you should remember Elijah. I was this way as a kid too." Christine started to sit up as she was looking around more. "Where is Daniel?" At that moment, Daniel arrived with Father Bernard close behind. By the look on the father's face, he already knew what would be discussed. "Please, Elijah. I don't wish to be any part of this." Father Bernard sounded terrified as his voice cracked.

"You lost that choice, old man." Elijah moved from the window so quick that John feared for Father Bernard's life. He quickly shot up to stand between the two. "Don't worry, *John*. I said we were only talking tonight."

Katie was awoken by their voices and looked confused as she noticed the priest was there as well. Everyone appeared on edge. Elijah took a moment before speaking, "I guess it's time to get started. I'm sure everyone here is confused by where I have been, why I came back, and what is going on. So, *father*, go ahead."

"Elijah, you know this isn't appropriate! I've already wrote a letter to the citadel! Your games are over, and it is time to settle up." He seemed smug as he spoke. Elijah calmly pulled a letter from one of his pockets and handed it to John.

"John, would you please tell us all whose seal is on the letter, who it is addressed to, and then open the letter and tell us what it says." As he looked the envelope over, confusion seemed to set in. He quickly opened the letter and read through it several times. "Well?"

"The letter is addressed to 'Let' and is sealed by Citadel." He looked over the letter once more before reading it aloud:

Dear Let,

> *We have confirmed that no communication has come from Father Bernard in Pneu, and we are deeply concerned about the information you have presented us. We are dispatching additional agents, and we ask that you do your best to handle the threat as discretely as possible. You do have permission to disclose certain information on a need to know basis, and we trust that you do so as little as possible.*
>
> *Regarding Father Bernard, this order hereby declares that he is a potential threat to the order and is to be arrested on sight until we can arrive for further questioning. We are granting Let temporary authority over the temple in Pneu until a new priest can be dispatched to the city. We hereby declare all public events within city be postponed, and the city will be placed in a mandatory curfew. In the event of a major incident, the residents are to be evacuated to the city of Kend where Father Richard is already preparing shelter.*
>
> *Until our agents arrive, Let is granted full authority over the city council and his discretion is fully supported by the Citadel and the Church. May the protection of Esprit shine on the city and its people as they go through this trial of faith, and our prayers will be for no further incident until more trained officials can arrive on scene. Please inform us once Father Bernard has been taken into custody, or should the situation change in any way,*

Lues Martenis
Keeper of Knowledge
Guardian of the Citadel
Holy Saint to the Order of Zosen

"Father Bernard?" John seemed lost as he read the letter out loud, "what is this?"

"Please John, you must believe me! This must be a lie! You know me! My intentions are here with protecting everyone!" Father Bernard stammered as he spoke. Beads of sweat forming on his forehead.

"John," Elijah's voice was soft, "this is a lot to take in, but you need to trust in what that letter says. Everything that *man* says is a lie. Don't trust him."

"Elijah," John was looking for some proof that this wasn't real, "Who are you?"

"I'm an agent of the church. Crusader is the official title. I am tasked with fighting the supernatural threats against our world. I'm still technically an apprentice though. Ten years ago, this man sold me to the church which is where I have been all these years. He can't even be honest with you all that he *sold* me."

"Is that true?" Katie spoke up in anger.

"It is true but not exactly—"

"You told us all that he ran away? You knew where he was all along?" Daniel too broke his composure.

"Look, everyone. You were all kids. He had a gift that the church seeks out, and we are sworn to secrecy!" Father Bernard pleaded with the group, "It would be sacrilege to speak of it! You must understand."

"We understand that we were kids who lost a friend. You could have at least told us he was safe!" Christine too seemed enraged, "We've been so angry at Elijah this entire time, but it wasn't his fault was it?"

"Father." John's voice was cracked, "What have you done? Why does the church want you arrested?"

"I've told you! This must be a lie! There is no way that they would be looking for me! All I have done is protect you!"

"You are being arrested under the suspicion of being an Arken-Priest." Elijah stepped forward as to grab the priest. "You are in league with the necromancer who has brought the demons into this area, and you are under suspicion for the missing individuals who recently disappeared in the city. You are both a heretic to the faith, and a traitor to the state."

"What about you Elijah?" The priest was now hostile. His gentle tone turned sour, and he spat as he spoke, "The demons and everything followed you here! It is your fault all this is happening! I kept things calm all this time! It wasn't until you and your master went snooping around where you don't belong! I'm glad that foolish man died!" Realizing what he said, Father Bernard quickly covered his mouth.

"How did you know that his master died?" Katie was the one to question him this time.

"Because he played a part in it." Elijah's voice was cold as he spoke. "We were sheltered here the week before we came across the necromancer and his cult. They knew we were coming, and my master died to buy time for me to escape. *He* was the only one who knew what our mission was."

Everyone was silent as they tried to make sense of what was going on. The silence was broken by the laughter of the old man. "You are such a clever boy, aren't you? Think you know so much, do ya? Well you are wrong! This city would have been wiped out so long ago if not for me! Who do you think keeps the Arken-Son happy? Who do you think gives him a reason not to come here? Who do you think keeps everyone nice, cozy, and safe while you are out running around without a care of what you break?" Father Bernard had lost his sense as he rambled. "He gives us protection as long as I give him my loyalty! The Arken-Son is more noble and holier than any in that God Forsaken church you so blindly follow!" He spit at Elijah's feet, "Thanks to you, they are going to kill everyone in this town! Because of you, no one can enter or leave the city without dying! Because of you, we are going to be isolated, tormented, and killed. Me along with all of you for not doing my job! It is all your fault you little bastard!" He charged Elijah but was caught quickly by Daniel. Twisting his wrist, Father Bernard dropped a dagger he had pulled from his sleeve.

Everyone remained silent as they tried to figure out what to do. It was Katie who spoke up first. "Didn't you kill the Arken-Son in the forest? At least that is who he claimed to be."

Father Bernard began to laugh hysterically, "That man was the first to learn how to conquer death, and his curse is to always return! Three days from now he will rise again. Three days the city will fall and you all will die!" Everyone seemed frozen in fear as the man's hysteria continued. It was finally ended by Elijah knocking him in the back of his head. Father Bernard fell to the floor unconscious.

"He brought up a good point though Elijah," Daniel turned his attention to him, "was this all because of what you and your master were doing? Is that what caused all of this?"

"No!" Katie jumped to her feet, "We crossed another Arken-Priest. It was Rufus from Kend," she looked to John for this, "he told us that I was always one of their targets. Elijah got to me before they could, or I would have been captured by them by now. To be honest, I think Pneu was always going to be a target."

"Why?" Christine was attempting to stand as she spoke. Daniel moved to her side to force her back in bed.

"Because they need my knowledge of the Elvish and Piet languages. After they got what they needed, they were most likely going to destroy the town so that no one could figure out what they are after."

"And what are they after?" John was moving Father Bernard to a bed.

"The revival of Quietus." Everyone took a breath as Elijah spoke, "They are looking for a way to break his prison."

"But..." Daniel was struggling for words, "There isn't a way to do that. Is there?"

Elijah was digging through his rucksack. He withdrew a bronze looking sphere that was covered in markings that could only be Elvish. "Although we haven't figured out how, this artifact is related to that. It's what me and Katie have been working on. I was trying to keep everyone out of this."

"Katie," Christine was still fighting with Daniel to stand, "do you have any other research that could help them? Anything else that could be used by them?"

"No." She seemed hesitant when she answered, "I don't think anything I have would help them unless—" She froze for a moment.

"What?" Elijah spun to her as she turned pale. "What do you have?"

"I was working on the locations of other sites. Sites that may have artifacts like that one. It's not pinpoints, but I made a map based on where they might be if they existed. No one knows about that though other than James."

Elijah suddenly grabbed her by the arms, "We need to go grab that! It isn't safe there!"

"But—" before she could finish, a large explosion rang out from somewhere within the city. The group ran towards the window. Looking out, they saw large spires of fire coming from library. They looked on in fear as the building burned in a black and yellow flame. They could hear shouting and screams coming from the people as they ran from the area.

"It's okay, though, right?" Christine was in shock as she watched the library burn. "That map would be burning in, there right?"

"No." Elijah sounded cold as he spoke, "James was one of them. He would have found that map before burning it down."

"How would you know that?" Daniel didn't look away from the church as he spoke

"You are wrong, Elijah," Katie fell to her knees as she watched her life work burn to the ground, "I took the map with me. I have it in my backpack. James has seen it enough to have it memorized though. They only needed him." A door suddenly slammed behind them. Turning around, Father Bernard was gone from his bed. Daniel and John chased after him, but Elijah ran to Abigail's bed first. Christine slumped next to Katie on the floor, and the two watched the fire in pain.

ᔕ

Chapter Twenty-One
Preparation

E lijah was sitting on his own at the bar in the guildhall as John approached. Before he was able to speak, Elijah called out to him, "John. You are the size of ten men. You can't sneak up on me."

"To be fair, that wasn't my intention. Do you mind if I sit down?" Elijah merely waved his hand for John to take the seat next to his. From the sight of it, Elijah had already had several drinks. "So, I'm guessing that Bryant didn't handle things well?"

"He is still just as nasty a man as he was ten years ago. Like, how have you been dealing with him for so long?" Elijah began to ramble, "Also, what's this about you being given titles? So, you are *Lord* John now?"

"I hate it, but the king insisted." John ordered his own ale, "You would not believe the amount of anger that went around the Kingdom that first year. I'm still surprised I have made it this long!"

"Yeah, but I also heard from Daniel that you are engaged? You?"

"Hey! Even I'm still surprised by this!" John took a drink as he spoke, "This girl is unlike anyone you will ever meet! Eyes like sapphires, hair like the sun, and she is worth so much more than a guy like me. I'm still hoping we can do the wedding here once this is all over."

"She's from the capital, right? What's her name? I might know her."

"No!" John was short as he answered, "Her name remains secret until after the marriage."

"Okay! No need to be so intense about it. She must be a pretty high up noble then if that much secrecy is needed."

"You have no idea." The two laughed briefly before silence fell over the pair.

"What happened with Amelia?" The room felt heavy at his question. "Daniel told me to ask you directly."

"It was the year after you disappeared. Amelia was eight when she got sick. For weeks she continued to get weaker until she wasn't even able to get out of bed. Father Bernard was even able to get Madame Jolie from the capital to come and look at her. She had caught some rare disease that is usually only found on some islands along the eastern coast. Normally, we wouldn't be exposed to it here. The only guess is that one of the rebel fighters brought it with them when they had attacked us. They don't know why it remained dormant for so long, but it was the only explanation they could offer. The worst of it though is that she was too far gone for the cure to help. Madame Jolie being the saint that she is still managed to get it to us, but it really was too late." John paused to finish off his glass.

"Me, Katie, Daniel, and Christine all took turns to be there with her, so she was never alone. We wanted to tell her to be brave, but, how could we? We wanted to tell her that she would be ok, but even she knew that she was dying. Story books make it seem easy and calm watching someone die; it wasn't. Every day was vomiting and seizures and crying. There would be times that she would beg us to help her get better. She didn't want to die, she was terrified; do you know who was there the day she finally did? Katie." John was shaking slightly as he spoke.

"There wasn't any last goodbye or a final exchange in words. She didn't just peacefully go in her sleep. Katie was reading to her. As she did, her eyes begin to harden and had another seizure coming on. This one wasn't like the others though. As Katie held her, she knew something was wrong. After some time, the seizure finally stopped. She wasn't awake, but that was normal. Katie realized that she wasn't breathing though. Madame Jolie came running in when she heard Katie screaming, but nothing could be done for her.

"After four months of going through that, she was gone. None of us knew what to do anymore, and I wasn't even there for her in the end. What kind of brother am I that I couldn't even be there with her in the end? What's worse is that it was supposed to be my turn with her. I couldn't bring myself to see her that day and asked Katie to go instead. I was so cowardice that she had to go without me."

"John—" Elijah was speechless as John continued.

"During that time, right after she died. I didn't sleep or eat. I was so angry and lost. How was I supposed to take care of everyone when I couldn't even protect her? After the funeral, I spent a while on my own. I traveled for a while, but, yeah. That's what you missed while you were gone. Which, I blamed you for. A lot. A part of me still hates you for it too. Even now, I know it wasn't you, but I still hate you for not being here. We needed you. Growing up, you were the one who kept us together. And you left us. The others may have, but I'm not ready to forgive you yet." He finished another drink that had been brought to him. "I don't want your sympathy, and I don't want you to think we are okay now. But I know you are trying to protect us, right? So, I will trust in that."

"You always were too proud for your own good, you know that?" Elijah finished his ale as well and stood to leave. "Don't worry. I'll be out of here once I know Pneu is safe. You don't have to worry about me anymore after that." He took several steps before making one last statement. "And about Amelia, she loved you more than anything else. The only thing she would ever hate you for is if you keep blaming yourself for her death. That girl never had the ability to hate someone. She was too good for the things that happened to her."

"Thank you."

Daniel was meditating near a large tree in the training yard. Too much had happened, and he knew that things were only going to get worse. As he thought back on everything, he heard someone approaching. He opened his eyes to see Elijah. "Mind if I join you?"

"Go ahead, but don't expect me to be good company right now."

"That is fine. I've been looking for you to ask about something."

"Which is?"

"What happened to the twins, Adam and Kimberly? They aren't here anymore?"

"They decided to leave and see the world. It was a year after you left, and none of us have heard from them since then."

"I'm happy for them then. They always seemed too big for such a small village."

"What about you, Elijah? You seemed to have gotten into something pretty big on your own."

"Too big if you ask me. I have managed to pick up quite a few things though in my travels."

"Like that golden weapon you were using?"

"Yes, actually, about that. I think I can help you with that bow you use. Do you know how it works?"

"Thanks to Katie, I know that it converts spiritual energy into wind, but humans don't have the same spiritual energy that the elves did so it can kill me after a few shots."

"That's partially right. If you learn how to control your release of spiritual energy, you will fire smaller arrows, but you can fire more of them." Daniel raised his eyebrow at Elijah.

"And how would I control the release then?"

"So," Elijah repositioned himself into a more upright pose as he sat cross-legged. "Without our physical bodies, our souls couldn't live here on earth. At the same time, without the soul, our bodies are just empty vessels. Spiritual energy is like the glue that holds the two together while on earth." As he spoke, Elijah closed his eyes and appeared to concentrate heavily. Suddenly, golden mist began to flutter out of Elijah's hands. From it, spiraling, twisting vines that appeared silver slowly worked their way from each hand to meet in the middle. The arch of silver vines solidified, and Elijah handed it to Daniel.

"Is this how you make those weapons you were fighting with?" He turned the arch over in his hands.

"Close, but once again not completely right. Crusaders fight creatures born from the rotting souls of a living thing. Spiritual energy isn't enough to fight most of them. We use that spiritual energy to sever pieces of our own soul away. We then harden the spiritual energy around it in the form of a weapon that we choose. When we just use spiritual energy, it looks silver like those vines, but when we use our soul," as Elijah spoke, a gold medallion with the symbol of Esprit embroidered upon it appeared in his hand, "they turn gold. As soon as we release our concentration, the gold returns to our soul, but the silver can stay permanently."

"That sounds painful and dangerous."

"It is. A broken soul cannot survive. If we don't reattach the piece of our soul, then it will cause our soul to corrupt and can spawn a powerful demon that is hard to kill. Every time I draw my weapon, my life and the life of those around me are in danger, but it is the only way to handle certain demons."

"That sounds like a lot, but what does it have to do with my bow?"

"It'll take more than three days to master it, but I think in that time I can teach you how to control the release of your spiritual energy so that you can fire more arrows, and change the size of them."

"Oh?"

"Meet me here for one hour each day starting today. I don't think help will come from the Citadel in time. I may need your help with that bow for smaller demons, and I can't have you falling out on me after only two shots. My drive for teaching you is rather selfish, but I will need your help. John's too."

"John? Have the two of you made up?"

"I don't think we ever will, but we understand each other enough to work together. We still haven't found Father Bernard either. John's sword is enchanted by the elves, and one of those enchantments allows him to be able to strike down demons. We are the only three here who will be able to fight them, but I don't know how many he will bring with him."

"That is fair enough. This is our city as much as it is anyone else. You won't have to try hard to convince us to fight with you. What will John be doing in the meantime?"

"He is preparing his guildmembers. At the first sign of an attack, John is going to ring the bell at the church. That will be the signal for the guild to move and evacuate everyone there. They may not be able to fight demons, but the Arken-Son has an entire cult full of people who can die just as easy as the next person. Their number one priority is getting themselves and the citizens to the church where John will keep them safe. Even if they can't kill the demons, there are still things they can do to help."

"Thank you, Elijah."

"For what?"

"This was all going to happen regardless, right? At least with you here we can actually do something for everyone."

"Don't thank me yet. I still don't know if this will be enough. If I am being honest, I am scared. I am on my own handling more than I ever have before. If we fail—"

"Well then let's not fail." Daniel reached his hand out towards Elijah. He took it and the two shook hands on their new plan, and Daniel started his first training session.

"Christine! You know Daniel will be mad if he hears you are sneaking about." Katie caught her as she was attempting to sneak out of the infirmary. "And Madame Jolie will never forgive a patient who leaves against medical recommendation. You really are playing with fire you know?"

"What about you then? Elijah will lose his lid if he hears you snuck away! He wants you here where he knows he can find you. Plus, you have that little girl to look out for! What will she think if she wakes up and not a single person she knows is there? You have some nerve to try and lecture me when you are leaving that poor little girl all alone!" Katie had forgotten how ruthless her lectures could be.

"I know…" Katie reached into her basket and pulled something out, "It's a sweet roll from The Long Way Home. Abby has never had one so I figured she may want to try it when she wakes up. Also," she placed the sweet roll on a table nearby to pull out a dress, "all her clothes were ripped apart when they were attacked. I wanted her to have something nice to wear. Oh, and," Katie returned the dress and pulled out a book, "this is just a blank journal, but it was supposed to be her present when she made it here. A journal for her studies when she started school after the festival. She may not need it for a while though…" Katie began to trail off. "She lost a lot and hasn't had time to really process it. I figured if I could keep her busy, she wouldn't have time to lose herself too."

Christine grabbed Katie and pulled her into a tight hug. "That girl is going to need you when she wakes up. If you need anything else, let me go and get it. Make sure you are here for her though."

"I will." The two moved back into the infirmary. Christine returned to her bed, and Katie took the chair next to Abigail. She pulled a brush from her basket and started to brush the girl's hair. "The library is completely gone. Whatever that fire was, it even burned the artifacts."

"I have never seen flames like that. It didn't spread anywhere away from the library either. I'm sorry you lost so much."

"It'll be ok. I documented everything in there in excruciating detail, and in duplicate. I haven't told you yet, but I was already speaking with the Citadel about making the Library a secondary location for knowledge. Should something ever happen to the Citadel, all that information would be gone. They have been working on duplicating everything in the Citadel, and we were going to keep the copies here. We were going to expand the library of course. Now we have solid ground to build from the bottom up. A second Citadel is what we are going to build."

"Katie that is…ambitious." Christine was awestruck by the news, "isn't there way too much information at the Citadel? How will they ever copy everything?"

"That's the good thing about apprentices, is what I was told." Katie chuckled, "They have been working on it for a year now and have over half the documents finished. Another year, and it'll start being delivered here."

"Well, now we need to rebuild the library, right?"

"Exactly, and it will be so much grander than it ever was before! I still get goosebumps thinking about it. They will be sending apprentices here to help learn and keep up with all the documents. We need to take care of our knowledge if it is to survive beyond us."

"You think humans are going to go somewhere?"

"Well, I'm sure the elves thought they would be here forever, but they aren't. I would be stupid to think the humans aren't at risk of disappearing too. I want to make sure our knowledge survives beyond that!"

"You never cease to amaze me Katie."

"No, that's not true. You are the amazing one. Speaking of, the first collection that will be coming here will be medical. Maybe we can start looking into a cure for you again?"

"No!" Christine shouted louder than she meant. "I'm sorry but everyone has already accepted this for what it is. I can't put Daniel back into that again."

"Christine…I'm sorry."

"Don't be. We all know what is coming. I feel it is best we just keep it as that. I just want to enjoy what I can, while I can."

"If it was me, I wouldn't give up. I know it isn't easy, and I can't imagine how hard it is to accept things as they are. That's why I think you're so strong, but maybe, for all of us, you don't have to give up just yet." The two sat in silence for a while. Suddenly, making both women jump, Abigail shot straight up in bed. Her eyes filled with tears as she held her hands over her mouth to keep from screaming.

Katie reached out grab her, and as she did, Abigail jumped from the bed and into Katie's lap. She buried her head into Katie's chest and began to sob uncontrollably. "I'll leave the two of you alone for a bit." Christine stood to leave, "Let me know if you need anything."

"I will. Thank you." With that Christine allowed the two girls to be alone.

Elijah found himself sitting alongside the old stump on Devil's Perch once again. He thought it was easiest to think here, and from this spot, he could see the entire town. As he sat and meditated, he found himself sharing energy with the stump once again, and through it, he was able to hear some of the stump's thoughts. Memories passed on through emotions. The elves truly were gifted in so many ways. He thanked the stump for sending the Great Elk to help them in the forest. He also thanked it for being here for all these years.

The stump in turn thanked him for returning to give him company again, for freeing his hill of the sickness, and for sharing something of the old elves once again. The stump could feel that something bad had been building, and its malice was aimed towards the city. Sensing that it was time for Elijah to leave once more, the stump thanked him for visiting, and Elijah left for the city. He had less pain in him than the last time the two departed. The stump hoped for him to continue getting better.

It was a slow walk back to the city. As he did, he reminded people of the curfew. Many of them were still upset or didn't understand it, but that was a problem Elijah had left for Bryant and Hugo. Bryant made sure to give him an earful when they were given the news as well. As he approached the guildhall, he took a moment to look up towards the infirmary window. He reminded himself repeatedly not to get attached again, but his heart longed to remain here.

To him, this was home, and his thoughts of Katie and the others were the only thing that got him through most of those years. This place was no longer his to return to. There was still so much for him to do. He knew that his path and his goals will never bring him back home, and he had accepted this. Being here again though made him long for a future where he could be here instead.

Don't go abandoning me now. You are stuck with me. We had a deal. Are you going back on your promise? Elijah quickly grabbed his forehead as though he were in pain. "Not now! I know my promise. I'm not going back on anything."

Traitor! You promised. Liar! You gave them up. Just give me up too.

"NO! I haven't given anything up. Now stop!" silence. His mind once again fell quiet. With that, he returned to the infirmary to check on Katie and Abigail. When he went into the room, he found Katie in her chair with Abigail asleep in her lap. On the nearby table was a half-eaten sweet roll, and Abigail was wearing a new dress that appeared just a bit too big.

Katie smiled to him as he approached, "This seems like it is going to be a lot more work than I thought." She chuckled as she spoke, "She doesn't want to let go of my sleeve or leg for even just a moment. It was torture just trying to go to the bathroom today."

"Sounds like you are going to be too tired then to help with the artifact tonight?"

"Absolutely not!" She slowly lifted Abigail to her bed and laid her down. She seemed to stretch out a few sore muscles in her back before meeting Elijah at the desk. "So now that we have the star map, how do you think it compares to the sphere?"

"I thought you were the expert. You know, I can still take it to someone else if you like?"

"Oh! So now you can make jokes? You really are getting back to your old self." Katie smiled to him. "Now, get my journal from my bag, and hand me the sphere." Elijah stared at her as though to remind her that he isn't her assistant. She ignored the stare and snapped her fingers. "Bring them to me and don't make me ask again." Faux-scornfully, he grabbed what she asked for and pulled up a chair next to hers.

"Ok, so we have this set of star systems here. We already guessed that these systems had to do with Esprit, and I had Christine bring me a book that we had here." She pulled the book from across the table. "See here? This star pattern is of the Goddess Esprit!"

"How does that help us with the sphere?"

"Stop interrupting me while I work! I'm getting there." Elijah was taken aback by how much fiercer she seemed than when they first started this project. "So those ruins where this was found, those ruins were a temple built for the worship of Esprit! I'm thinking that—" She began to trail off as she began to turn dials and wheels atop the sphere. She continued for a while without saying a word as Elijah sat quietly watching. He watched as her hands delicately turned each dial, and he watched how focused her eyes were as she looked at each move methodically.

"There!" She quietly shouted. "Look!" She pointed to a section of lines and shapes. Although she clearly understood what it was, he was entirely lost. Rolling her eyes, she traced the lines of several patterns. "This is Piet for Esprit. Well really it is Piet for Goddess, shield, bird, wood, and a bunch of other things. BUT, Piet through the perspective of Esprit, is the Goddesses name."

"Yeah, I'm still not fully getting it."

"I think, I need to write each one of the constellations in Piet around the dome of the sphere and in the same order that they are in the stars."

"There are hundreds of turns you can make though. How are you supposed to do that?"

"Give me some time. I bet I can do it tonight!"

"Go right for it. I'll be sleeping in here with the two of you tonight so wake me up if you figure it out."

"Who gave you permission to go to sleep while I work away at this? Go get us some coffee. You're staying up until we figure this out." Elijah felt his blood begin to boil. He was going to make sure she understood who he was in all of this. Somehow though, he found himself running for coffee instead.

Several hours had passed, and Katie still diligently worked the dials and wheels on the surface of the sphere. Every so often she would get excited at landing another mark only to look ready to throw the thing out the window. Elijah dozed off from time to time only to be hit with a book.

"Finally!" She shouted too loud. The pair checked to make sure Abigail was still asleep who didn't seem to have moved since laying her down.

"What has you so excited?"

"I did it! There is only one dial left to turn, and I will have finished the pattern. And so..." She gently turned the last dial. As her hand stopped, a click was heard from within the sphere. Suddenly, gears and wheels begun to spin from within the device. Finally, even the surface started turning and spinning. The device rolled off the table with a loud thud. It danced back and forth across the floor as it continued to turn, and the pair tried to catch it. Finally, it started to slow down as the device finished shuffling itself.

They picked it up from the floor, and at first it didn't seem any different other than the patterns had been reshuffled again. Katie began to look flustered as they turned it over in their hands. On the bottom, was a small hole in a strange shape. "A key?" Elijah said. Katie seemed to have an idea as she ran to her bag. She pulled out the necklace that the Elf had given her on her first visit to the ruins.

"When she gave me this, she told me it was the key to everything!" She removed the object from the string, and she gently placed the piece in the hole on the sphere. It seemed to click into place. With that, the other side of the sphere twisted and opened to reveal a folded piece of paper and two pyramid shaped objects that were small enough to fit into a ring. Katie quickly opened the paper which revealed a map of their continent. The map showed the outline of the Elvish empire as well as territories belonging to strange beings that Katie didn't know how to translate.

The most important revelation on this map, however, was the precise locations of all eight Holy Temples. The temple of Esprit sat right where it should be. Katie spent several minutes tracing her finger to each temple on the map. "Are they close to where you predicted they would be?" Elijah asked.

"Four of them, yes! Three of them are somewhat close, but there is one that I was incredibly wrong about."

"Which one?"

"This one! The temple of Magi. If I'm reading the map right, it is in the sky, but I'm not quite sure how."

"Maybe it's flying?"

"I mean, it is built in honor of the Goddess of Magic. I guess that is possible."

"I'm sure I don't need to tell you how dangerous this thing is?"

"Incredibly! For now, I am just excited we figured it out. I think it will be best if everyone just assumes, we still don't know and keep the map a secret. We should also hold onto that sphere. I have a hunch that we will have to use it the same way for each of the Gods."

"It may be safe not to pursue the others, if I am being honest." Katie looked at him quizzically. "If this has something to do with releasing Quietus, and each one of those locations has something to do with releasing him, I think it would be safest to keep them all separated."

"Except, whoever these guys are, they are probably going to use James and what he knows to find them. There are six more they will be able to find with my map. The Temple of Magi is a tricky one, but we have the eighth and they know that! If they get all the others, all they need is to steal ours and it's over. I think after this, we need to go find the others to be safe!"

"I am not letting you get dragged into this further. It is out of the question. I'll go and look for them if you think they are dangerous and bring them back here." The two stared each other down for several minutes. Abigail suddenly began to cry in her sleep. They ran to her, but it seemed as though she was only having a nightmare. Remembering the doll, Katie retrieved it from her bag and placed it under Abigail's arm.

"I think we both should get some sleep while we can. She wants to see you again too you know. You'll have a busy day tomorrow." Katie gently brushed Abigail's hair from her face.

"Why does she want to see me?"

"She watched you save us. She wants to thank you. When she can that is."

"When she can?"

"She won't talk." Katie grabbed the journal that she had gifted to Abigail, "she has been writing to ask when she wants something, but other than that she won't make a sound." She showed Elijah the pages they had been using for Abigail to ask for things. "Madame Jolie said it is a trauma reaction. She might talk again, or she might not. It's all going to be up to Abby. Here look, she wrote about you a lot today!" Katie showed him the page, and it was just as she had said. Lines filled with questions asking about Elijah. He quietly read through them as he sat down on the closest bed.

"Tomorrow is the funeral service. It's going to be hard on her." Elijah handed the book back.

"That's why I am expecting you to spend plenty of time with her. She is terrified and has no one else."

"She can't depend on me. I have to leave when this is over. I can't be a support for her."

"I know you do. I'm not asking you to be here. She is. Stay here while you can, and when it's time to leave," she paused, "just make sure to say goodbye this time. As long as she has that, she will be okay."

"I think...I think I can do that." He walked towards Katie and pulled her hand into his. She blushed as he quietly ran his fingers across the top of her wrist. Before she could ask what it was he was doing, a faint golden light began to emit from her wrist. She watched as silver vines begun to wrap their way around her wrist into the shape of one of the most beautiful bracelets she had seen.

"I can sense my spiritual energy if it is close enough." He motioned to the silver tulip he had given to Abigail, "As long as you have this on you, I will be able to find you." He left her sitting there in her own daze as he pulled himself back into the bed he was sitting on. "For now, sleep is needed. I'll wake up if anything happens so be sure and get sleep yourself." With that, the two fell asleep.

⑤

CHAPTER TWENTY-TWO
PREFACE TO THE ATTACK

E lijah had slept harder than he had in a long time that night. The shining sun through the window woke him, and he was worried about having slept as long as he did. A small bit of panic sank over him when he noticed Abigail wasn't in her bed. He went to wake up Katie only to find that Abigail had made her way into bed with her. She was still awake, but she stayed quiet so that Katie could sleep.

As she watched him approach the bed, she withdrew into the covers so that all he could see were her eyes. He could tell she was both scared and curious as he sat down in the chair next to the bed. Elijah was at a loss of words as the pair stared at one another.

He felt that the two should be okay long enough for him to go and get breakfast for them all. He stood back up and as he walked towards the door, the small pattering of feet behind him made him aware of Abigail having followed him to the door. She stood there timidly with the journal in her hands. She had quickly scribbled out a question for him: *Where are you going?*

"I'm just running to get us all some food." He kneeled so he could talk to her easier. "Is there anything you want?" She quickly scribbled away in her journal before turning it back to him, *Can I come with you?* He smiled at the question. "I don't see why not. Do you have shoes?" She ran to her bed where a pair of boots had been sitting. He took notice that they were the same farm boots she had worn when they rescued her.

"Do you still have the flower I gave you?" He asked her as she returned. Gently she pulled out a string from around her neck that had the flower tied to it. "Good! As long as you keep that on you, I will always be able to find you. Just sit tight, and I will come to you if we get separated, okay?" She nodded her head in response, and with her journal tucked beneath her arm. The two headed out of the guildhall.

It didn't take long for him to understand what Katie had gone through the day before. As soon as they were out of the building, she had clung to his arm rather tightly. The pair wandered for a bit until they had made their way to a shopping part of the town. Still early, there weren't many people out. The whole town had been put on alert with the events having happened the way they did. Most people didn't even open their shops. He could feel the fear that was seeping through the town as they wandered near-empty streets.

After going down several streets, Elijah finally found the shop he had been looking for. He was met by a strange look from Abigail as they knocked on the door. He knocked again after a few moments to which he still received no answer. A third knock finally warranted an answer. "What is it you want? We are closed until this mess is cleaned up!"

"I was hoping to get some shoes made. Not for me. I have a girl here I was hoping to get them made for." The door finally opened just enough for the woman to look out at the pair. She took notice of Abigail who was lifting her foot to look at her own boots. The shop owner looked the girl once over and opened her door fully.

"You can't have a girl in a dress like that wearing boots as dirty as those." The woman sighed, "Come on in. I might actually have something I could get her in now." Abigail pulled herself in behind Elijah's arm as they entered the lady's shop. "Now, let me get a good look at the girl's feet so I can see what size I am looking for."

She was hesitant at first, but Elijah had finally convinced Abigail to take a seat and remove her shoes. "You don't have stockings on this girl either? I'd swear it was your first-time taking care of the girl!" The shop-keep looked suspiciously over Elijah. "I'm guessing she isn't your daughter?"

"No," Elijah answered gently, "I'm helping look after her for the time being. Katie will be taking care of her."

"Katie from the library? She wasn't in that big fire, was she?"

"No. Fortunately, the dorms were evacuated before the fire spread from the main building. She is pretty upset over losing it though."

"I am sure she is. That was her life work after all. I couldn't imagine what would happen if I ever lost this place." She had been going through various places in her shop as the pair spoke. Abigail simply followed the woman with her eyes as she worked. "So, what is your name little one?" She had stopped to look back at the girl.

"Her name is Abigail."

"She can't talk for herself?" The woman spoke rather sharply to Elijah.

"She currently isn't able to speak."

"I can tell that, but that doesn't mean she can't talk." She pointed to Abigail who had pulled out her journal and had started writing her name for the lady. Elijah caught on that he was wrong for talking in her place. The woman stepped in to speak again to Abigail. "Abigail seems like a pretty big name. Can I call you Abby instead?" She quickly nodded her head. "Good! Well Abby, sit tight and I'll have some shoes put together that will go great with that dress you are wearing."

Nearly an hour had passed as the woman worked, and Abigail had wandered over to her and watched. Finally, the woman seemed to be finished with the shoes. She had put together a pair of slide-on dress shoes. The backs rose slightly with a strap that wrapped around the front of her ankle. To go with the shoes, the woman even had a pair of white stockings for Abigail.

"Well Abby, what do you think?" She walked around the shop for a few minutes before running back to the shop-keep and giving her a hug. "Well, I think she likes them." The lady laughed. Elijah thanked her for taking them in and settled the bill for the shoes. As they left, Abigail waved goodbye before taking back her post at Elijah's side.

"Now that we have you in some proper shoes, why don't we go and get breakfast now?" She nodded back to Elijah as they began to walk back to the guildhall. They could have easily got breakfast there, but Elijah was wanting to get her out and in some better shoes that morning.

He felt a small tug on his shirt, and when he looked down, she was scribbling away in her journal again, *Can I have another sweet roll?* Elijah laughed as he read it and nodded his head. He had only passed it once, but he was able to recall a bakery that sold some.

Katie had been pacing back and forth in the guildhall when the pair finally returned. Worried, she quickly came after the two. "Where have you been? I was so worried when Abby was gone!" She had already grabbed Abigail and was hugging the girl. She noticed that Elijah was carrying a basket with The Long Way Home Bakery logo on it.

"I was just getting us some food. Also, Abigail needed some better shoes, so we made a detour." Katie pulled away to look at Abigail's feet. "Well, also at the bakery, as soon as I mentioned your name, I got lectured in how you finally seemed to find someone. Oh, and I was lectured on not being a deadbeat like her late husband, *God rest his soul.*" He joked towards Katie as her face seemed to glow red. "I figured we should get one of the rent rooms here. No sense in staying in the infirmary anymore nights. Plus, I'd rather talk about certain things somewhere not so open." He looked around the guildhall which was filling with many people.

Abigail had started pulling on Elijah's arm with the food. He wouldn't let her eat on the road and she was ready to eat. The remarks about the bakery seemed to put Katie at a loss for words as the trio ate in silence. "So, for that thing to take care of today. It was just going to be us. I figured it would be easier that way." It was Elijah who spoke first. Katie knew he was referring to Abigail's parents. "Thanks to John, and the other council members, we don't have to worry about any of the citizens right now. We should just take the day and handle things here."

"I don't think it's real for her yet." Katie was gently stroking Abigail's hair as she spoke. "It will be. Am I a bad person for wanting to drag this out a little longer?"

"No. But the sooner she can have the—" he was cut off by Abigail tapping on her journal. He could hear her sniffling; *you are talking about mom and dad, aren't you?* Katie and Elijah exchanged looks as Katie looked about ready to cry as well. Abigail was still looking down towards her journal. Elijah borrowed the pen from her hand; *It's ok for you to cry. Me and Katie are both here so you can cry as much as you need to.* With that, Abigail threw herself into Elijah's chest and began to sob. She cried harder than she had with Katie the day before.

Abigail had fallen asleep on Elijah the way she did Katie the day before. "Where did you learn how to get along with kids so well?" Katie was watching the two as he gently moved her to one of the beds. The room he had rented for them was spacious with two beds and a table. Food was still spread out from their breakfast, but Katie had already started to clean up.

"In the capital," he kept his voice quiet as he spoke, "I help with some kids I know there. I'm not perfect. I learned just enough so that I can help without scaring the kids."

"You don't have your own kid, do you?"

"No!"

"A family at all? Is anyone waiting for you back in the capital?"

"I don't live in the capital." Elijah's voice sounded distant as he spoke, "I don't have anywhere to call home. I belong to the church, so I go where they send me. The only thing I had close to a family was my master."

"I'm sorry you lost him." Katie was sincere in her statement, but she was only met by Elijah's laughter.

"I don't mean to laugh." He calmed himself again, "I hated the man. His death was one of the best things that could have happened. I only wish he were here to help handle all of this. He was a horrible person, but his knowledge was unlike anyone else. We could have really used him."

"I don't mean to speak on things I don't know a lot about, but things seem really bad in the church. Are you okay staying in all of that?"

"Like I said. I belong to the church. My only way out is death, and before you ask again, I will not drag you into this world."

"I wasn't going to ask that!" She quickly thought to change her question, "I just was wondering how you plan to let the church allow you to stay on this task. You aren't a full crusader, right? Won't they just take everything you did here and give it to someone more experienced?" Elijah seemed to distance himself as he looked for an answer. "You didn't think of that did you?" He again didn't answer.

"I will figure it out. I need you to hold to your promise." Elijah had grabbed Katie's hand, "I don't want you in this world that the church put me in. If you get dragged into this, it'll feel like this has all been for nothing."

"And what does that mean?"

"Just…" Elijah looked intently to Katie, "hold to your promise. Let me go when it is time for me to leave." She finally nodded her head.

Seeing the loss in his eyes as he spoke, she was reminded of how much she didn't know about him anymore. "thank you." He turned to look at Abigail, "When she wakes up. It will be time to head to the church." With a nod, the two waited together while the girl slept.

"John!" Christine called out to him as she jogged to catch up to him.

"Christine," he smiled as she approached, "I am surprised that Daniel let you out of his sight. He's going to be upset next you see him."

"Let him! I'm tired of always being treated so frail. Anyway, where are you heading to?"

"I'm heading back to the guildhall. I've been meeting with people all day upset that they can't leave town. People seem to be split in half over all of this. Some are panicking and refusing to even open their windows. Others are angry that they are having to give up the festival and follow curfew. They don't seem to believe they are in danger and think this is all a joke."

"Well, most people are afraid to accept the truth. Because as soon as they do, it means they are really in danger. If I had to choose between accepting danger with no control over it, and accepting that this is some sort of joke, I would rather this all be a joke." Christine spoke as though she were talking about something else.

"So, you are saying that people are accepting what they want because the reality of what is happening is more than they are willing to accept?"

"In part. I think we all have things we would like to believe rather than accept the truth of it. I think all of us will have to face a truth that goes against everything we think we know. I can't fault someone for wanting to believe in the route that causes the least amount of pain." John was staring at Christine as she spoke, "I am sort of just rambling. I don't think any of that really made sense."

"No, it did." John quickly answered. "It made more sense than I wanted it to."

"Oh?"

"Anyway, where are you off to?"

"I am heading to meet Katie. They should be taking Abigail to the church soon. I wanted to see if there was anything they needed when they got back. They are going to have their hands full the rest of the day."

"We all know what that little girl is going through. I wouldn't wish that on anyone."

"You know I can tell when you are angry, right?" John seemed to tense up as she addressed him, "You don't seem angry at her though. Do you still blame Elijah for all of this?"

"Not him directly..." John was trying to find the right words, "I know that this isn't his fault. If he wasn't here, I think we would be worse off. It is hard though. To just accept everything as what it is. Father Bernard did so much for us. Is he really the bad guy here? And Elijah. He was gone for ten years and just shows up to play hero at the right time?"

"I think we all have things we would like to believe rather than accept the truth of it." Christine smirked at him as she repeated herself to him. John was silent as the pair continued to walk. "All things aside, none of us know what will happen tomorrow. Not even Elijah. Until this is resolved, we can't afford to doubt one another. Besides, for the last ten years, you are the one I have looked for to keep us all safe. That isn't going to change just because one person showed up. I still believe in you John so make sure you take care of all of us, ok?"

She was smiling at him genuinely as he felt a knot in his chest. "You are one of my oldest and best friends, Christine. I don't know how I would handle things if you weren't around."

"Hey! Being all sweet on me now won't make a difference." She seemed to be teasing John, "I chose Daniel, remember? Don't you have someone now anyway? When will I get to meet her?"

"You will meet her when everyone else does!" John seemed to bolster himself as he spoke, "There has never been a woman more beautiful than her. Truly more than I deserve. I am worried that you will try and talk her out of it if you meet her too soon." He gave a loud laugh.

"Someone needs to warn her of what she is getting into."

"Seriously, does no one think more of me than that?" John seemed worried, "I may say the same thing, but it would be nice if just one of you didn't act like she was in danger." Christine began to laugh as she grabbed onto John's arm as though she were struggling to keep herself up.

"I'm sorry John," She wiped tears from her eyes as she stifled her laughing, "I am honestly happy for you. None of us thought you would ever tie the knot. We are all just excited for you. Let's get through this so that we can finally meet her."

When they arrived back to the guildhall, they met Elijah, Katie, and Abigail on their way out. Abigail looked lost as she held both others hand. The next few hours would be tough for her. Christine quickly ran to Katie and Abigail to give them both a hug before the trio headed out. John couldn't think of anything he could say or do that would help. He chose to leave this one to Elijah.

The church was lit by the setting sun, shining brightly through the stain glass window. The chapel was silent except for the sounds of their footsteps as they entered the hall. Near the pulpit rested the two coffins for Mr. and Mrs. McKenna. Abigail squeezed both Katie and Elijah's hands tight as they began to walk towards the front of the hall.

With each step, she seemed to begin shaking. She let go of Elijah's hand and clung tightly to Katie's arm. Elijah looked down to see her face puff up as she tried to hold back her tears. She was sniffling hard, and as they drew closer to the caskets; she began to slow her steps.

Placing a hand on her back, Elijah kept her moving. He hated to put her through this, but he knew that she needed closure on this. If he had buried her parents without her getting the chance to say goodbye, there were a variety of emotions that wouldn't be settled for her. He remembered Katie when she was going through this. They had finally made it to the front of the chapel.

Abigail was immediately drawn to the sight of her mother. She managed to let go of Katie's arm, and walked to her mother's side. She gently placed her hand on her mom's shoulder. Quickly looking away, she turned to her dad. She repeated the same here. She shook her dad's shoulder several times. Throughout the interaction, Abigail seemed to do her best to hold back tears. After seeing her father not moving before her, she began to sob.

She collapsed to the floor as the tears overwhelmed her while still holding on to the side of her dad's coffin. Katie and Elijah moved quickly to either side of her. They let her stay there as long as she needed. She cried and cried, while the other two stayed there on either side, reassuring her that she was not alone. When the time finally came, Elijah carried Abigail as she said goodbye to her parents for the last time.

He carried her as she sobbed with Katie following close by. Daniel had been waiting by the door for them. He had agreed to seal the coffins and move them to a wagon so that they could be buried back in Kend. He would take care of it so that Elijah and Katie could spend the rest of the evening with Abigail.

They returned to their room at the guildhall where they quickly fell asleep while caring for the mourning girl. Night moved fast, and third day finally arrived. Elijah, Katie, John, Christine, and Daniel all awoke with an uneasiness in their chests.

§

TWENTY-THREE

ATTACK

The sun rose and set again on the third day. As it did the fourth, fifth, and sixth day. The city had been untouched during these days and the eerie quiet that had settled over the city felt more unnerving than the mysterious fire that destroyed the library.

In the guildhall, Elijah, Katie, Daniel, Christine, John, Hugo, and Bryant were all seated along a table that had been set for their meeting. Anger was apparent on Bryant's face as the group sat in silence. The city was still under curfew and the gates were still closed to keep people from leaving.

"Financially, our city is ruined!" Bryant finally let out, "This lockdown *you* ordered has proven to be for nothing just as I told you it would!" He was spitting as he directed his harsh words towards Elijah who was going by his travel name Let for official purposes.

"Bryant," Hugo had placed a hand on his friend's shoulder, "I understand your anger right now, but you have to admit how strange it is. Not a single letter has come by either air or rider since the fire. We have sent out plenty to have heard something back too."

"Still…" Bryant searched for a reasoning, "how long are we going to have to keep everyone here? With work at a near standstill and housing the refugees from Lake Town, this is taking a massive toll on the city's treasury. It is going to be a struggle to pay our taxes without something changing soon!"

"The church will provide aid to the city, if it is needed." Elijah's voice was flat as he spoke, "It was our inability to control the situation that put the town in this position. If you keep a proper ledger of expenses used to take care of the town, I will make sure the church compensates you for it." This seemed to quell Bryant's anger some. Elijah quickly turned his attention to John, "How are your men doing? Has there been anything on Father Bernard?"

"Still no sign of him." John seemed distant as he spoke, "My men seem a bit anxious that nothing has happened. Is there any way to know if the threat has passed?"

"We won't know that until either the church arrives, or the attack happens. They should be here in another day or two, so I am hoping that there isn't an attack before then. The only real information we must go off is what Father Bernard said before he ran away. There is no way to know what the truth is. Our number one priority should be finding him and hoping he hasn't left town."

"Some of the people have been getting pretty restless," It was Daniel to speak up this time, "yesterday we had to disperse three groups that were trying to demand that they be allowed to leave the city. I feel that two more days will be more than some of them can handle."

"I can help out with that." John spoke up quickly.

"After your incident in the training yard," Christine sounded worried as she spoke, "People have lost a lot of confidence in you. I think Katie and I should take this one."

"Yeah?" Katie spoke up quickly. She hadn't been paying attention, and hearing her name quickly brought her back to the conversation.

"Katie, what's on your mind?" Elijah had reached over to grab her hand without thinking about it. An action everyone took quick note of.

"I was just thinking. Abigail has been eating too many sweets the last few days. I think she needs to eat something a bit healthier tonight." Everyone stared at her for a moment before breaking out into laughter. She looked from person to person confused before she remembered why they had all met today. "I'm…I'm sorry! I just don't really have much to add here!"

"I think this is a good place to end things for tonight." Hugo chimed in as he stifled his laughter, "In the morning, Bryant and I will meet with some of the individuals who have been causing the most trouble." Turning his attention to Christine, "I'll trust in you and Katie to handle any outbursts that we missed. Our best strategy right now is just trying to keep everyone calm until this ends." Everyone agreed one by one as they wrapped up their meeting for the evening.

"I'm going to go take a tour around the city." John still looked rather distant as he spoke, "I can't really keep my mind focused anyway." He strapped his great sword to his back as he headed for the door. He was followed soon by Hugo and Bryant.

"Daniel," Christine was holding tight to his arm, "Can we take a walk too? Just the two of us?" He stared into her eyes for a moment before planting a kiss on her forehead and nodding. They too left the guildhall. Distracted by his wife though, he had forgotten to grab his bow as they left.

"Well," Katie turned her attention to Elijah, "we should go and check on Abby. I'm surprised we were able to keep her in the room as long as we did." Grabbing his hand, she began to pull him towards the room they had been renting. Slowly, Elijah had been letting his guard down around her. He began to feel like he was back home again as she pulled him away by his hand. Even if it wouldn't last, he enjoyed being there with her again.

The sight of Abigail fast asleep in the bed informed them as to how she had been comfortable enough to be away from them as long as she was. They decided to let her sleep and returned to the main hall. "Elijah," Katie kept her back to him as she spoke. The pair were alone in the hall, "I'm in love with you. I know you must leave again, but I'm not someone to keep things like this to myself." She finally turned back to look at him. He was as stoned face as he was the day he had returned to Pneu.

"No matter what you think or what you have to do, this is your home." She had grabbed both of his hands as she spoke, "Whatever happens, I am here for you to come home to, Abby too. You mean the world to both of us, and the only thing I can say is that I love you."

Elijah didn't change expressions once as she spoke, but he also didn't pull his hands away from hers. He noticed how red Katie's cheeks were glowing as she spoke as well as the few beads of sweat that began to roll down the side of her face. He took notice to how much her eyes shined as she looked to him for an answer to her sudden confession of love. Her lips looked soft, and the longer he stared at her, the more of her features he observed carefully.

Feeling a knot wheeling within his chest, he moved his eyes to look past her. He could feel his heart racing in his chest as she stood there silently waiting for him to answer her. Against the wall towards the door though, he noticed Daniel's bow that had been left behind. "Katie," he turned his eyes back to hers.

"Y...yes?" Her voice shook as she answered him.

"Can I give you a proper answer once all of this is finished?" He was gripping her hands tighter now, "I have a bad feeling about something." He returned his stare to Daniel's bow, and Katie followed his gaze to it.

"Daniel never leaves that bow." She pulled her hands away and began walking towards the bow, "Do you think something is going to happen tonight?"

"I don't know, but we should bring that to him just in case." The pair collected the bow and quickly ran out the door of the guild hall.

John had been wandering the streets for some time lost in his own thoughts. He wandered around without any real place in mind, and before he realized it, he was standing before the church. He gave a small chuckle as he thought about Father Bernard, and he decided to visit the man's study once more.

Entering the room, it was just as it had been the last time they had looked for him. John knew he wouldn't find the Father here. He ran his hand across the desk as he thought of all the conversations he had here. The man he felt closest to had been named most wanted in the town, and John felt torn between duty and respect. Without Father Bernard, he would not be the man he is today.

The sound of the door opening behind him made John quickly reach for his sword and spin around on his heels. Standing there in the doorway was none other than Father Bernard. "Wait, John! Please let me speak with you." The Father pleaded.

"Why should I let you speak?" John filled his voice with anger to hide his indecisiveness.

"I once told you that you were like a real son to me." Father Bernard's voice sounded sincere as he spoke, "Please. There is something you *must* know." John relaxed his posture as he moved his hand from his sword.

"Thank you!" Father Bernard slightly bowed his head as he spoke, "First, I need to show you something. Something Elijah has been hiding from you." He moved passed John to stand near the bookshelf which rested just behind the desk. Pulling on one of the books, the entire case pulled away from the wall to reveal a hidden door. "There is something down here that means the difference in protecting the town and ending it."

Against his better judgement, John followed Father Bernard down the dark staircase. They walked for only a short time before the stairs came to a long hallway. Towards the end of the hall was a single door that was illuminated by two small torches. Feeling uneasy, John returned his hand to his sword as he continued to follow the Father.

Inside was a single room that was lit by strange green stones that were glowing on the walls. In the middle of the floor was a drawing. Old and faded, the drawing was shaped in a variety of geometrical shapes and symbols. It looked like elvish, but it felt slightly off to John. "What is this?"

"This is a seal that keeps demons from entering the town." Father Bernard walked from crystal to crystal checking them, "This was made back when the church was founded to protect the village when it was still small. It has been connected directly to me ever since I took the vows as priest to this temple, but it is too weak now." He was tracing the lines on the floor now.

"I truly meant it when I said that I care about protecting everyone." He was now standing before John, "I only want to keep you all safe. My involvement with the Arken-Faith is purely as another way to protect everyone. You *must* believe me!"

John felt torn. He didn't know what was right anymore. "If I were to believe you, why did you bring me here? Even if it is weak, it should still help right?"

"As soon as two or three demons try to enter the town, this barrier will be broken, and we won't stand a chance." John could see tears filling Father Bernard's eyes. "I can establish a new, stronger barrier but this one has to break first. I cannot do that myself. I need your help for this."

"You are asking me to help you break some sort of barrier that is supposedly protecting us even though I know that you are part of the Arken-Faith?" John's head had begun to hurt.

"I know. But John, Please! You have known me your entire life. All I have ever done is protect you all. I love you as much as any man would love his son. I have no one else to turn to." Father Bernard pleaded heavily for John to trust in him, and it pulled hard in John's mind.

"What would I need to do to help you?" John ceded to the man who had raised him. He chose to trust the Father.

"Thank you, John. You truly grew up into a great man." Father Bernard wiped the tears from his eyes. "The barrier is weak enough that by removing just one of the green crystals will break the barrier."

John had moved to one of the nearest walls. He felt something was off. "And you are sure that this will help everyone?"

"I am positive! I cannot set a new barrier until the old one is broken." Waiting no further, John grabbed hold of the green crystal. It felt warm through his glove as he held it in his hand, and the crystal somehow seemed to be suspended in front of the wall without anything mounting it. With very little effort, it pulled away from the wall, and all the crystals began to flicker as they all slowly extinguished their light.

For a moment there was silence. In the next moment, a voice that sent chills through his body rang out. "Wow! John, you really did it!" Instantly his heart sank as his adrenaline began to pump through his body, "You really are the best brother in the whole world!" It was hard to see in the darkness, but the sudden tugging on his sleeve told him exactly where his sister was standing.

A sudden, deep throated laughter from near the door made John horribly aware of the mistake he had made. "John, you really are the golden knight you always try to be." Father Bernard sounded ecstatic as he spoke. "I have a riddle for you!"

"What is this?" John continued to feel his sister bouncing on his arm as many thoughts began to race through his head.

"Yay! My big brother loves riddles!" She answered for him.

"How does a rare disease from far away find its way into such a sweet little girl?" John couldn't keep up with the events happening before him. "Come on John. You are a smart man. Tell me! How did your sister contract such a deadly disease?"

"Come on big brother! How did I die! Guess! Guess!" The girl was bouncing merrily on his arm.

"What…I…" John looked for an answer. Any answer besides the one that was in his mind.

"Oh John." Father Bernard sounded disappointed. "You are thinking too hard on it." John heard the footsteps begin to move away from him. In the dark room he could make out the silhouette of the Father near the door. "I gave her the disease!"

John's heart felt as though it left his chest as he sank to his knees. He heard what the Father had said. He knew each word and what they meant in the order that he had said them, but he couldn't accept it for what it was. This reality was too harsh for him. He couldn't find words as Amelia began laughing at him kneeling on the floor beside her.

"Thank you for giving us the final thing we needed to get into the city." Father Bernard was laughing as he spoke. "Enjoy your time with Amelia. We'll be upstairs taking care of your friends if you would like to join us. Ihave a feeling you and your sweet sister have time to make up for though." With a quick slam of the door, John was left alone in the dark with no one besides Amelia.

"John!" She wrapped her arms tightly around his neck. "I missed you so much! I'm sorry you went through so much, but I'm here now." Her arms kept wrapping tighter as she spoke, "Soon, you will be with me and none of this will hurt anymore! Father Bernard will take great care of us." He finally noticed that it was getting harder to breath.

Everything finally made sense to him. Amelia was murdered. It was Father Bernard who did it. He belonged to the Arken-Faith and their goal was to kill them all. John was used to break the barrier that kept demons from entering the town, and right now demons were probably ravaging the city. Father Bernard was the one who was controlling Amelia's spirit now through some form of necromancy, and he was using her to kill him here. John accepted this and figured his death would be better for everyone. It is his fault, and this was his punishment.

"I can't wait for us to be together forever!" She whispered in his ear, "No one here loved you anyway."

I love you.

A voice rang out in his mind. A sweet voice that he hadn't heard in too long. The voice of a woman who swore to spend the rest of her life with him.

"No one here wants you around!" His sister's voice was bitter. "I hate you for letting me die so come and be with me forever!"

That girl never had the ability to hate someone

This time it was Elijah's voice that rang out in his mind. It was getting hard for him to breath and tears filled his eyes.

Amelia, she loved you more than anything else.

"This isn't it…" John's voice was hoarse as he spoke. He gripped Amelia's arm tight as he began to pry himself free from her grip.

"What are you doing? Don't you want to be with me? It's your fault I'm dead! I hate you John!" Amelia was shouting as she tried to tighten her grip again. She was stronger than an eight-year-old should be, but he was still stronger.

"I am sorry." John was crying as he faced her, "I wasn't able to save you when you were alive." He managed to grab hold of both her wrists. His hands were large enough that he managed to restrain them with one. His free hand drew the sword from his back. "This is all my fault, but it changes here."

"No!" She was crying now, "What are you doing? I'm scared John! What's happening to me?" She jerked hard against his grip as she desperately tried to escape.

"I couldn't save you when you were alive, but I can at least save your spirit now." Eyes swollen with tears; he drove his sword through the girl's chest. "I'm so sorry! Goodbye Amelia."

She had been fighting him until the sword pierced her chest. He couldn't see it in the dark, but her eyes were swollen with tears as she lost consciousness. With a smile, she finally stopped fighting. Her body fell and turned to ash as it hit the floor. John had freed his sister from the hold of Father Bernard. He laid on the ground where she had collapsed crying, "I'm sorry. I'm so sorry." He cried out to her. Soon though, a new feeling began to rise within him. A fiery hot anger began to boil within him. "BERNARD!!" His cry was so loud that he was certain anyone still around the church would have heard it. "BERNARD!!" He shouted once more as he forced himself from the ground.

Both the door to the underground room and the room to the study had been securely locked. John's brute strength was enough to shatter the doors into splinters. He was unstoppable force seeking out the focus of his boiling rage. Standing in the courtyard out front of the church stood Father Bernard.

"I never expected you to kill your own sister!" He sneered at John, "How truly heartless you are!"

"I WILL KILL YOU HERE!" John screamed, venom coating every syllable. He could feel the heat rising in his chest as he gripped the hilt of his sword tight. He prepared himself to charge Father Bernard.

"I would *love* to see you try!" As he spoke, Father Bernard pulled a medallion from beneath his robes. The same that John had seen in the forest a week prior. From the medallion, several shadowy figures immerged. They took no form and appeared to be nothing more than a dark mist that began floating around him. "Most of the other's hate dealing with the Shapeless. They aren't the easiest to control and against the Crusaders they are nearly useless."

The dark mist around him began to form into the shape of a large bow and several arrows. "This will be far more painful than if you had just let yourself die below!" He let loose one of the arrows which flew too fast for John to see.

John felt a deep burning in his leg that brought him to his knees. Looking down, the arrow had pierced into his left leg. The shapeless arrow transformed again into a black fire that began to burn his leg where it struck. Pain racked his mind so hard that he nearly collapsed. The pain in his leg though was not enough to quell his anger. He found his way back to his feet and began to walk towards Father Bernard.

"Oh John! You really should have just stayed down." He fired another arrow which struck into John's shoulder. He screamed out in pain as the fire set in there as well. His feet kept moving. "No!" Father Bernard screamed out, "You must die here!" John was only steps from him now. The Father began to take steps back as he readied the third arrow.

Walking backwards, his foot caught a small stone causing him stumble as he fired the arrow which narrowly missed John's head. Realizing John was too close, Father Bernard transformed his bow into a knife. "You are in too much pain, I know it! Now Die!" He drove the knife straight for John's chest. The Shapeless dagger landed squarely in the center of John's hand which he had brought to stop the blade. "No!"

"I said," John's voice was strained, almost a whisper, "I will kill you here." He drove his sword through Father Bernard's chest. The medallion was caught in the strike and shattered as it was driven through the Father's body with the blade. The medallion which was imbedded into his chest began to leak out all the souls which had been trapped within. Screaming in agonizing pain, souls began to burst from within the Father's chest. After only a few seconds, the Father was dead and the fire on John's body had been extinguished.

John collapsed onto his back as he watched the lights of all the different souls begin to drift away. He reached out towards them wondering how many of them were people he had known. As he laid there, a new light caught his attention. A bright red light lit up the sky to his left. There was a fire burning from somewhere within the city.

He forced himself back to his feet and into the church. He needed to ring the bell which was the signal for everyone to evacuate there. "I'm sorry for all of this." He cried out as he worked his way to the bells. "I can do at least this much." He pulled hard on the rope. *DING* He pulled again and a third time *DING DING DING.* He let himself collapse to the floor once more. "Elijah. The rest is on all of you now. I'm sorry."

Chapter Twenty-Four
SCATTERED FIGHTING

The moon was brighter than most nights and with the clear skies, the city streets were well lit. Christine held tight to Daniel's arm as they enjoyed the quiet streets. He smiled as they walked down the moonlit street. He looked down towards Christine who was smiling with her head laid on his shoulder. Despite everything that was happening, she appeared as relaxed and calm as ever. She looked at peace would be the right way to describe it.

They were crossing over one of the bridges in town when she pulled him to the side. They stood there together looking out at the moon which aligned perfectly with the river. The water was flowing smooth enough that the moon cast a perfect reflection upon it. She was humming to herself as she looked out over the river.

Daniel didn't pay any mind to the river. He stood there and watched her. He thought back to all the years they have been together now, and he thanked the Gods for all the time that he had had with her. He still cared about the others, but none of them could compare to her. If it ever came down to it, he would turn on any of them just to keep Christine safe.

She suddenly turned to him, "We've been so busy lately that we haven't had a lot of time just me and you, have we?" The smile she gave him made it feel as though he could float away.

"I guess not." He leaned against the bridge and peered out across the river, "All the trouble we've been going through has taken a lot to deal with. I don't think I've asked you, but you're still doing okay right? You aren't pushing yourself too hard?" He was always worrying about her health. Over the years, her health had declined faster than the others, and he was worried about what kind of time they still had together.

"I told you silly. You don't have to worry about me." She grabbed his hand and placed it on her left cheek. "I'm doing fine. I don't have any plans on leaving anytime soon. Besides, there is still a promise you have to keep." She gave him a very stern look as she said this.

"You still have never taken me on a honeymoon you know." She had made a sour face at him as they spoke, "You keep promising me you will, but something always seems to come up." Her face had changed from 'upset' to 'sad' as she began to speak again, "Unless you just don't love me anymore. I guess that's only fair. I can't expect you to understand the needs of a woman. I should just let you go free and enjoy your wonderful youth while I wither away reminiscing of old times." She melodramatically placed a hand over her face as though she was hiding tears, sarcasm ringing high in her voice.

"You really are something you know." He chuckled as he wrapped his arms around her. He couldn't see her face however he knew that she was smiling. He felt her bury her face into his shoulder as she placed her arms around him as well.

An uneasy feeling began to creep over him. It felt as though they were being watched. *Damn, I didn't bring anything with me.* Christine had squeezed him twice before whispering in his ear, "Someone's here." He nodded his head letting her know that he knew as well.

He turned his head slightly so that he could view the end of the bridge. Standing there was a tall hooded man who wore a dark metallic amulet around his neck. He didn't need to see anymore to know who this was. He broke their embrace to look towards the other end of the bridge where several more hooded men were standing.

Sharp laughter pierced through him as they stood there defenseless as the one of them began to approach. He shoved Christine behind him and cornered her against the edge of the bridge. "I don't want you to even think about it." His words were sharp with worry. Very few people knew of her special ability. It was very powerful however it was also the cause of her illness. Each time she used it, it had shortened her life and damaged her body greatly. The last time she had used it, she almost wasn't able to return to who she was. "I'm not ready to lose you so please don't use it here. I'll find a way to keep you safe."

Daniel racked his brain for a way out. These were just normal humans, and he knew he could probably handle them fist to fist, but what about their demons? As he desperately tried to think of a plan, the one who had been walking forward spoke, "We are here to cleanse this city in the name of the Arken-Son. You should consider yourselves fortunate to be the first to be sacrificed in his honor!"

Daniel refused to let them have her. He made the decision that he would throw Christine into the river so that she can get away while he holds them back as long as he was able. As he was preparing himself to do so, he felt Christine's soft hand on his shoulder. He turned to face her, and she placed a gentle kiss on his cheek. "It's okay. I promise I'll come back to you." His heart sank as she suddenly placed her hand on his chest and forced him over the edge of the bridge.

As he fell towards the river, he watched as the skin ripped away from around her. In place of her face grew a large snout and sharp teeth. Where her arms were sprung two large paws, and her torso grew over twice its size. He felt the water engulf him as her beast form took full shape. As the water rushed around him, he could hear her howling. *No!*

DING, DING, DING. The Church bells rang out to signal the evacuation of the people. Columns of smoke were rising from all over the city. "Damn! They're here." Katie clung tightly to Elijah's arm as they watched more smoke begin to rise from some buildings only a few blocks over. Katie Tugged on his shirt, and when he looked towards her, he realized where it was that she had her eyes set.

From where they were standing, only the top of the guildhall could be seen with smoke billowing from around the spires of the hall. They were unable to see if the smoke was coming from the hall or buildings nearby, but all their thoughts were of the little girl they had left asleep in the room.

He grabbed hold of Katie's hand and started back towards the hall as fast as he was able. He knew he was probably hurting her hand from how hard he had grabbed it, but he didn't want to lose her in the madness that was quickly growing in the city around them.

He could feel tears swelling in his eyes from frustration which he tried choking back. Nearby, they could hear someone screaming, but he couldn't bring himself to stop and help. The guild can help them. He felt Katie stumble a couple times as they ran but, she would regain her footing and keep running. If she was hurting, she wasn't going to let herself show it. She was as worried about Abigail as he was. The only thing either of them could think about was getting to her and keeping her safe.

As they turned onto the main street to bring them to the guild, they came face to face with seven hooded figures and several demons. He pulled Katie behind him as to guard her however they soon realized there were more standing behind them as well. Katie gripped tight to Elijah's back as one of them stepped forward. "Crusader! Scholar! We are here in the name of the Arken-Son who demands the world fall so the God of Death can once again rise. The demand for your sacrifice, however, is greater than any other sacrifice which will be made tonight. Please, die in peace knowing that this is his will."

As the man raised his arms, several more demons emerged from his amulet. There now stood eight demons before them: each one unique and terrifying in its own way. Behind them stood four more. Katie's grip began to tighten even more. Her fingernails were digging into Elijah's back, and he felt a couple drops of blood begin to stream down his back. "YOU TELL YOUR GOD, THE ONLY SACRIFICE HE'LL GET TONIGHT IS YOUR OWN SOUL!" Elijah's sudden outburst had startled Katie. He had felt her jump when he spoke out, and he felt her grip loosen just a bit. "Katie, take this." He had created a shield like the weapons he used in the forest. It had a golden gleam to it and had appeared so quick that Katie didn't even notice it form. "You don't have to worry about fighting with it. Just block anything that tries to grab you. No matter what though, don't let go of it or it'll come right back to me."

Hands shaking, she had taken the shield. He could tell by the surprised look on her face that she didn't expect it to be as light as it was. Weapon's made from the soul have very little weight to them and are easy to handle. He knew that this was more demons than he had faced before, but he needed to protect Katie and get to Abigail.

With a crooked smile, the man lowered his arms and the demons began to swarm them. Elijah had summoned a spear as the demons closed in. Watching them move, he decided to take a defensive stance. With this many, he would wait for openings and strike. As powerful as demons are, it only takes one solid strike of a soul weapon to destroy one.

The first demon that had made it to him was an exceptionally tall one. It stood nearly eight feet tall and carried no weapon. On each hand was three long claws, each the length of a dagger. This demon had a single eye, and its lower jaw was missing. Its tongue hung down where it's jaw should be, swaying back and forth with each step. The demon made a rasping gargling sound as it breathed.

Beside it was the next closest demon. This one bore seven eyes. The eye in the middle of its face was glowing a deep, crimson red. It had small straps of flesh stretched across its lips leaving them exposed. Each tooth was sharpened to a point, each bite capable of tearing a man in half.

As they had reached him, Elijah used his spear to deflect the claw strike of the first demon. With the same motion, he drove his spear through the mouth of the second. As it fell to the ground in ash, the third drove itself through the collapsing remains of the fallen.

This new demon had no face. Where its mouth should be, muffled screaming could be heard. It was missing its left arm, its right arm shriveled and small. The hand was where its elbow should have been. As it approached him, its chest split open in a v shape exposing rows of flattened teeth.

Elijah was still recovering his stance from striking the other demon and knew he wouldn't regain his balance before it bit into him. Around his right foot spawned a sabaton which formed to a sharp point on the toe. Elijah used the momentum from his forward strike to bring his leg around in a wide kick. The point of his sabaton struck this third demon in the neck. Knocking it to the ground and decapitating it however, not destroying it.

It flailed around on the ground as it tried to bring itself back towards him. He heard a small shriek from behind him. He adjusted his head slightly to see one of the demons striking the shield that Katy was holding. *Good girl Katie, keep blocking them.* He brought his foot down through the chest of the third demon. He pivoted on this foot, causing it to be destroyed, and this allowed him to turn and drive his spear through the chest of the one that had struck at Katie.

He heard Katie scream and when he looked down, the first demon that had come for him had wrapped its hand around her leg. She brought her shield down hard against the arm, severing it from its body. The arm turned to ash as the demon attempted to shriek. The only sound that had come from the demon was a foul gargling noise that caused bloody bile to discharge from its throat.

Elijah grabbed Katie and spun her around as he drove the spear down, impaling the demon through the head and into its chest. As the demon turned to ash, three more had reached them. Two from behind and one from ahead of them. The first demon from behind them, walked on frail legs, with bladed arms, and white blind eyes. The other with it was short, barely standing at five feet tall, wielding a large dagger. The demon that stood alone was the one that worried Elijah the most though.

This demon was rather large both in height and in size, and unlike the others, this one was rather proportionate. His body was covered in a dark purple flame and wielded a great sword that stood as tall as it did. The sword was engulfed in the same flames as the demon however it dripped molten flesh upon the ground, decaying where it fell.

Elijah turned his spear into a broadsword as he felt his heart sink. This was the largest demon he had ever seen, and he was intimidated by its size. He steeled his heart as he repositioned Katie behind him. "I need you. Don't get yourself in a bad spot but keep those two off us for as long as you can." He suddenly realized that she was shaking and when he looked towards her, she had tears streaming down her face. Her eyes were swollen red and she looked as though she was on the verge of breaking.

He was so used to fighting at this point, he didn't even think of how terrified she must be right now. He placed a hand on her shoulder and brought his mouth towards her ear. He whispered to her, "I'm not going anywhere. Just keep holding on and I'll keep you and Abigail safe. Don't give in yet." he brought a hand towards her face to wipe away some of her tears. She nodded her head and readied her shield with a renewed will to hold back the demons from behind them.

He repositioned himself to prepare for his fight against this giant demon. He didn't have much time before the rest of the demons were on them as well. Not wanting to waste time, he changed to an offensive stance as he moved forward to strike the demon. It didn't move, guard, or even try to stop his strike. Elijah drove his sword through the demon down to the hilt, having no visible effect. It reached down and grasped Elijah's hands with one. His hands felt as though they had burst into flames as the demon's grip tightened around his wrists.

The demon raised its sword high above its head and brought it down with terrifying force. Elijah released his sword and put all his energy into summoning a shield over his left shoulder which protected him from the demon's strike. It may have saved his life; however, the strike was so powerful that it threw Elijah to the ground. His head was spinning as he tried to regain himself. Katie was screaming in terror as the giant demon had grabbed her around her waist. "No! Elijah, No!" She was screaming out for help however he couldn't get himself back to his feet. That strike left his head spinning to the point he couldn't even hold himself up.

She had dropped the shield as well which brought it back to him. *No, you can't have her.* He fought hard to try and stand again but to no avail. "Katie, I'm coming. I swear I'm going to get you." He desperately pleaded knowing that he couldn't bring himself from the ground. He heard the men begin to laugh as they watched him struggle to stand.

He watched as the demon carried Katie away. "I can still save her if I can just get up." His head began to level out again as he regained his balance enough to stand. He stood in time to watch as the demon charged off towards the guild hall.

One of the men stepped forward, "She still has a purpose to serve our God before her death. You though have served your purpose. Go now, and let your life be an offering!" He was now surrounded by the remaining demons. He brought forth a short spear and hand sickle this time. "I'll kill you all. Every one of you will die tonight!" He felt himself beginning to crack again. He didn't have time to keep himself. He needed to save them. He began to feel his eye twitch as his senses began to numb. He cackled as he readied himself to fight.

He suddenly heard a loud howling from his left, and then from an alleyway burst a giant beast. The creature was on all four paws and stood nearly ten feet tall. The creature had a wild look in its eye that made it seem as though it only wanted blood. It was a senseless animal driven by its bloodlust. Elijah stood in awe at this terrifying beast as he wondered where it came from and whose side it was on.

"Damn!" Daniel sat along the riverbank for a moment while he tried to think up a plan. "You know that you can't control yourself in that form. Why did you push me off?" He squeezed out as much water from his clothes as he could before he headed back to the street. He knew he needed to be careful. Unarmed, he could do nothing against the demons. DING, DING, DING. This was the signal for the citizens to evacuate to the church.

"I'll head back to the guild for my bow. Once I have that, I need to find Christine. If she hurts someone, she'll never forgive herself." He also worried about if he could even get her back this time. It took over a month for her to turn back into a human the last time she transformed. He heard footsteps coming towards him.

He quickly ducked behind some crates near the shop he found himself next to. Soon the footsteps came into view. It was Stephanie. She had come close enough that with the moonlight he was able to see that she was crying and in pain. A shadow scurried across the road and wrapped itself around her leg making her trip. She didn't attempt to stand again. She laid there sobbing.

Another figure came into view from where she had come. The hooded figure was of the cult which Daniel could tell from the medallion that hung from his neck. He continued to approach Stephanie who still had not moved from her frozen state. *Get up! Run! I can't fight for you here!* Daniel pleaded in his mind for her to move. He started looking around for something. Anything. There was a single stone that was loose from the side of the building he was next to.

The stone was heavy, but he would be able to throw it. *If you don't move woman, I'm going to do something really stupid, now move!* She stayed as she was, sobbing on the ground. The man was laughing now as he neared her. *Damn, don't make me regret this.* He stepped out from behind the crate and threw the rock as hard as his arm would allow. The rock struck the man hard in the top of his head. The stone caused the hood to fall back, and the face that was seen made Daniel shudder.

The man did not have a normal head. It was the decayed face of a man who had been long dead. One eye was missing with the flesh rotted from around it. The other eye was stone black. The lips of the man had been ripped from place exposing black, rotten teeth. The man stopped and turned its head to face Daniel. The empty face let out a haunting laugh, and Daniel knew he needed to move.

He ran straight to Stephanie's side and forced her to her feet. He knew his grip would be hurting her, but he didn't have time to consider how she must be feeling. He needed to get them as far away from this evil figure as fast as he could. Soon his nose had filled with the smell of charcoal and ash. The street ahead was bright, and he could see smoke coming from nearby. He figured that there would probably be more people to fight on the next street, but this was the fastest way back to the guild. He needed to get his bow. He could fight as soon as he had that. As they turned the next corner, nearly every building that could be seen was on fire.

Several shops that he would visit often were now nothing more than ash. The bakery that Katie would bring them to laid in ruins. In front of the bakery was a demon. He could only see the demon's back however this was not a demon that he wanted to draw attention from. With four large arms that sprouted from his miniscule body, it stood on the twisted hands of large, bulging arms. Despite its appearance, Daniel couldn't look away from what had the demon's attention.

The demon had two hands plunged into the body of a shoemaker from another store near here. It was eating her as it ripped bit after bit from her innards. Daniel felt as though he would be sick. He couldn't afford that though. A single noise may draw it to him, and he needed to get by as fast as he could. For a moment, Daniel had even forgotten about Stephanie. Her presence was made very clear however by the echoing scream she had let out upon seeing the demon feasting on the shoemaker.

Daniel quickly wrapped his hand around her mouth as he forced the two of them against a nearby wall. The demon heard the scream as well as he turned to face the two of them. The demon didn't have any eyes. Instead, there was a second mouth sitting where its eyes should have been. It let out a shriek with each mouth producing a different sound.

Daniel felt Stephanie shaking, but he refused to loosen his grip on her mouth. Watching the demon, he realized that it couldn't see. Watching the demon turning its head frantically, he knew that it was listening for them.

The demon used its arms to lift itself from the ground and was soon standing where they had been standing only a moment before. Stephanie's tears had Daniel's hand soaking wet. When Daniel had pressed them against the wall, he didn't pay attention to the building that they were resting against.

His back was growing hot, as he realized it was burning behind him. This wall wasn't in flames yet, but this didn't stop the heat from the other side from being felt. A hot coal had fallen from above and landed on Stephanie's shoulder. Through his hand, she had let out a muffled scream, and he quickly flicked the coal from her shoulder however it was too late. The demon was aware of their location now as it turned its head towards them. It began to let out another shriek.

"Run!" Daniel shouted as he pushed the two of them away from the wall. They ran towards the guild hall as fast as they were able. From behind them, he could hear the demon's hands as they slapped upon the ground. "It's too fast!" He could hear the slapping growing closer to them. Stopping now though would absolutely mean their death. He refused to stop or even look back. Just keep going.

The demon sounded as though it was behind him now. He clenched his eyes shut as he prepared himself for the strike that was soon to come. "Daniel, drop down!" He knew that voice. He never thought he would ever be so happy to hear the deep, annoying voice in his life. Without wasting a step, he let his knees buckle beneath him. He opened his eyes as he collapsed to the ground to see a heavy log being dragged from either side by Bryant and Hugo.

The log made solid contact with the demon hard enough to drop it on its back. Followed closely behind the pair were several guild members. They took advantage of the demon being on the ground to drop several more logs on the creature's arms. "We may not be able to kill it, but that should hold it there for a while." Hugo sounded proud of himself for their plan.

"Get Stephanie and yourselves to the church now! I need to get back to the guildhall!" Daniel shouted the orders harshly, and the guild members wasted no time.

"Gee, a thank you would be nice." Bryant sounded as frustrated as he usually did, but he too followed close with the other guild members. Not wanting to be around when the demon freed itself, Daniel began making his way to the guildhall once more. He needed to find someone to help him fight before things got any worse.

Chapter Twenty-Five

GATHERING FIGHT

Katie felt a sharp pain in her leg. She tried to move her arms however something around her wrists were keeping her from being able to move her hands. Her eyes were struggling to adjust as she tried to open them, and she could smell something burning. It was foul smell that was mixed with the smell of charcoal.

There were several large lights that she could see as well as several shadows that she tried to focus on. Looking up, she could see a large building behind her. She realized it was the guildhall. She started to remember what had happened before she was here. A demon had taken her, here. "Abigail!"

A voice started to laugh from in front of her, "So you have finally awakened scholar." As her eyes focused on one of the shadows that was standing in front of her, she was able to clearly see the man who stood before her with his flaming red hair and red eyes. She felt her eyes fill with tears as she realized who the man was, and she was terrified that he would be standing before her. They were in the courtyard of the guildhall, and there were about twenty others standing nearby. Some had their hoods up, and some she was able to see their faces. Also, around the courtyard were many dead bodies. Some were guild members; others were just normal citizens who were unlucky.

The one who was speaking in front of her though was the reason she felt panic growing inside her. The man was the very same man Elijah had killed in the forest that day they had saved Abigail. She couldn't find a way to speak. This man came back to life just as Father Bernard had claimed.

"I'm glad you remember our time together Katie. This wouldn't have been fun if you didn't recognize who I was." He spoke with a mad look in his eye. "I'm ready to watch you die, but first, there is something I need from you." She looked around the courtyard at each of the bodies. She wanted to be sure that Abigail wasn't here anywhere. All the bodies lying around were adults, allowing some of her fear to dissipate.

"Katie, I'm offended. You can't even bring yourself to look at me." He moved as though he was floating as his body rushed towards her own. His hand grabbed her by the chin, and she found herself staring straight into the cold eyes of the man. His hand was as cold as ice, and his breath burned hot and smelled of death. "You have the key I need. Give me that and we won't touch the little girl you are hiding inside of this building."

Her heart stopped. They knew where Abigail was. They intentionally hadn't gone for her. What they were asking for though, she couldn't let them have it. "I…don't know…what key?" She tried to lie however this angered the man, striking her hard across her left cheek.

"Don't insult me woman! The day you discovered those ruins you were given a key! We need that key. It wasn't in your library and it's not on you now so where is it!?" The man's face grew hard and angry. It felt as though the man would burst into flames as his anger roared around her. "The little girl you so desperately tried to save is currently crying and hiding in one of the rooms right now. If you can't remember where the key is, then perhaps I should take that girl's soul. It'd make a fantastic demon don't you think?" As he asked this, the others began to laugh.

"How do you know about the key?" Katie trembled as she spoke. She knew that the man would kill Abigail no matter what. Katie desperately tried to think of a way to get out of this and protect her. "The only ones who know about the keys are dead so how do you know?"

"You see, Katie. I don't only have the power to control demons. I can control those who have died." As he said this, one of the hooded figures had stepped forward and lowered its hood. Katie began to weep as she realized who it was. The reptiliad that was now standing here looked as though part of his face had been crushed. His eyes were now empty. This was the reptiliad that she had traveled with when she discovered the ruins.

"Your old friend here has told me everything about your little quest. The people you met, and the things you learned." The man raised his arm and as he did, his shadowy arm had extended. The arm gripped itself tightly around the reptiliad's body and ripped the heart out of the once dead companion. As it did, the reptiliad collapsed to the ground. "I don't have a need for him anymore." The man laughed.

"How could you? He was so nice. He didn't want to hurt anyone! Why would you do that to him?" Katie cried out in anger seeing her late friend's soul being tormented. She thought back to her first journey and how that reptiliad was the first friend she had made outside of the village. Despite his race, he was one of the gentlest people that she had ever met. She lowered her head as she spoke, "Why are you doing this?"

"We only want to finish our Lord's work. The God of Death wished to turn this world into a wasteland, but we can't do that on our own. We need the keys to finish what he started. You're amazing apprentice has given us the map to the others. We just need your key so that we can complete His work!"

Katie felt defeated. She unknowingly gave the Arken-Son all the pieces he needed. "I watched you die. How are you even here now?" She was desperately trying to stall for time.

"I can raise the dead. What makes you think I can't do that for myself?"

Katie couldn't think of anything else to stall. She was running out of time and needed something fast. "Time's up Katie. Bring the girl! I knew you wouldn't talk so I already had them fetch her for me." Katie looked towards the guild hall and saw a demon dragging Abigail towards the courtyard.

"No! Leave her alone, Please!" Katie was desperately pleading with the man. This only seemed to bring the man joy as he watched her struggle. Abigail was in tears as she was being dragged. She was pulling against the demon however it didn't even seem to notice. Soon, Abigail was thrown to the ground before the Arken-Son.

"Just remember Katie, everything that happens to this girl is because of you. Her death will be never ending as I keep her soul tormented for all eternity!" The man howled with laughter as he raised his shadowy arms. Abagail looked terrified and was crying so hard that she couldn't even open her eyes. Katie didn't know what to do. "Please! Someone!"

The man suddenly froze in place as a loud howling rang out across the courtyard. Suddenly a giant beast sprung into sight. The beast stood over Abigail, and Katie saw Elijah dismounting from atop the beast. Katie was both confused and happy to see them standing there. She knew about Christine's transformation, but she didn't have any control in that form. She wondered why she seemed to be in control this time.

§

As the beast stood there before Elijah, he tried to understand where it had come from. He had never seen anything like this before. One of the demons went to strike the beast. Its attack appeared to not even affect it. The beast turned to the demon and began to snarl. It quickly gripped down upon the demon with its teeth. In a single bite, the demon was torn to shreds. The other demons as well as the men turned their attention to the beast however, they were all too weak in comparison. One of the men were thrown down near Elijah. The hood fell back, and he was able to see his face.

The man's face looked as though it had been ripped apart and pieced together again. His eyes were stone black, and there was no life to be seen within his actions. Elijah came to a sudden realization that most of the people attacking weren't alive.

Elijah summoned a dagger and removed the man's head. Soon, all the demon's and corpses had been disposed of by the beast. Elijah gave a shout of victory towards the beast whose attention was now on him. Elijah's confidence in this fight was fleeting. As the beast stared at him, he realized that it had no sense of who it was. Before it could attack, Elijah made a quick dash from the road they were on.

He could hear the beast pursuing him, and it was moving fast. He decided that if he could keep this beast chasing him, it would take care of any demons they came across. He knew that he needed to reach the guildhall for Abigail's sake, and ran as fast as his legs would carry him.

He soon found himself surrounded by another group of demons. Just as he had hoped, the beast was still chasing him and joined the fray. These demons stood no more chance against it than the others. Elijah planned to continue his chase as soon as these demons were dispatched.

He suddenly felt a sharp strike along the left side of his body. The beast had struck him with its paw. Fortunately, due to the beast's size, he was only hit by the pad. The claws had all missed him.

He saw the beast ready to strike down upon him. There was a spear lying next to him that had been dropped. He didn't want to use his spirit wielding against it. Using the spear, he managed to strike the beast along the left of its face, and its mouth came down next to him. Looking into the beast's eyes he had a familiar feeling course through him. "Christine?"

He jumped out of the way before the beast could regain its balance. A demon had taken advantage of this moment and jumped on the beasts back. This demon had a single eye in the middle of its face, but it lacked any other facial features. Its arm grew into a large spear that it drove down into one of the beast's shoulders.

The beast let out a painful roar as it tried to bite at the demon. Its head could not reach around far enough to catch it though. The demon's other arm had grown into a spear as well and it began to strike into the beast with both its arms. "No!" Elijah jumped onto the beasts back as well and drove his spear through the demon's head. He withdrew the spear, and with a wide sweep, removed the demon's head.

The demon crumbled as it fell off the beast's back. The beast managed to grab hold of Elijah's spear with its teeth and ripped it from his hands. In doing so, Elijah had fallen forward and was lying atop the beast's face. Looking into its eyes again he knew for sure this was Christine. She shook her head to attempt to throw Elijah from her.

Elijah gripped firmly to her fur so that he would not be dismounted. He needed to bring her senses back to her. Using something similar to what he did with the old stump, he flowed energy into her in hopes that she would remember who she was. He placed his head firmly against hers as he flooded his own spirit into the spot where their heads met.

She continued to throw her head around. However, after a few moments, the bucking had stopped. He opened his eyes and lifted his head again. Looking into her eyes, she had begun to weep. Releasing himself from her fur, he fell to the ground on his feet and she stood there staring at him.

"Christine, that's you right?" The beast whimpered as she nodded her head. He reached his hand out to her, and she brought her paw forward to meet his. "I'm glad I brought you back." He smiled to her as he stroked her fur. "Katie is in danger; will you be ok like this to help save her?" She snarled as she turned her head towards the guildhall. Her sense of smell allowed her to find Katie right away. Elijah smiled towards her as she kneeled. He was able to climb onto her back. Once he had a firm grip on her, she bolted down the street towards the guild.

She moved so fast that it was hard to see anyone they were passing. She suddenly came to a quick spot where Daniel had been standing. Without wasting any time, Elijah flung the bow to him. "Get to the guild quick! Katie is in danger! Bring anyone you can find that can fight!" Before Daniel could respond, Christine had taken off once more.

They were approaching the guildhall, and the courtyard was coming into view. Elijah could see Katie tied up in the courtyard, and in front of the guildhall, Abigail was being carried by one of the demons.

Christine must have seen this as well. She began to howl as she leapt into the courtyard. She stood over Abigail to guard her while Elijah dismounted. He stared down the Necromancer who he had killed in the forest. The two of them stared each other down.

The man laughed as he spoke, "You are a foolish boy if you think you will be enough to stop me." Elijah remained stone faced as he stared down the man.

Elijah had drawn his twin daggers. He readied to strike against the man however he had grabbed Katie to use her as a shield against Elijah. He stepped away from them as the other hooded figures had stepped between them.

Christine snarled as she looked around at the demons which were spawning in around them. "No matter what, protect Abigail!" Elijah barked at her sharper than he intended to. She didn't seem to take offense to it though, at least not from what he could tell. It was hard to read the facial expressions of such a large beast.

The man spoke out from behind the figures, "Do you really think the two of you will be enough to stop this? I can control the dead and as long as I live there will be an endless swarm of soldiers at my dispense." At this, he raised one of his hands and the dead bodies that were around the courtyard began to stand. Each one taking up a weapon near them. Even the ones who were just citizens now stood armed between Elijah and Katie.

As confident as Elijah wanted to be, they were now drastically outnumbered. Even if Christine wasn't having to guard Abigail, he wasn't too confident about their chances right now. Suddenly, he heard a strange whistling sound. One of the demons was struck in the torso. As the arrow hit its target, it began to unravel and twisted the demon's body in half. The demon crumbled as it collapsed.

Daniel was standing at the edge of the courtyard with his bow drawn, and several of the guild members were standing behind him as well. The Arken-Son began to grimace. This was the first time since Elijah first met this man that he was not smiling. "This is it!" Elijah focused on the bracelet he had made for Katie. Since it was made from his own Spiritual energy, he could still manipulate its shape as long as he could see it.

He turned the bracelet into a spear which drove its tip into the Arken-Son's shoulder. Simultaneously, the other end of the spear cut the cords that were wrapped around Katie's wrists. "Grab it Katie! Keep yourself safe!" Elijah shouted out towards her. She did as Elijah shouted, and she ran from the Arken-Son as fast as she could. They were still separated, but at least for now she wasn't a hostage.

"Damn you all! I'll kill every last one of you!" The man shouted out in anger. Soon the demon's split; some headed towards the guild, and the rest towards Elijah and Christine. The first to reach Elijah was one of the reanimated guild members. The man carried a sword which Elijah avoided with ease. He plunged one of the daggers through the man's chest however instead of puncturing the man, he phased through the man. As his arm came out through the man's back, the deceased man's soul was clung to the dagger. The body collapsed as its soul was ripped away, and the soul quickly lost its form. It became a single orb of light that floated around its now fallen body. "Good, I can still give them peace when this is over."

Elijah ran forward to meet the next man who was brought down the same way. Next up was a demon. This demon had no head, with a disfigured face upon its torso that vomited blood as Elijah approached. Its body was fat, and its limbs were thin. With a solid kick, Elijah forced the demon to collapse under its own weight. Elijah had summoned a chain that connected his daggers. He threw one forcefully which had struck another demon in its back. Elijah gave the chain a solid pull which caused the demon to fall backwards onto the fat one. The dagger had extended into a spear which pierced through both demons causing them to crumble.

Looking back, Christine still stood guard over Abigail. She had a demon in her mouth as her paw was striking down another one. There were several bodies lying around her. He looked down at Abigail. She was standing now however she was clutching tight to one of Christine's back legs. Tears filled her eyes, and she was staring at him. Elijah wished he could go to her, but right now he needed to fight.

He looked back ahead of him, and there was a new demon approaching him. This one was small and fast. Elijah was barely able to pull his spear up in time to block. The demon wielded a short sword in both hands, and while Elijah had blocked the first one, the second was still free.

He watched as the demon readied its strike. It would catch him in the gut, and he didn't have time to put a shield up. "Damn!" Before the demon could land its strike though, an arrow had pierced the demon. It crumbled before him, and he looked over to see Daniel with a smug look on his face.

Elijah skimmed the courtyard to look for Katie. She was standing near the front of the Guild hall. She still held his spear however she now also was holding a shield. She was doing good to use the spear for the demons, and the shield for the reanimated. She was doing fine, but he noticed that the Arken-Son was heading towards her again.

Elijah needed to get there first, and he charged headfirst towards them. He summoned a large shield. He didn't have time to waste fighting each one, so he had decided to force his way through. He was nearly there when before him stood the large demon from before. This is the one that had taken Katie. Staring it down, he wasn't sure the best way to attack. He needed to make this quick, but he wasn't very good with such large opponents. He heard heavy footsteps coming from behind him. I can't take a fight from both sides. Turning, he realized it wasn't a demon coming from behind; it was John. He ran past Elijah and crossed swords with the large demon. "Go, you have to get to Katie!" He shouted as he threw himself into another attack against the demon.

Elijah nodded and ran quickly past the demon. It tried to strike as he ran past, but John blocked the strike with his sword. "Thanks John!" Elijah pressed on and soon he was standing between Katie and the Arken-Son. He stared down the man with a hardened glare. "I think it is time we have a rematch from the forest."

The man smiled as he stared at Elijah, "I suppose you think you can take me by yourself then?" The man laughed.

"You wouldn't have needed all these bodies if you could stand on your own."

"Oh, I believe you may have misread my actions boy. I didn't use them because I needed them. I just didn't find any of you worth me fighting myself. You have succeeded in pissing me off though, so I think I'll let you taste how strong I am for yourself."

Shadows began to swallow the man as his body was engulfed by them. Soon he was sheltered deep within the demons that provided him with a body larger than anything Elijah had ever seen. His large, clawed hands began to swing at Elijah which he was able to deflect with his shield. As the man's strike landed against his shield the second time, Elijah felt a sharp pain course through his entire body.

This pain brought him to his knees and the shield he held had returned. He realized he was at his limit. He had been ripping apart his soul too many times. Using every ounce of his strength, he managed to summon back a great sword. The body can only stand having its soul in fragments for so long before it begins to break down. He was running out of time before his body began to devour itself, but he couldn't think about that. He's been through worse pain than this, so he had to keep pushing forward.

As the man brought down another strike, Elijah pierced the arm through the palm of its hand. The shadowy arm remained for a moment before crumbling. This only lasted a moment before a new arm had sprouted. "I have a nearly endless supply of Shapeless. Do you think you can even manage a few of them?" The man shouted at Elijah with a smug look upon his face.

He heard Katie scream from behind him. He turned his head slightly as he felt himself growing weaker. Just as he had worried, Katie's spear had disappeared. There were three demons that now had her pinned.

Knowing it wasn't the best decision, he turned his back on the Arken-Son and charged towards her.

He struck out with his great sword and pierced all three demons at once. "No!" Katie shouted out. As she did, Elijah felt a burning pain pierce his leg. Looking back, the man had drove his arm through Elijah's leg. His sword returned and Elijah laid their defenseless. "Run, Katie. Get out of here now!"

Katie shook her head and threw herself over Elijah. The man was now laughing as he raised his other arm. "I'll just kill you both and search through the ashes for that key!" They braced themselves for the impact. From nearby they heard Abigail screaming out, "No!" As she screamed, a bright blue light flew past them and struck the man. In an instant, his shadowy body had turned to ice.

The man screamed out in pain, and when the ice broke away his body was exposed. "You stupid little girl! I'll kill you; I'll kill you all!!" The man was being surrounded by shapeless again however an arrow struck into his side and blew away the demons. He had a look of desperation on his face as he saw John running towards him, sword drawn. Knowing that he wouldn't have time to avoid the strike, the man formed his arm into a single blade. Maybe he had thought John would deflect the strike and give him a chance to counter, but John kept his sword straight.

He drove his sword deep into the man's chest. Although the Arken-Son was seriously injured, he let out a sinister laugh. The man's arm had pierced through John just as deep. Elijah, Katie, Daniel, and Christine all stood in shock as the watched John collapse. The Arken-Son was still laughing and was still standing there.

He once again tried to surround himself in Shapeless. Daniel couldn't get another shot off and was soon being attacked by a demon that had gotten too close. Elijah was lifting himself again, but he couldn't get another weapon to summon.

Katie threw herself into the man causing the shadows to disperse for a moment. He was still severely injured from John's sword making it easy for Katie to get several solid hits against him. The man let out a bellowing yell as a shapeless shot out of him and threw Katie back. With every bit of strength he had, Elijah was able to summon a trident in his hand.

The man was pushing himself back to his feet as Elijah threw the weapon. It struck the man through his chest. Just as it did with the reanimated from earlier, the trident had stuck to the Arken-Son's soul and ripped it from his body. The trident struck into the ground near where the man's body was. His soul screamed out in a terrifying shriek as it was trying to drag itself back to his body.

Elijah rushed over and drove his hand through the man's soul to grip the weapon. "Don't come back again!" Elijah let out a scream as he squeezed the handle. The man's soul suddenly dispersed, and his body collapsed to the ground.

Around the courtyard, nearly every demon and body had collapsed. There were a few remaining hooded figures who had tried to run as fast as they were able. Daniel found each one with his arrows. Everyone ran to John as fast as they could.

"John!" Elijah was the first to reach him, but it was too late. He was already dead. The strike had pierced his heart and there wasn't anything that could be done for him. The others soon reached them as well. They all stood around him in silence as the mourned their lost friend.

Abigail had made it to them now, and she threw herself into Elijah crying. She buried her face into his side, "Why did you leave me alone? You promised you wouldn't leave me alone?" She gently hit him a couple times before letting herself just rest against him. He wrapped his arm around her as Katie came over and wrapped herself around Abigail.

Christine was now lying on the ground next to Daniel. As he stroked her head, she began to turn back into her human form. She passed out from exhaustion and laid there in Daniel's lap. *Tomorrow will be a hard day, but for now at least things are over.* Or, this is what Elijah had thought.

CHAPTER TWENTY-SIX
RESOLUTION

As the sun was rising, smoke could still be seen from various parts of the city. Most of the fires were now extinguished however the damage was far from dealt with. The people were currently looking for anyone who was missing and preparing the dead for burial. Standing along edge of the forest watching the sun rise on this unfortunate city was a single man. He sat on that old oak stump that gave him a clear view of the entire city. The man wore a dark cloak that covered his head, and around his face burned a dark purple flame mask.

As he stared out over the city, a scratching sound could be heard from behind him. "Oh? You're getting better at that." The scratching grew louder, and soon a hand had burst from the ground. The hand was soon joined by another, and the hands began pushing dirt away as the man dug himself from the ground. The necromancer had emerged from the dirt, but his body was still incomplete. The flesh was missing from around his left eye and cheek leaving the bone and teeth exposed. His right hand was missing the skin as well as three fingers, and there was blood dripping from the nubs.

Clinging to him was an old lady. She appeared to have held on to him as he brought himself back from hell. The old woman had wiry grey hair that was rather thin in several spots. She was more complete than the Arken-Son however the flesh was still missing from her lower jaw leaving the teeth exposed. The man sitting upon the stump was unphased by the two as he continued to stare out over the city. "So, I see you succeeded in finding her finally." The man's voice was flat and expressionless.

"You were supposed to protect me! They shouldn't have been able to kill me you bastard!" his voice cracked and weak as he shouted at the man. "I guess you just found it fun to sit here and break your promise!"

"Not once, but three times you have failed us. Yet you sit here and accuse me of betrayal?" The man's voice remained unchanged, and he still refused to look at the necromancer. "You were supposed to kill the boy, but you failed. You were supposed to get the key, and you failed. At least though, in your latest death you were able to bring us the witch finally."

The Arken-son stared at him brimming with anger. He spit on the ground near the man. The man finally turned to look at the Arken-Son as he burst into laughter, "You truly are a pathetic creature. Still, you served some purpose to us. Take the witch and return home. Wait there until we decide what else you are good for."

"That place is no home to me. I brought you the witch now I'm free to do as I want." He walked past the man making sure to strike his shoulder as he did. "I'm not finished with them yet."

"We could care less now that your job is finished, but if you decide to head back on your own, we can't provide you with protection anymore." The man's voice had gone flat again.

"You couldn't protect me to begin with. I'm beginning to doubt if you all are a bunch of frauds to begin with. Leave me alone and take your witch."

"Believe what you would like but remember, there are still creatures in this realm seeking souls that don't belong. Mind you don't attract them to you." With that, the man and the witch had disappeared. The Arken-Son stood there in disgust, "Say what you want. No matter how many times I die I will always find a way back."

As the sun began to peak over the city walls, many of the buildings that had been ablaze were finally down to coals. Most of the fires were gone, but the scars left from the night before would take some time to heal. A wagon had been brought to the courtyard of the guildhall to keep logs of everything. The buildings that had been destroyed, people who had died, people who were still missing, and a collection site for anything that may have been left by the Arken-faithful. Most of their items though were the amulets.

These amulets had to be destroyed properly so that the souls from within would be released. According to Elijah, if they weren't destroyed correctly then the souls within would remain in torment for eternity. Katie was laying in the back of this wagon with Abigail asleep on top of her. She gently stroked the girl's hair as she slept.

Abigail had wanted to try and stay awake to help as much as she could. The others told her that she was too young to have to help with all of this, but she still wanted to. They let her help with writing down names so that she didn't have to be out around any of the bodies. It didn't take long though before she was falling asleep on Katie. She had someone else take over and laid down here in the wagon with her.

Abigail had done something no one had ever seen before. Katie was curious how she froze that man. Elijah told them all that there were rumors of magic users in the east, but he also admitted that he had never seen it himself. No matter what it was, that little girl continued to surprise everyone. They would have to go to the capital once everything was cleaned up, and they had agreed to bring Abigail with them to see if they could find an answer.

"This is all my fault." Katie began to cry as she thought about everything. Elijah was involved because the Arken-Son was looking for her. Daisey, the reptiliad, was ripped from his grave because of her, and the city was attacked because of her. John is dead now because of her too. These were all the thoughts and blame she put upon herself.

She knew that Elijah was going to be dragged into more trouble that she had started. "Thank you for coming back. We wouldn't have made it if not for you," was the silent thanks she offered to him. She looked down and gently ran her fingers through Abigail's hair. "I'll find a way to keep both of you safe like you did last night for us." There was a sudden clank that had made Katie jump.

"Sorry! I didn't mean to scare you." Elijah spoke softly so not to wake Abigail. He had dropped several more amulets into the wagon. He climbed in and sat against the side as he closed his eyes for a moment. "You could be sleeping too while she is. Its ok to rest now." His voice was cracked from his own exhaustion which spurred her not to sleep even more.

"No, I'm fine. I couldn't sleep even if I wanted to right now." Katie watched him for a moment as he sat there. With his eyes closed and head back, she had thought he did fall asleep. She was about to speak, but his voice reached out first.

"After we visit the capital, I want to take Abigail east. Someone there should be able to give us real answers about her. I'm sure the capital could, but I don't trust anyone there. I think it'll be best to keep her a secret while we are there. When I go, I want you to join us as well." He had lifted his head and was now looking at Abigail.

Katie could see how worried he was about her. She felt guilty to be happy that he had asked her to come with them, but her heart was ready to stop hearing him ask her. "Of course, I'll go. I want to protect her too, but I'm also not ready to lose you again."

"I want to make one thing clear." He moved his eyes to meet hers. "I still don't want you there. This world is filled with things I want to protect you from, but you were right that you are one of the best people to have around while we figure all of this out."

"I know," Katie sounded sad as she spoke, "I don't think I want you to leave me again. You can't leave me again. I meant what I said last night. I love you."

"Katie," He sounded troubled as he spoke, "there are things I need to tell you about before we get to the capital."

"What? Are you about to tell me that you have a family there?"

"No, I don't have a family—" The two of them were interrupted by Daniel and Christine. They had brought food for them all. It wasn't much, just some bread and broth. They were happy to see it though.

"Christine, are you sure you are okay to be walking around?" Katie was worried about her friend. Although she was up and walking around, Christine couldn't hide her exhaustion. The night before, she had beast-changed which usually took days or weeks to turn back. Elijah had brought her back somehow, and no one could figure out what he did.

"I'm ok, thank you though." she stated, smiling. "I'm a little tired, but everyone else is too. I'm just trying to help as much as everyone else is."

"Yeah, but you're the only one who was physically exhausted the way you were."

"Oh, Daniel, you worry too much." Christine smiled as she gave him a gentle push. "I promise you all, I'm fine." She looked towards Elijah, "Thank you for saving me last night. I don't know how you did it, but I was able to act on my own." She smiled again before picking up her tray to head out, "There are still more people who need food, so I'll be going."

Daniel stayed behind for a moment. When Christine was out of earshot, he spoke to Elijah, "Thank you for helping her last night. Each time she transforms, we never know if we'll get her back. How did you do it though?"

"There were times in the past when we would wander into an animal's territory when we shouldn't. It wasn't their fault, so it would have been wrong to kill them. My master taught me a way to communicate with nature and animals. I didn't know if it would work, but that is all I did. Once the beast was calmed, it allowed Christine to take back control."

Daniel stood there for a moment before speaking, "Do you think you could teach me how to do that? I don't want her transforming again, but if she does, I would like to be able to help her." Elijah simply nodded, and with that, Daniel looked as though he were about to follow Christine before turning back to Elijah. "Will *he* be back again?

Elijah seemed lost in thought as he searched for an answer. "If I'm being honest, he shouldn't be able to come back at all." Daniel waited for Elijah to continue. "Just as Eimput has angels to bring souls to Earth, Zosen has reapers to bring souls to the afterlife. I have been trying to figure out how the Arken-Son has been avoiding the reapers."

"Could it be some sort of magic," Katie spoke up this time, "like his necromancy?" Daniel seemed to nod at this assumption as well.

"It's possible, but that would mean there is a limit to it as well. Even if he has the ability to do a lot, he can only do so much before he slips up and the reapers find him." The group sat in silence for several minutes.

"Well," Daniel spoke to Elijah, "I will leave you to figure that one out. I need to catch back up with Christine." With that, Daniel bounded off after his wife.

Katie looked in awe at Elijah which he took notice of, "What is it?" Elijah looked at her quizzically. She didn't say anything. She simply smiled at him. He looked as though he was going to say something however there seemed to be a commotion coming from the city somewhere.

"You stay here with her. I'll see what's going on." Elijah stood to head out where everyone was drawn to. As he left from sight, Katie worried. *Everything is done right? There isn't something wrong? Please be safe Elijah.*

Rushed towards the front of the city, Elijah had met up with Daniel who had a worrisome look upon his face. "Do you know what's going on?" He looked at Elijah with a face a panic. "What is it?"

"Someone claimed that they saw the Arken-Son walking towards the city. He's dead right? We killed him for good?" Daniel's fear was warranted. It took everything they had to kill him this time. If that man was back, Elijah didn't know if they had the strength to fight him again.

Soon they were at the front gate of the city where Bryant and Hugo were already waiting. As they stood out front the city, they were able to see the outline of a man slowly drawing nearer. "This can't be happening." Cried Hugo. Although the man's face was rather grotesque, it was the Arken-Son. Elijah looked back towards some of the guild members standing nearby, "Get everyone into the city and close the gate. I'll take care of it here."

The man had looked terrified. He had been one of the ones that fought in the courtyard last night making him fully aware of how powerful this man was. He nodded his head, and he began ushering everyone back into the city. Daniel, however, did not waiver.

"If you are going to stand against him then so will I." Daniel stood firmly next to him. As the man approached them, they were able to see just how disfigured he was. His physical body though wasn't what made him powerful. Elijah knew that they shouldn't consider him weak because of how he stood. The man soon stopped to speak.

"You think that I can die just like that?" Blood dripped from the man's mouth as he spoke, "I am death reborn. In our God's absence I have come to fulfill his role. You don't have what it takes to kill me. I can keep coming back. No matter how many times you kill me, I will always come back to haunt you." The man was pointing his decayed hand towards Elijah.

"How many times do you think Zosen will let you escape? I'm sure he doesn't find your little act to be very amusing." Elijah tried to sound confident as he spoke, but he has never seen anyone come back before, not like this. "I'm sure he has his reapers looking for you now."

"Don't try and scare me boy." He began to cough as he vomited blood. "I'm already beyond the reach of his pets and soon I'll be more powerful than Zosen himself! All I need is that little key your scholar is hiding from me." He laughed maniacally, seemingly lost all sense of himself.

"You don't have your amulet. You don't have your weapons to fight for you. You are going to die here, again." Elijah shouted out.

The man began to laugh as more blood dripped from his mouth, "I control the dead." He raised his arms and after a moment, the ground around him appeared to be moving. Bodies began to rise from the ground all around him. "You think I can only summon my own soul from the dead?"

Elijah began to smile. "I figured as almighty you claim to be that you would be able to summon more than that!" Elijah taunted the man.

"Elijah what are you doing? I don't have my bow, and we're all too weak to fight. I don't know if we can take the one's here now!" Daniel sounded panicked as he spoke.

"It's ok. The more he summons, the less energy he has to hide himself from the reapers." Elijah looked nervous as he spoke. "I hope..." The man was enraged by Elijah's challenge and screamed out as more and more bodies began to rise from the ground.

Daniel caught on and began to taunt the man as well, "You really did come back weaker than before. You might as well go back to hell on your own!"

"How dare you all mock me! Every one of you are dead. Dead. DEAD!!!" As the man shouted, even more bodies began to rise. Seventy, eighty, no, the man had managed to raise nearly one hundred bodies from the ground.

"Elijah, if you are wrong, we are going to die, you know that, right?" The bodies began to move. First at a walk, then running. As they closed in, the bodies were in various levels of decomposition. The man must have been rather weak to not be able to complete his own body. This many must have him at his limit which meant that he wouldn't be able to hide himself from the fiends.

The bodies were closing in, and Daniel was getting shaky. "Just wait." Elijah's voice was calm as he spoke. They couldn't see it, but he was worried that he may be wrong about this himself. The bodies were nearly to them when suddenly there was a loud crack that came from where the man was standing.